Valley of Dreams

Books by Lauraine Snelling

*Golden Filly Collection One**
*Golden Filly Collection Two**
*High Hurdles Collection One**
*High Hurdles Collection Two**

SECRET REFUGE
Daughter of Twin Oaks

DAKOTAH TREASURES
Ruby • *Pearl*
Opal • *Amethyst*

DAUGHTERS OF BLESSING
A Promise for Ellie • *Sophie's Dilemma*
A Touch of Grace • *Rebecca's Reward*

HOME TO BLESSING
A Measure of Mercy • *No Distance Too Far*
A Heart for Home

RED RIVER OF THE NORTH
An Untamed Land • *A New Day Rising*
A Land to Call Home • *The Reapers' Song*
Tender Mercies • *Blessing in Disguise*

RETURN TO RED RIVER
A Dream to Follow • *Believing the Dream*
More Than a Dream

WILD WEST WIND
Valley of Dreams

*5 books in each volume

Wild West Wind • BOOK I

Valley of Dreams

LAURAINE SNELLING

BETHANY HOUSE PUBLISHERS
a division of Baker Publishing Group
Minneapolis, Minnesota

Valley of Dreams
© 2011 by Lauraine Snelling
Cover design by John Hamilton Design

Published by Bethany House Publishers
11400 Hampshire Avenue South
Bloomington, Minnesota 55438
www.bethanyhouse.com

Bethany House Publishers is a division of
Baker Publishing Group, Grand Rapids, Michigan.

Printed in the United States of America

Library of Congress Cataloging-in-Publication Data
Snelling, Lauraine.
    Valley of dreams / Lauraine Snelling.
        p.   cm.
    ISBN 978-0-7642-0921-5 (hardcover : alk. paper)
    ISBN 978-0-7642-0415-9 (pbk.)
    ISBN 978-0-7642-0924-6 (large-print pbk.)
    1. Single women—Fiction. 2. Frontier and pioneer life—South Dakota—Fiction. 3. Black Hills (S.D. and Wyo.)—Fiction. I. Title.
PS3569.N39V35 2011
813'.54—dc22   2011025218

11   12   13   14   15   16   17   7   6   5   4   3   2   1

To my friend Woodeene, who has pulled me out of the fire so often, especially, but not only, when my computer would eat a chapter. Computers mind for her, mastermind that she is. Besides that, she listens closely, gives wise advice as we wade through life's many challenges, and makes me laugh when technology makes me cry. God gave us each other, and we live and share His unconditional love. To God be the glory.

Who am I, daughter of the wind,
The wind that brings rain,
The wind that brings life?
I am she who breathes deep of that wind,
Drinks until full of the rain,
Lives so that others
Yearn for the wind.

—Lauraine Snelling

1

*J*ust get through today," Cassie told herself, as she did every October first.

As far as she could figure, hard work was the only antidote to the grief that threatened to paralyze her. So far, on this day that had started, as every day, before dawn, she had given her trick-riding pinto, Wind Dancer, a bath, brushed him dry, and made sure not one tangle remained in his black-and-white mane and tail. She had cleaned and polished his hooves and would have brushed his teeth, if that were possible.

Her tent on the grounds of the Lockwood and Talbot Wild West Show would meet military standards for order and cleanliness, the supplies in her trunk all folded or placed precisely. Her guns gleamed from polishing; no trace of gunpowder or dust would dare adhere to stocks or barrels. All were wrapped in cotton cloths and returned to their cases.

If George had allowed it, she would have scrubbed him too, but while the ancient buffalo bull enjoyed a good grooming, he didn't care for bathing. Even Cassie knew better than to push her friend too far. Her dog, Othello, on the other hand, had been scrubbed to the point of nearly losing his wiry hair—and his dignity. While he stayed near her in the corral, he kept his head turned the other way.

It was only three o'clock. If there had been a show today, she could have handled the memories better. Digging into the grooming bucket, she pulled out a carrot and fed it to George. The crunching brought Othello over to sit by the bucket, hinting that he'd like one too but was too miffed to ask.

She broke a second carrot in half and fed part to the dog and the rest to Wind Dancer. Between the pinto and the buffalo, where no one else could see her, she let the tears that had been burning behind her eyes all day pour forth. Othello abandoned his resentment and came to sit at her feet as she cried into Wind Dancer's mane. George snorted and shook his head but stayed right beside her, as he had ever since she bottle-fed him as a calf after his mother died.

Would the tears never cease? Such was the case every year, no matter how hard she fought to control her emotions. All the other performers had learned to leave her alone if they didn't want to lose their head.

Her mother and father had both died on October first, five years apart. For Cassie Lockwood, at age ten, losing her mother had taken the light from her world, but when she was fifteen and her father died, her life nearly went with him. Each of the five years since, she had struggled through this day of memory, praying for peace and comfort, feeling that God had left her right along with her parents.

After what seemed like hours she wiped her tears on George's dense coat and heaved a sigh that came clear up from her toes. She rubbed his favorite spot, right above his eye and onto his forehead, turned to Wind Dancer and did the same, then leaned down and ruffled Othello's ears. "Maybe I should just give up and cry it out at the beginning of the day. You think it would be easier?"

George nudged her with his broad black nose, so she petted him some more too. Safe between her three animal friends, she wiped her eyes on her shirttail before tucking it back into the waistband of her britches. With her mother no longer around to force her into the niceties of womanhood, Cassie wore pants to work around the animals. As the star of the show with her trick riding and shooting, she pretty much did as she pleased, but when she entered the arena, she was all professional. Her mother and father, who headlined before her, had taught her well.

"Miss Cassie." Micah—he never had given a last name— waited patiently for her outside the corral.

"I'll be along soon."

"You are all right now?" While slow of speech and movement, Micah had a way with animals that bordered on legendary.

"Yes, thank you." *Or at least I soon will be.*

"The supper bell rang."

Really? I didn't even hear it. "Long ago?"

"Food will be gone soon."

Cassie heaved another sigh and picked up her bucket. She gave each of her friends another pat and exited the corral out the swinging gate. Othello remained at her knee, and Micah fell into step beside her. He took the bucket and went to set it inside her tent before catching up with her again. Sometimes she wondered who was guarding whom. Years before, she had come upon two of the young roustabouts deviling him and lit into them like a swarm of bees. Micah had assigned himself to her service ever since, along with taking care of the show stock of Longhorn cattle, buffalo, and horses. He'd arrived one night, skinny and starving, and grew into the length of his feet, but while strong, he had a whipcord stature. He saved his rare smiles for Cassie and the animals.

"You hungry?"

Cassie thought a moment. *Yes.* That rumbling in her belly was most likely hunger now that the pain of grief had retired to await another vulnerable time. "I guess. You know what's for supper?"

"Smells like pork chops."

Othello whined, so Micah dropped a hand down to the dog's head. "I'll save you my bones. Don't worry."

Cassie knew that Micah carried on more conversations with the animals than he did with humans, and she no longer let it bother her. Others were not so tolerant. Since Micah listened more than he talked, he usually knew what was happening in their confined world of travel and performing. October was usually the final month of the show season before they headed south to winter in warmer weather. When her father ran the show, they did enough gigs in the winter season to keep all of the cast and crew employed. Not so with Jason Talbot, her father's former partner and Uncle Jason to her, an honorary title for the family friend she'd known all her life. He'd promised both her and her father that he would see to Cassie's care as long as she needed him.

"Something strange going on." Micah held back the flap for her to enter the cook tent ahead of him.

"I know." *But what?* Cassie thought back as she returned greetings, making sure she smiled to let her friends know she was all right. When had she first sensed the feeling?

"You're lookin' better, honey," Miz Mac, the seamstress and costume designer and keeper, said, concern darkening her fading blue eyes. She and her husband, Mac, had taken Cassie into their tent and hearts when her father died. Cassie had opted for a tent of her own when she turned eighteen, two years earlier. "We saved you a place."

"Thank you. We'll be right back. How's the food?"

"John Henry is back."

"Good thing." Cassie grinned and headed for the serving line. John Henry had left the troupe to return home for a few days to bury his father. His second in command could make good soups, but the quality slipped on other entrees.

With their trays full, Cassie and her cohort made their way back to the table without incident, but several conversations had hushed as they passed. Folks always thought she belonged more on the management side, a slight cut above the performers. She'd never be able to disabuse them of that notion. She might call him *Uncle* Jason, but he never shared business information with her, still thinking of her as that cute little pigtailed girl who used to sit on his knee. At least that was Cassie's take on things.

Halfway through her meal, weariness rolled over her like a huge wave, leaving her foundering in the backwash. The conversation around her faded as she fought to stay awake.

Two nights of little sleep had a tendency to do that to a person. She set the remainder of her plate on the ground for Othello, bid the others good-night, and headed for her tent. Tomorrow would be a show day, a better day for sure. Maybe her sense of apprehension was on high alert because she was so tired.

2

*O*thello growled from the door of her tent.

A string of profanity and the thuds of a fight jerked her from a deep sleep the next morning. The degree of light coming through the tent walls told her it was time to get up. The fighting reminded her that something in their show world was indeed wrong, or going wrong, because fisticuffs were rare on the lot. A body crashed into the tent wall, setting the tent poles to screeching.

"All right, you two, break it up before you get a broken head," someone called.

"He said—"

"I don't care who said what. Keep it up and Talbot will dock your pay or send you down the road. You both been here too long to let some stupid little argument bring you down."

Cassie recognized the voice. Shorty Simmons, second in command, could easily take the two miscreants and knock their heads together had he so desired. But he rarely used his superior size when common sense would do, like today. As the sounds of the three faded, Cassie threw back the covers on her cot and, sitting up, swung her feet to the rug to find her slippers. Dressed in a matter of minutes, she made her bed and neatened the already pristine area. As she inhaled, she realized the cloud of grief had again passed and she was back to being herself. She whistled for Othello and caught herself whistling a tune on the way to the cook tent. Micah would have already fed and watered her animals, along with all the others. Sometimes she wondered if he ever slept.

A cut lip on one and a swelling eye on the other told her who had been fighting without her needing to ask.

"Sorry if we woke you." The dirtier of the two turned to her in the chow line.

"You better get cleaned up before Jason sees you." She picked up her tray. "You gone crazy or something? You know the rules."

"I know." He glanced at her over his shoulder. "You heard anything? The tension around here can be cut with a sword."

The other members of the cast thought she had an inside track to Jason Talbot, but she didn't, and no amount of explaining had changed their minds. "Any thoughts on it?" she asked.

"Nope. Nobody has."

Cassie filled her tray with bacon, scrambled eggs, and two biscuits, and then added a dollop of applesauce. One of the cook's helpers would be bringing the coffeepot around to the tables. She settled down at the end of one of the tables and bowed her head for the table grace she'd learned from her Norwegian mother.

Every once in a while, she allowed herself to dream of going to Norway, the land of her mother's birth. But more often she dreamed of the valley her father had created for her in her mind. At first the valley was his dream, but through the years it had become hers as well. They would leave the world of the Wild West shows with enough money tucked away to build a ranch in that Black Hills valley he'd discovered and raise cattle and fine horses. His big stallion, Lobos, was to have been the stud. Then Lobos had to be put down because someone fed him too much grain and he foundered. Sometime after that, her father died.

Do not think of that today, she ordered herself as she spread butter and jam on her biscuits. *"Yesterday is gone, tomorrow not yet here, so live today the best you can"* had been one of her mother's favorite sayings. And today was show day. She glanced around the tent, but Uncle Jason was not at his usual table. If she allowed herself to think about it, she had to admit he didn't make it to breakfast much anymore. Rumor had it he was sleeping off the night before, but sometimes not knowing something for sure made acceptance easier.

Was it her place to confront him? She mopped up her eggs with the biscuit. Surely not.

The feeling was even stronger that afternoon, an almost palpable miasma. Something was wrong—but what? And where could she go for answers?

Wearing her red-fringed skirt and white shirt, Cassie Lockwood studied the performers of the Lockwood and Talbot Wild West Show as they lined up for the opening parade around the wide open arena. The United States flag snapped in the breeze above the uniformed riders waiting for the big wooden gates to swing open. The snorts of horses, the jingle of harnesses, the laughter of performers, and the tuning of instruments were all normal sounds. She glanced down at the scruffy dog sitting placidly by Wind Dancer's right knee. If Othello wasn't picking up on it, then surely the feeling was only in her head. He scented trouble faster than he did birds.

Ignore it, her mind commanded. *Concentrate on the parade and getting through this performance.* She went through this ritual before every performance— butterflies vaulting in her middle, her mouth as dry as a desert. At least she'd progressed to the point that her hands no longer shook. *Think about something else.* Her father had said he always thought of his valley, and that calmed him down. But she'd never been there. All those years he promised they would go to the valley in the Black Hills of South Dakota. But he died before he was able to keep the promise. So she'd promised him she'd go there herself. Were deathbed promises breakable? How could she ever get there, wherever *there* was. The thought clenched her throat. *Think on something else.*

The drums crashed, the trumpets blared, the gates swung open, and the performers of the internationally known company burst into the sunny outdoor arena, led by horse-mounted flag bearers. Jason Talbot, decked out in cutaway frock coat and wide-brimmed white hat, welcomed the crowd that filled not only the wooden bleachers but overflowed to line the far fences. This final afternoon performance of their stay in Dickinson, North Dakota, was off to a sparkling start. The crisp fall breeze was finally breaking the heat spell that had nearly drowned the region in stifling humidity.

As the mounted Indians nudged their horses into a gallop, Wind Dancer waited for her signal to join the racing parade. Three chuck wagons were lined up behind them, their horses tugging at their bits. The excitement was as contagious to the animals as to the human performers.

The applause swelled when Cassie passed through the gates. Some called her the Darling of the West and others the greatest sharpshooter since Annie Oakley, but her official title was the Shooting Princess, since her mother had been a member of the Norwegian royal family. Whatever the name, people flocked to watch her perform. Between trick riding and sharpshooting, she always fulfilled their high expectations. She circled the arena, waved to the crowds, and then exited the gates to wait for the pioneer and Wild West scenes to be presented.

Knowing it would be about an hour before her turn in the ring, Cassie dismounted in front of her tent and tied her pinto to the hitching post. She leaned against his shoulder, waiting for her heart to return to normal. Giving him a good brushing would soothe both of them. She pulled off Wind Dancer's saddle and breast collar, setting them on the other end of the rail, and went for a brush and currycomb.

Othello flopped down in the shade of the tent after scratching one ear with a long hind leg. He was not the most handsome dog around, but he more than made up for his looks in the brain department. He often knew what she was going to do next before she did. Between Wind Dancer and Othello, Cassie knew she had the most stalwart and faithful friends anyone could have. And George, of course. Wouldn't that be a lark if she let him in the arena to follow her around like he did in the corral? The big bad bull buffalo. Her smile at the thought released some of the tension in her neck.

After a brushing, a wipe-down with a cloth, and a nuzzle from her horse, she checked her guns and ammunition. When she heard the applause after the attack on the settlers' cabin, she replaced her tack and mounted to head back to the arena, her heart rate kicking up again, no matter how many deep breaths she sucked in to try to keep it from happening.

"You have everything?" Micah asked, picking up the leather satchels that contained her guns. Though Micah spent most of his time caring for the animals, he made it a point to recheck Cassie's gear and make sure it was where it was supposed to be at showtime.

"Thanks, Micah. Don't know what I'd do without you."

As a matter of habit, and to help her calm down, she let her gaze rove over the performers and back-lot hands as they went about their assigned duties. The performance was proceeding as normal, but something was wrong—she was sure of it. If only her father were there to talk this over with. After her mother died, her father often said he didn't see how he could live without the wife he adored, so it wasn't entirely unexpected when he had an attack of pneumonia while they were touring in England and soon died. Cassie had stayed with the Lockwood and Talbot Show because she knew no other life, and Uncle Jason had pleaded with her to stay and promised he would always watch out for her, just as he'd promised her father.

The exit gate swung open, and the performers poured out.

"Easy, boy." Cassie tightened the reins as she and Wind Dancer waited for their signal to enter. Never sure who was more impatient, she or her mount, she swallowed again, counting the beats of the fife and drum so they'd enter at exactly the right moment. "Six, five, four, three, two, one. Go!"

Wind Dancer leaped forward and hit his stride as they breezed through their mounted shooting act. Wrapping the reins around the saddle horn, she drew her revolvers and nailed the targets as they galloped by. Then, coming around the far side of the arena, she swung down to the side and shot from under the pinto's neck, setting a line of bells ringing. Horse and rider slid to a stop in the center of the ring, and slipping her pistols back into her holsters, she waved to the crowd, turned, and did the same again.

As the horse kept his hindquarters in one spot and spun around with his front legs, she pulled the rifle from the scabbard at her left knee and downed each of the clay pigeons that shot into the air, then nudged Wind Dancer into a lope and blew the heads off three puppets as they popped up from behind a wooden wall. Had her equine partner been off even a whisker, she'd have failed. Cassie hated failure worse than anything, fighting anger if she missed a shot and spending hours practicing so it wouldn't happen again.

Cassie absolutely forbade any trickery in her act. No one was ringing the bells if she missed or breaking the glass balls if her shots were off. She had a reputation to uphold, much like her hero, Annie Oakley. Cassie started trick riding at the age of six on the back of her pony with her trick-riding father and mother as her coaches. The three of them had been billed as the Dashing Lockwoods after they introduced her into their act when she was seven. She'd been the darling of the Wild West Show ever since.

Growing up in a world-renowned show gave Cassie a different kind of education than most young people received. Her father insisted she learn reading and arithmetic, but touring the great shrines of Europe also gave her an up-close view of history, art, and geography.

Wind Dancer again slid to a stop in the center of the arena, and both of them bowed after she dismounted. She gave him a pat on the rump and waved him toward the exit, through which he galloped, applause following him. Cassie continued her act by shooting an apple off her dog's head and the ashes off a cigarette smoked by her current assistant, Joe Bingham. After reloading her six-shooters, she split plates and performed a variety of other shooting feats before the black-and-white pinto tore back into the arena. She caught the saddle horn to swing aboard and executed several more riding tricks while galloping around the arena, waving her hat before once again bowing in the center. This time as her horse raced toward the exit gate, she stayed mounted and rode out to thunderous applause.

"And that, ladies and gentlemen, is our final act for today," Jason Talbot shouted over the cheers.

Three chuck wagons suddenly burst into the arena.

"Pardon me, folks, but those cowboys insist on a chuck-wagon race, so hang on to your hats."

Cassie barely heard Uncle Jason's voice, but she well knew what he was saying. She dismounted by her tent and let Wind Dancer rub his forehead against her shoulder, all the while telling him what a good horse he was and inhaling deep breaths to calm herself.

"Great, as always." Joe Bingham slapped his wide-brimmed felt hat against his thigh. "Working with you has made me a real believer in not smoking."

"I saw you flinch. Not much but enough for me to notice."

"Just can't get used to a bullet flying that close to my nose. The urge to duck and run . . . it's all I can do to stand there."

"At least no one else would know that." After unbuckling the chest collar, she uncinched her saddle and pulled it from the horse's back. Joe took it and carried it into her tent to place it on the stand built especially for it. Cassie removed the silver-studded bridle and buckled a halter in place instead. Brushing Wind Dancer helped her relax after the high tension of her act.

Her father had always told her to take care of her own horse and equipment, to not give the job to someone whose life did not depend on top performance from everything associated with her act. Micah had stepped in to help her, as her backup. It never hurt to have a second pair of eyes and hands to make sure nothing was forgotten.

She'd never gone a day without thinking about her father, and after her act even more so. They used to replay their acts in their minds to see if there was any place that needed tightening or if there was something new that could be added. While she enjoyed the competition of shooting matches in both the States and in Europe, this kind of show took another type of preparation and practice. When she was shooting in a match, it was just her and her guns—and her competitors, of course. But a successful show involved all the other performers and support personnel around her.

"Father, if you could give me an inkling of what I'm sensing, I'd sure appreciate it." She wasn't sure if she was speaking to her dead pa or to her living heavenly Father, whom she'd met early on at her mother's knee.

"You going to the meeting?" Joe asked.

"What meeting?"

"In the food tent. A sign was posted at breakfast."

"What's the meeting for?"

"I have no idea. Didn't you read the sign?"

"Didn't notice it. Who called the meeting?"

"Jason, I'm sure. Who else would?"

The little worm of concern popped up its head again. "Receipts were good, weren't they?"

"A crowd like we had today should help make up for the last couple of shows." People hadn't come out as much in the rain like they had in Bismarck the week before. They should have put up the big tents, but the days had started out sunny. Performing in the open arenas made the show seem more realistic.

Why did the idea of a meeting bother her? Perhaps because so often Uncle Jason used a meeting as a place to announce bad news.

Prescient, her mother had often called her. On days like today, prescience was not a comfortable trait to have.

"You need some help, or should I go check on the others?"

She knew Joe had a sweet spot for April, one of the women who played a white settler during a staged Indian attack as well as a pioneer woman on the Oregon Trail. Joe played the part of the wagon master on the trail and was a Union soldier in the attack by Indians. Most of the actors played various parts. The more they played, the better their chances of staying on for more than one season. Headliners like Cassie were paid better wages for a week than most men could earn in a couple of months. Cassie happily gave Jason most of her earnings so that he could reinvest them in the show. He always promised her that when she needed her money, it would be there for her.

"You go on. I'm going to clean my guns before supper." She didn't add "and the meeting," but it hung there between them. Joe was concerned too, but he tried not to show it.

"Okay."

She watched him walk away, the slight limp he'd earned from being stomped on by a bucking bronco more obvious when he was tired or upset. As they'd added more rodeo-type events to the program, more of the men were bearing the scars of flying falls. Calf roping and steer dogging weren't quite as dangerous.

After Micah had taken Wind Dancer back to the rope strung between several trees where the horses were tied and fed, she brought out her cleaning supplies and, using the top of her trunk for a table, set to cleaning her guns, starting with the pistols and finishing with the twenty-gauge shotgun. Her favorite was her Marlin lever-action rifle, with the etching of a valley on the silver-plated receiver on the stock. Her father's valley of dreams had become her own. Someday she would find that valley and make his dream of breeding horses, particularly the Indian Appaloosas, and raising cattle come true.

Someday they would have a home.

When the gunpowder and lead residue were cleaned out and her guns lubricated, she wrapped them in soft cotton and laid them in the leather satchels, ready for the next performance. The ringing of the supper bell brought Othello to his feet. He stretched and glanced over his shoulder to make sure she got the point.

"I'm coming." She set the satchels inside the tent and, after making sure nothing was out of place, set off for the dull gray mess tent that once had been white. As she walked, she glanced at the painted wagon her father and mother used to live in. Uncle Jason had appropriated it after the funeral, sending Cassie to live with an aging pair of performers, Mac and Miz Mac. The gilt was in need of polishing, and the paint could use some freshening up, but everyone still called it the Gypsy Wagon, as her father had christened it many years ago. The name, Lockwood and Talbot Wild West Show, arching over a charging buffalo, still stood for quality and fair treatment for all members of the organization.

Lately, however, she'd heard some grumblings, especially from the show Indians, most of whom were hired on a seasonal basis. A few had become permanent members, like Chief, who drove the Gypsy Wagon in the opening parade.

Why did these thoughts keep plaguing her? "Come on, Othello, let's get our food and go eat." She broke into a dog trot and laughed when he gamboled beside her. "We need to go hunting one of these days. You think Micah would like to go along?"

"Go along where?" Joe asked, falling into a jog beside her.

"Hunting. Othello said he wanted to go hunting. For birds, of course." Cassie had never shot anything larger and had no intention of ever doing so.

Joe rolled his eyes and shook his head. "How come no one understands that dog but you?"

"Friends are like that," she said, slowing to a walk. "He doesn't flinch when I shoot the apple off his head."

"I told you—"

She raised a hand to stop him. "I was just teasing."

"Oh." Joe glanced down to see Othello staring up at him. "I didn't yell at her, so don't go glarin' at me." He muttered more under his breath but stopped when Othello bumped his leg with a sturdy nose.

"You know his hearing is far stronger than ours."

"And his nose and—"

"What set you off?" A grin broke across her face. "April didn't want any help—is that it?"

He stepped back and motioned for her to enter the tent before him.

She tossed a grin over her shoulder. "Sorry."

"You are not." He stepped back again when Othello paused and his tail stopped wagging. "All right."

After the last person was served and before the early diners got up to leave, Jason Talbot stood up from the table off to the north corner that had become his. "Folks," he called. When the din continued, he raised his voice and clapped his hands. "I have an announcement to make." He paused and waited. Slowly the troupe quieted and stared at him, waiting.

"Much to my sorrow, I have to tell you that this has been the final performance of the Lockwood and Talbot Wild West Show. Pick up your pay envelopes. We are just not making enough money to cover expenses, and there is nothing else I can do but close the doors."

Cassie stared at him, her stomach wrapping around itself. Surely this couldn't be.

Not like this.

3

Why didn't he tell me how bad things were?
    "You think he means it, Cassie?" Joe poked her elbow to get her attention. She nodded as she turned. "Did you know anything? No, from the look on your face, I guess this is as big a shock to you." He thumped his fist on the table. "I knew we'd have a winter break, but this . . ." Tipping his head back, he exhaled, the sound effectively describing his feelings.

Cassie looked over to Micah, knowing she might have to explain this to him. Where would he get another job? Half his life had been spent here. *And all of your life.*

The little voice inside made her want to scream. What about all the money her father had invested in the show? What about all of her wages that she'd returned to Jason to invest in the show? Was that all gone too?

Feeling as if she were slogging through watery mud, she pushed herself to her feet. The only way to find any answers was to confront Uncle Jason. Most of the troupe and the back-lot hands were lining up at a table set up at the opening to the outside, where darkness was creeping around the tents. Leaving Joe, who was heading for the tail end of the line, she made her way outside and strode over to the Gypsy Wagon.

Right now, instead of calling Jason by his familial title, she wanted to scream at him. That would shock him for sure. He still thought she was the biddable little girl who doted on her uncle Jason. Somewhere along the way in the last couple of years, she'd left that child behind and was developing a reputation for a strong will.

Othello sat as she stopped at the bottom of the three steps leading up to the door and took a deep breath. "Uncle Jason." She could hear someone moving around in there, so unless it was someone else . . . She raised her voice. "Uncle Jason."

"Come back later, darlin'. I have things to do."

"No. We need to talk right now." She started up the steps and nodded when he opened the door and motioned her to come in. The first thing she saw was two carpetbags on the lower bunk, pieces of clothing trailing out. "What are you doing?"

"Gettin' ready to move on, just like the rest of you."

"So soon? I mean what about all the animals and the tents and all the gear?"

"There's a man comin' for it all. I suggest you take your horse and whatever else you need and hit the road yourself." He stuffed more shirts into one of the bags.

"But what about the money my father invested in this show?"

"Gone. All gone. Too much competition, too many

expenses, just couldn't keep ahead of it all. Then when I borrowed more money, the creditors demanded it be paid back right away."

"And my money? All my pay that you said was safely invested back in the show?"

"Same. I'm sorry, darlin'."

She noticed an open bottle of whiskey sitting on the table. He made a move for it but then stopped. She'd wondered at times if he had a drinking problem but had turned a blind eye, since there was nothing she could do about it.

"So you are just leaving it all?"

"That's the plan, missy." He stopped his feverish packing. "I got something to tell you that I been puttin' off these last couple of years. Good thing you came by."

She nodded encouragement. Who was this man, and where had her genial uncle Jason gone?

He pulled a lockbox out from under the bed and flipped it open. After rummaging through some papers, he pulled out an envelope. "This is it."

"What?"

"The deed to the show. When your father was dying, he had this will drawn up. When you reached the age of adulthood, you were to take over his half of the show."

"Age of adulthood, meaning what?"

"Oh, eighteen, nineteen, I forget. You'll find it in there." He handed her the envelope. "I'd make sure that bank man doesn't see that, or he'll expect you to pay half the bills too."

Then what good is this to me? "Unc—" Never again would she use that word in regard to this man. "Jason Talbot, you mean I've owned half this company for possibly the last two years and you never told me? That's thievery."

29

"Ah, honey, I was tryin' to get it back to its former glory, and then I was going to tell you. You've had a good life here. I saved you a whole lot of heartache. Worrying about payroll, booking enough shows—ever since your pa died, it's been too much, too hard." He ignored her and grabbed the bottle from the table. "Sometimes I fear that he was the brains behind this. All those glory years." He stopped and took a drink. "Now, you listen real close here. You know the company owns everything, including . . ." He shook his head and, taking a handkerchief from his back pocket, blew his nose.

His pause gave her time to think. "Wind Dancer?"

"No. Your pa bought him for you, but if you want that horse, you better get him out of here. Take this wagon, the team, and git." He took another swig. "Go find that valley your pa always went on about. Somewhere down in the Black Hills. I hear there's a road of sorts that the stagecoaches and the dray wagons use. You follow that and go find his valley." He pulled a roll of bills out of his pocket. "You take this too. Help you get started."

She took it, shaking her head. "But surely all this show is worth more than the money you owe."

"It would be if they would give me more time. But banks are like that. Happy to loan you money, but things get tight and no matter what, they want their blood share." He snapped the lockbox closed and tossed it on the bed. "You go get Micah and have him bring around the team. I think Chief would be glad to go with you. His reservation, Pine Ridge, is somewhere down there. He's always talked about going back home 'to die,' but he's got some more good years in those bones of his."

"Wouldn't I be stealing?"

"The wagon was your pa's too. Got a bill of sale here somewhere."

"But you said they own it all."

"Forget what I said. Just do as I say. They'll get plenty out of it all—call it my half. What they can't find can't be accounted for. You watch, most everyone will be gone in the morning, and I ain't gonna be here to supervise who takes what. That's just the lay of the land." He stuffed some books and papers into the last bag and snapped both closed. "You go tell Chief I want to see him. He can take George and the Longhorns. Micah needs a horse, and he can harness up the wagon team. You get a move on, and you can be in the Black Hills before winter sets in."

"Would you have just gone off and not come to say good-bye?"

"Why, a'course not. I'd never do that to you." His whiskey breath made her cringe as he put his arms around her and pulled her to his chest. "You just do what your uncle Jason said, and all will be well."

Her mother's words coming from his mouth made her tighten her jaw. She half hugged him back. "What will you do?"

"I don't know, darlin'. I just don't know. But something will come along. It always does." He paused and then forced a smile. "Do this for your pa. It'd mean a lot to him."

Cassie nodded and left before she burst into tears. Was what he had told her to do legal? According to the will, she did own half of everything, which at this moment really was half of nothing. But she couldn't sacrifice Wind Dancer, and who would hire Micah?

With a heavy heart she paused on the steps, setting a plan to follow Jason's instructions. "Othello, find Chief." Othello sniffed the air and then trotted toward the Indian encampment, Cassie following. He stopped in front of a tepee and yipped. Chief bent over to come out and stood in front of her. "Jason wants to see you in the Gypsy Wagon."

Chief thought only a moment before nodding and striding off, with her at his side.

"He wants me to take the wagon and head down to the Black Hills to my father's valley. He said you'd talked about returning to your reservation." She left off the *to die* part.

He paused in front of her tent. "I would go with you."

"You think Micah will go too?"

"Micah will always go where you go."

"I hoped so."

"I will return here after I talk with Jason."

Cassie headed to her tent. What did she really need to take with her? What would fit in the wagon? Was she crazy to be doing this? But what were her choices? She didn't have enough money to go to a hotel and wait to contact some other shows to see if they would hire her. This show had been her home, her family, her life. She sank down into the folding chair and covered her face with her hands. How could she ever make it on her own? Othello nudged her hands and licked her cheek. When she didn't respond, he put a paw up on her knee and whimpered.

"It's okay, fella, just a moment of stark, terrified weakness here. Like Mor always said, *'All will be well.'*" She heaved a sigh at the same moment as someone cleared his throat at the tent door.

"Come in."

"Okay, we are set." Chief nodded to Micah, who had joined him. "We need to be on the road before daybreak, so we need to get moving."

Within minutes the two men were going about their chores. There was a party going on in the dining tent. Several of the other tents were all dark. Had some of the others left already?

She packed up her personal things, filling the trunk, making sure that all her costumes and clothing were packed in the wardrobe. There was no room in the wagon for it, but they could load it up on top. Some things she rolled into her bedroll before heading for the wagon. Jason had left a light on for her, leaving the wagon looking like he'd just stepped out and would return momentarily. She took off his bedding and spread out her own, tucking the sheets under the plush mattress and thick feather bed. Jason Talbot had liked the better things in life. How much had that desire caused the demise of the show? She ordered herself not to think along those lines and headed back to her tent, Othello at her side. She grabbed the handle on the side of the trunk and leaned into the weight to drag it back.

"Can't you ever ask for help?" Joe asked, grabbing the other handle between mutterings.

"I didn't know there was anyone around to help me."

"Well, we haven't all left. What are you going to do?"

"Head south to the Black Hills and see if I can find the valley my father always dreamed of."

"Do you have a map?"

"Sort of. He drew it years ago."

Joe stopped in his tracks. "Does it have a name?"

The sudden weight jerked her backward. "I don't know."

"Let me get this straight. You are going off all by yourself

33

to find a valley that your father discovered maybe twenty years ago and you don't even know exactly where it is?"

"That's right, except for the fact that Micah and Chief are coming with me."

"I see. That makes it even better. You and two men—"

"Joseph A. Bingham, get your mind out of the mud. You know as well as I do that those two would take on the entire Sioux nation to protect me." She started to drag the trunk again. He grabbed the other side, and when they got to the wagon, he grabbed both handles and heaved the trunk up the steps. "Where do you want this?"

"Under the table." He put it away and she extended her hand. "Thanks, Joe. I hope you find a good place to work."

"Whatever I find, I most likely won't have to stand still for a cigarette to be shot off under my nose." He looked into her eyes. "Take care of yourself, princess. Maybe someday we'll meet again."

Cassie swallowed hard. "Thank you. I hope so." After Joe clattered down the three stairs, she inspected the cupboards. Pretty bare. Jason had eaten in the mess tent like all the rest of them had. She snatched a couple of burlap sacks off a hook on the wall and headed for the kitchen. He had said to take what she needed, and they would definitely need at least the staples. But since she'd never cooked a meal in her life, she wasn't too sure what to take.

While the party was still going on in the dining tent, the kitchen lay dark and still. When her eyes adjusted, she could make out shelves and bins but could only determine their content by feel. Beans, flour, sugar, perhaps rice. She felt around and finally found a scoop to use to fill her sacks, but how to tie them off so the contents wouldn't spill? If only she dared light a lamp.

"Miss Cassie." The low voice definitely belonged to Micah.

"Yes. I'm trying to get us some supplies."

"I'll get bags of flour, sugar, and beans from the storage. Can you find bacon or ham? Cook kept them in the icebox on that far wall. Better be quick. Those partying are getting restless for more to drink. They'll search here first."

"Drink. Hadn't they better be footin' it out of here instead?"

"Drink does bad things to a man's mind."

"I know. What else should we get?"

"Coffee, rice, eggs—if there are any. Tomorrow is when Cook buys supplies."

"How do you know all this?"

"I help in here when they need me."

"Oh." There were so many things she didn't know. Surely she'd been living a protected life. Just taking care of her supplies for her act and herself. From the looks of it, that was already changing. "Thanks, Micah. You find whatever you think we need."

"Are there cooking utensils in the wagon?"

Cassie thought for a moment. "There used to be, but I didn't look in all the cabinets."

He thrust a frying pan and a cast-iron Dutch oven into her hands and then added a coffeepot. "The plates, cups, and utensils are over there." She went to the shelf and took the essentials. So instead of food in her bags, she returned to the wagon with household gear.

Chief grunted when he saw her. "Micah?"

"Raiding the cook tent."

The old Indian strode off in the direction of off-key singing and shrill laughing. The party was definitely deteriorating.

Cassie thrust her booty into the lower cabinets of the wagon and checked each of the doors and drawers to see what else they needed. Candles and matches in one drawer sent her on a search for kerosene for lamps. A half-full can hung on a hook under the wagon, along with a couple of pails and a water barrel.

When Micah carried supplies up the stairs, she asked, "What about grain for the horses?"

"They'll have to make do with grass. This bucket has eggs. I used kitchen towels to cushion them. Meat's in the other sack."

"I'll stow the supplies. You and Chief get whatever else you think we need."

"Do you have ammunition? Knives?"

"Not much. Un—" She stopped herself. "Jason always brought the ammunition to me. I don't know where he kept it."

"Chief knows everything. Ask him when he returns." With that, Micah faded into the darkness.

Why were the cooks not on duty? Had they left with their pay in hand like the others? She heard glass breaking and wild laughter. Without more contemplation, she buckled her holster belt in place and dug two revolvers out of the bag she kept them in. She already had bullets on the gun belt, but she stuffed a couple more into her shirt pocket.

She'd just finished finding places for the supplies when she heard a gunshot. Without a thought she slammed the door shut and leaped down the steps. The crash of things breaking came from the dining tent, where the laughter had turned to shouting. Two men slugging it out stumbled from the tent opening.

"Hey, how 'bout the pet here?"

She headed for the voice and saw two men holding Micah by the arms while a third slugged him in the belly. Stepping into the tent, she drew both guns and cocked the hammer. "That's about enough, boys."

The slugger threw another punch, and she shot a round into the dirt beside his right foot.

"Hey, watch what yer doin'." He swung around, fists raised, and then his face blanched. "Come on, princess, we don't mean nothing by this."

"Then leave right now before someone really gets hurt."

He narrowed his eyes and took a step forward. "You don't shoot people. You just aim for targets." His hat flew up as the revolver cracked.

"One more step and the next shot will be in your foot. Hard to find work with a shot-up foot."

He stared at her, trying to judge if she was bluffing.

"Come on, man, let's get out of here." The two holding Micah's arms faded away, and the third man decided retreat was a better idea than pushing Cassie again.

"We was just havin' a bit of fun."

"Take your fun down the road. Next time it won't be just your hat."

Micah tried to take a deep breath and bent over coughing. "S-sorry."

"Let's get our things and head out. Can you walk?"

"Yeah." He turned around and grabbed two sacks that had fallen to the ground. With a grunt of pain, he stumbled toward the outside of the tent.

Feeling a touch foolish, she kept her guns drawn and followed him, wishing she had eyes in the back of her head. What if the *players* were waiting just beyond the edge of the light?

No matter whether they had all they needed, they were leaving now, not waiting for first light as she'd intended. Why had she not planned for such a contingency as this? Why would she even think she needed to plan for things like this? Nothing was in any plan or dream of hers since Jason announced the end of the Lockwood and Talbot Wild West Show.

4

"hank you."

"You are welcome, Micah. Sorry I didn't think ahead and prepare for such as those three." She inclined her head toward the drunken men now skedaddling down the road.

"You can't—" he coughed again and gasped for a breath— "th-think of everything." Micah set the bags down beside the wagon steps. "Where you want these?"

Cassie touched his shoulder. "Are you seriously hurt?"

He shook his head. "Bruised and the breath knocked out. Thought they was friends."

"Liquor does strange things to people." She started to reach for one of the sacks, and he gently pushed her to the side.

"I'll do it. Put them where?"

"Under the bunk. Wish we could put the food in barrels, but there's no room for that." She climbed the steps and entered, at the same time watching carefully for intruders. If someone thought she had money, he might be waiting for her. But the wagon was clear, so she beckoned Micah in and breathed a sigh of relief at the same time. Good thing Othello was on watch or she'd have missed the supposed *fun*. And Micah might be dead or at the very least severely injured.

She was now responsible for not only herself but two other people. And a small herd of animals. She who had never had responsibilities beyond her own act in the show. The thought hit like a punch in the solar plexus.

Othello rumbled a deep growl and then whined when he heard Chief's gentle voice. Cassie's heart settled back from leaping into her throat. She heard a knock at the door and Chief's whisper of introduction.

"Come in."

Chief, wearing his standard black felt hat and vest, fur side out, over a faded red shirt, paused in the doorway, took one look at Micah, and closed the door behind himself. "Visitors?"

"Yes, you might say."

Chief glanced at her. "Your guns?"

She nodded. "I didn't like their games. If you could call three against one a game."

"I see." A glint of a smile lit his dark eyes. "We go tonight?"

"I think we're going to have to. Don't you agree?"

The chief nodded.

She stood with her hands on her hips, surveying the wagon. "More supplies?"

She shook her head. "We'll make do with what we have. Can you think of anything else?"

Chief emptied his pockets onto the bed where the bullets bounced on the quilt. He set a box of shotgun shells beside the booty. "No time to find more."

"I have some, so we should be okay." After all, what did they need bullets for? This was no longer the days of the Wild West, when a man's gun was the law. She'd heard tales of the early days from listening to her father swap tales with other performers, mostly the men.

Both men stared at her, shook their heads, and settled their hats more tightly on their heads.

Cassie thought a moment before turning and pulling one of her rifles from the show pack. "Take this with you, in case we need it."

Chief took the proffered gun and checked the magazine. "Full."

She nodded. "I'm sure you know how to use it."

The look he gave her questioned her intelligence.

"Just checking. Micah, have you ever shot a firearm?"

He shook his head.

"We'll rectify that down the road."

"I get livestock ready," the chief said. He hurried down the steps, Micah behind him.

Cassie glanced around the wagon and blew out the lamp. Surprised at herself, she locked the door behind her and tucked the key into a pocket of her leather jacket. The roll of bills Jason had tossed her gave her a cushion of comfort. At least they had something to start out with.

When the livestock were ready, she swung aboard Wind Dancer and followed Micah to the corral where Chief had sequestered the stock they were taking. Her old friend, George, snorted when Micah slid open the bars on the gate, but he trotted out the opening, followed by the rest of the herd. With the Gypsy Wagon in the lead, the entourage slipped as silently as possible out of the lot. One of the cattle bellowed, and another from the remainder of the herd answered, but none tried to turn back.

Cassie swung her open loop and kept her focus on the small herd as they made their way down the road heading south from the sleeping town. Only a sliver of a moon hung in the western sky, but the starlight grew brighter as they left the buildings behind. They crossed the train tracks, the wheels clattering a mighty racket.

She hung back, watching to see if anyone showed up to question their exit. A dog barked but Othello never answered, trotting along just ahead and to the side of Wind Dancer's prancing feet. The thudding of cattle and horse hooves and the creak of the wagon all sounded loud in the stillness.

They kept at a steady pace hour after hour until she realized the sky was indeed lightening and a widening band of pale yellow cracked the eastern horizon. She trotted up to the wagon and rode beside Chief. "We better stop and water them, wouldn't you say?"

"I'll find us a place with water and grass, and we'll let them rest."

"All right."

"Tell Micah to trade places with me."

Cassie nodded and reined her mount away from the wagon. She dropped back and gave Micah the message.

Hills and rocks came into view as the daylight woke the birds and set the crows to announcing their passage. They passed a road that turned off to the right. *Bar S Ranch* was carved into the top half log of a three-log sign. As the dust from the hooves floated westward through the gate, she wondered how many ranches they'd passed in the dark. The ranch road curved between two hills, leaving her pondering who lived there and how far they were from town now. About an hour later, with the sun climbing well above the horizon, Chief returned from his place in the lead.

"Good place to stop a mile or so ahead."

"Good." While she'd not mentioned it, her legs, so used to quick rides and flashy moves, were grumbling at this new protracted riding. While she was not sure what time they'd left the show grounds, her body was telling her she'd been in the saddle far longer than it was used to.

With daylight, she counted the herd. Three buffalo, eight head of cattle, and two horses, besides the team pulling the wagon and the two they were riding. Fairly sure she'd not requested more horses, she figured Chief had a reason for bringing them. If only she had her father's stallion, Lobos, but he'd been put down sometime before her father died.

Cassie shifted in the saddle. Discomfort was quickly escalating to actual pain.

"Up ahead and to the right. There's a gully to shield us from the road."

She followed Chief's instructions and brought up the rear. Her lack of endurance was quickly becoming evident when she tried to dismount and could barely swing her leg over the saddle. When her feet hit the dirt, she crumpled, her dignity saved by hanging on to the stirrup leathers.

Micah came up behind her and, putting an arm around her waist, helped her over to sit on a rock.

"Thank you." She let out a puff. "I've never had that happen before."

"You never rode this long."

Chief sat on his horse, watching the cattle and buffalo

drink from the stream and then set to serious grazing. "I watch. You rest."

"But . . ." Sometimes taking advice was the better part of wisdom. This time when she tried to stand, her feet came back to life and carried her over to the wagon and even climbed the steps. She collapsed on the lower bunk bed, with only her hat coming to a rest on the table.

A knock on the door brought her out of a dead slumber. She stared at the wall across the narrow room where the horizontal door had been raised to let in fresh air. Not knowing where she was for a moment set her heart to racing, but with a deep breath, all the events of the night before came roaring back to her awareness. Her stomach grumbling sounded louder than the creek outside. What day was it? Had she slept through the day as well as the night? Throwing back the blanket, she tried to remember if she had covered herself, but nothing came to mind.

She sat up, careful to keep from banging her head on the upper bunk. Bare feet. Either Micah or Chief had taken her boots off and covered her. Her hips and knees groaned when she stood up. Her mouth felt like George the Buffalo had tromped through. When she opened the door, the dew sparkling on grass and rocks told her the light meant morning, not evening. No wonder her stomach was complaining. She'd slept the clock around.

Clamping her hat on her head, she sat down on the steps to pull on and lace up her boots. She knew exactly where her other boots were, her practical ones rather than these designed to go with her riding and shooting costume, but right now she didn't have time to dig them out. Chief had meant for this to be a brief stop, not a twenty-four-hour one.

The fragrance of coffee and bacon made her stomach rumble again. Following her nose, she found a campfire on the other side of a couple of boulders with Chief turning bacon in a skillet and the coffeepot steaming on one of the rocks set in a circle to hem the fire in.

"You feel better?" he asked.

"Thank you, I do. I thought we were moving on last night."

"Temperature is dropping."

"I can tell. Where's Micah?"

"Out with the stock. Eat and we saddle up." He handed her a plate of bacon, two eggs, and a piece of toast. "Coffee's ready."

"Where did we get eggs?"

"Mess tent."

Cassie remembered the basket of eggs Micah had brought out. But she had a feeling Chief had managed to pack more things than she realized. At that point, she wasn't prepared to argue, settling herself on a rock to inhale the plate's contents. He handed her a cup of steaming coffee before fixing his own plate.

"Good day for travel."

She nodded, her mouth too full to answer.

Micah strode around a rock. "Othello has them bedding down. I could smell the coffee on the way in." He picked up the third tin plate, dished bacon and eggs out of the frying pan, and leaned against a taller rock to eat.

"Thanks to whoever tucked me in." Cassie looked from one to the other. Micah stared at his plate, a flush of red climbing his neck.

"I'll get the team harnessed while you clean up." Chief nodded to her. "Make sure the fire is out."

For a moment Cassie wondered who was in charge here but kept from responding. The one with the most experience needed to be in charge—at least for the moment. "Yes, sir."

Micah snorted and then coughed as food lodged in his throat. He bent over, but Cassie wasn't sure if he was laughing or choking, especially when he straightened and wiped his mouth with the back of his hand. Mischief danced in his eyes.

"I'm glad someone can see the humor in this situation." She stood, stretched, and then looked around for a pot of hot water to wash the dishes. Bacon grease in the frying pan—what to do with that? She set her plate and fork down on a rock and stared around. A wooden box sat off to the side. Checking that, she found kettles, the basket of eggs, and other supplies. Surely she shouldn't put dirty dishes in with the clean. Did they have any soap for washing?

"Ah . . ."

Micah brought his plate and utensils to the fire. "I'll saddle the horses."

She nodded, studying the contents of the box.

"You wash things in the creek, scrub with sand," Chief said as he walked up behind her.

She tried to smile. "I do?"

"Pour the grease into a mug or jar if there is one."

"How do you know this stuff?"

"I grew up traveling, and I pay attention."

She did as he suggested, scouring the grease off the plates and frying pan with sand and small rocks from the creek, flinching at the grease on her fingers. Setting the frying pan filled with tin plates on a rock to dry, she hauled water in the cast-iron kettle to drown the fire. The steam made her step back, realizing she needed to make several trips. She should have grabbed one of the pails hanging under the wagon. The smoke and steam made her eyes run, her nose chasing the former.

How to feel dumber than stupid in the space of minutes. They should have brought some soap along. Perhaps she had some in her toiletry bag, at least for a bath—if she ever got to a place that had a bathtub again. Scrubbing dishes and pans with sand. Had her mother ever been forced into such primitive behavior? Did it matter? Why did he tell her to save the bacon grease?

It took another trip with water splashing out of the kettle and onto her pant legs before the coals and black pieces of wood lay in a soggy puddle. One thing accomplished. She pushed a lock of loosened hair back behind her ear and glared at the wooden box. It wouldn't pack itself, that was for sure. The box wouldn't close after she'd packed the utensils in, so she pulled them all out and tried again. Surely it didn't take a genius to pack the box. The kettle waited beside the fire rocks.

"Well . . ." She thought of several of the words she'd heard spoken around the back lot of the Wild West Show but refrained from using them, as her mother had convinced her, via a mouth full of soap, that ladies did not use such language. But then her mother had most likely not been caught without such basic survival necessities either. Not that a member of the royal house of Norway had been wilderness camping. At least not without an entourage. Her mother had left that life to become Mrs. Adam Lockwood. The thought of her mother brought on an ache for the father she had adored and depended on so fully after her beautiful mother had died. She tried to blink back the tears but, failing in that, rubbed her shirtsleeve across her face. It must have been the smoke from the fire.

She repacked the box, including the frying pan, and succeeded this time. She dragged it back to the wagon. Once inside, she straightened her bed and dug out her comb and brush. Upon hearing the jangles of the harnessed team, she stuffed them back into the drawer, flipped her braid over her shoulder, and clapped her hat back on. So much for her feminine toilette. Glancing around to make sure everything was in its place, she stepped outside again and closed the door tightly behind her. After locking the hinged steps up and into place, she lowered the long hatch on the side of the wagon and slid the hasps in place for locks.

Wind Dancer, fully saddled, studied her from where he was tied to the front wagon wheel.

"I know. I'm coming." But when she tried to put her foot in the stirrup, the ride of yesterday nicked her knee.

"Stretching is a good idea."

She looked up to see Micah smiling down at her from the back of his horse. "Thanks."

"You want some help?"

"No, I do not want help." She concealed a yelp with the curt words. *Cassandra Marie Lockwood, behave yourself. It's not his fault you aged forty years in one night and a day.* She bent over into a stretch, easing down until her legs screamed at her. But by the time she'd done that three times, she could tell it was helping. She stretched every day before her performances—why should today be any different? When she returned to Wind Dancer's side, she stuck two fingers between cinch and horse to make sure he'd not blown up his belly when saddled and swung aboard, this time with only a minor flinch.

She looked up from checking her scabbard to find both men watching her. "I'm sorry, gentlemen, am I detaining you?" She too heard the caustic tone to what had been a simple question. Of course she was detaining them, but at least they had the wisdom not to laugh at her.

Chief hawked and spat over the wheel and pulled back on the reins to back the team and wagon. The horses snorted and shook their heads but did as he ordered. With enough space to turn around now, Chief flicked the reins and they started out. Within a couple of minutes they were back on the trail, or road, if one could call it that. She dropped back to help Micah with the stock, and they headed south.

Sometime later when a wind kicked up, dropping the temperature instead of warming it, she glanced back to see black clouds piling up behind them. The sun was fighting a valiant battle, but the clouds soon won, turning the blue sky gray.

The first snowflake on her face made her realize she'd been dozing in the saddle. Jerking awake, she saw Micah across the plodding herd, hunched over on his horse. Othello ranged ahead of her, the spring gone from his step. Nudging Wind Dancer, she trotted up even with the painted wagon. "Hadn't we better find a place to camp?"

Chief nodded. "Been watching."

"Isn't it early for snow?"

"Snow can come anytime in the Dakotas."

Cassie shivered at a fierce blast that seemed to slice right through her. If Jason Talbot had been riding with them, she would have given him more than a piece of her mind, that is, if she could break any off. "Cold clear through" now had a new meaning for her. She thanked God they had the wagon when they finally did stop. The snow swirled around them, dancing on the freezing wind.

5

*S*hrieking wind, driving snow, bitter cold.

Blizzard was no longer just a word in a diction-ary or a scene in a story to Cassie. In the past, the Wild West Show had always moved south to somewhere warm, both for wintering and for added shows. They would always leave before winter came to the northern Midwest.

As soon as the herd huddled together and bedded down in the lee of large boulders, Chief told Micah to unhitch the team while he went searching for firewood.

Cassie had no idea how he would find anything when she could barely see her hand in front of her face. When her fingers were too stiff with cold to undo the cinch, Micah told her to get in the wagon and let him take care of Wind Dancer. For a change Cassie didn't argue.

Chief managed to find a downed dried tree somewhere, so feeding the stove became her job. Cassie learned that chopping wood with a hatchet did a good job of keeping her warm. The knowledge that they had no idea how long the storm would last made her far more thrifty with the fire, especially after a reprimand from Chief over wasting wood by keeping the stove too hot. Hot enough to keep the pot of beans and chunks of bacon simmering but not bubbling was her new guide.

Micah stumbled up the steps and let Othello enter ahead of him. When inside, he put his shoulder against the wall to pull the door shut against the howling wind. The dog shook, snow flying in every direction. Cassie pointed Micah at the woodbox for a chair and grabbed a rag to help dry her dog.

"Where's Chief?"

"Checking the cattle. The buffalo are doing better than any of the others." He held his hands over the top of the stove, and then rubbed his arms. "Bad out there."

Cassie lifted the lid on the kettle and gave the beans a stir with the wooden spoon. Then it was back to chopping wood by the door, being careful to sweep up the chips and dump them into a basket. Chief had already taught her the value of dry fire starter. She would never look at a chunk of firewood the same again.

"How are the horses?"

"Tied so that the wagon shields them from the wind." Micah took off his hat and slapped it against his thigh to rid it of snow, then hung it on a peg on the wall. "Let me." He held his hand out for the hatchet handle. "I need to get warm too."

Cassie handed it over. "Keep the pieces short enough to fit in the stove." When he stared at her, she added, "Chief said that."

"Oh."

Why did she have a feeling that while she'd always

understood that Micah was often slow to respond because he was so painfully shy, in this situation he was far more competent than she? Since she was no longer working to keep warm, she moved closer to the stove. As small as this wagon was, it had to be mighty cold outside to be this cold inside. She knelt by Othello, who had curled up in the corner right behind the stove, and stroked his head and back. His tail thumped but he stayed curled tight.

"I don't suppose you had time to grow a winter coat, traveling in warmer weather like we've been doing."

"Least he can grow one." Micah stacked the wood he'd chopped in the box next to the stove, then swept up the chips for the basket. "When will the beans be done?"

She shrugged. How did one tell when the beans were done? Obviously they couldn't get up and talk. "Take a taste." She pointed to a drawer. "Spoons are in there."

Othello's ears went up and then his head when he heard Chief mutter something as he entered the house-wagon. The dog stuck his nose back under his tail and closed his eyes again.

"Beans done?" Chief asked.

"Some crunchy but taste good." Micah reached for a bowl off the shelf, dipped it into the bean kettle, and licked the drippings off the side. He caught the astonished look from Cassie and shrugged, his face pure guilt. "Sorry. Don't know where the scoop spoon is."

Chief did his half snort, half chuckle sound and then took a bowl and used the wooden spoon to scoop some beans into his bowl. "You want some?" He looked to Cassie.

"Not yet. I'll keep chopping while you two eat. The coffee-pot is hot too." She rose from beside her dog and jerked the hatchet out of the chopping block by the door. They certainly should have brought something better than this, but she grabbed the branch she'd been working on and started chopping again. At least she kept warm this way. Her stomach grumbled as she inhaled the fragrance coming from the cooking pot. The thought of crunchy beans did not sound appealing.

Right about now she wished they were on the train heading east. At least there would be a dining car and plenty of hot food. Potbellied stoves warmed every car that held humans and kept a coffeepot hot. And the Gypsy Wagon would have been inside a railroad car, protected from the elements.

If only Jason had been a better businessman.

She knew it came down to that. Her father had been the brains behind the outfit, while Jason did the announcing and glad-handing to gain new venues. How she knew that she wasn't sure, but most likely it came from listening to all the meetings around this table when she should have been asleep in her hammock. She paused her chopping as memories swirled through her mind. Her mother and father laughing together, her mother kissing her little girl good-night and sharing prayers—some in Norwegian, others in English—her parents discussing new additions to their act, plans for the future of the show, for their future as a family. The tales her father told about the valley he had found in the Black Hills of South Dakota.

Blinking back tears, Cassie returned to her chopping. Keeping busy was far better than sniveling over the past. After all, the past was gone and would not come again—except in her dreams. Now she had to think about the future. And making sure they all made it to that valley. Somewhere there

54

must still be a map showing the way to it. She remembered her father talking about Hill City, a town somewhere near Rapid City, South Dakota. Amazing what things came to her mind when she'd not realized they were part and parcel of her now, living in her head.

She stopped and stood up straight. "The wind has stopped."

Chief nodded and then poured himself a cup of thick coffee.

She glanced over to see Micah leaning against the wall, sound asleep. The night before, the men had slept outside under the wagon. Tonight that was impossible. "Chief, there used to be a couple of hammocks in that bag up on the top shelf. If you find one there, we can string it between those two hooks, and Micah can sleep there."

"I will use the floor by the stove." Chief reached for the bundle and sneezed at the dust that flew when he brought it down. He did indeed pull out a hammock and held it up. "Short."

"Try the other one." A pang thrust through her chest. That was her girl-sized hammock. Had Jason not thrown anything out of the wagon when he took it over? Sure enough, the second hammock was adult sized. Together they slipped the rings over the wall hooks.

Cassie walked over and shook Micah. "We have a bed for you. Do you have a quilt or some blankets?"

Micah stared up at her, as if unsure who she was or what she was asking.

"Quilt or blankets?"

He nodded slowly. "A box under the wagon bed."

"I'll get it." Without waiting Chief plunged back outside and returned with a blanket, a fur-lined elk hide, and something else furry. He thrust the blanket and a sort of blanket of fur-lined animal skins at Micah. "Roll in these."

"How do I get in that thing?" Micah stared at the canvas contraption hanging limply from the hooks in the opposite walls.

"It is a hammock. Sailors sleep in them all the time on ships. They use up less space. You sit on the edge and roll into it."

The hammock dumped Micah back onto his feet, and he staggered almost into the stove.

"The floor is fine."

"No, let me show you." Remembering how her father had taught her, she demonstrated, then got up and held the edge for him. Glancing over her shoulder, she caught a look from Chief that made her stifle a grin herself. Holding the hammock steady, she waited for Micah to try again. He wrapped his blanket around himself and sat on the edge, then leaned over until his body was in the hammock before pulling in his legs.

"What if I fall out?"

"You won't. Just get out again like you got in." She tucked the furry hides over him and went to sit on her built-in bed. Her stomach reminded her she'd not eaten yet.

"You eat while I check the animals." Chief slipped out the door.

She spooned bacon and beans into another bowl and sat down on her bed. Once again, it looked like the only things she'd be able to remove were her boots and jacket. And maybe even that was not a good idea. The warmth of the beans going down, even though some did still crunch a bit, felt comforting and stopped the gnawing sensation. She scraped the bowl clean and sat down to unlace her boots. Tomorrow

56

she would dig another pair out of her trunk. She climbed in bed and spread her coat over her feet. With both a blanket and a quilt, she should be warm enough.

She heard Chief come in and put wood in the stove before wrapping himself in his robe and lying down on the floor. Within seconds he was snoring softly.

Sleep took longer to claim Cassie. Her thoughts were spinning inside her head. Chief seemed to know the general direction they needed to go, and since he'd been with the show years longer than she, she let him lead. Something made her think he'd been a friend of her father's long before the show came into existence. But that was years ago, putting him at about a grandfather's age. How could he remember the way after all those years? Where might her father's map be? What if it had been thrown away? If only she could remember some landmarks her father had mentioned when he used to tell her stories about the valley of dreams.

Something else hovered on the edge of her mind. Something about three huge rocks at the end of the valley, like fingers pointing to heaven. When they saw these, they'd know it was the right valley.

The only thing she knew for sure was that she could, if need be, either join another show or send out word that she was looking for shooting matches to compete in. If only she knew who to contact. *If only. What if?* Two two-word sentences that led her nowhere but in circles. Her mother had always said God had a plan for her life, but if wandering around in a blizzard was part of it—

Stop it, she ordered herself. Why was it she could control her rifle shots but not her mind, at least not in the lonely hours of night when everyone else was fast asleep?

The clattering of stove lids pulled her from a deep chasm of writhing black monsters that clawed at her when she fought to escape. She lay still, not even opening her eyes. With the wind gone, the wagon held some heat from the stove so her nose was no longer icy cold.

A string of strong words assaulted her, accompanied by a thump and a thud as Micah disengaged himself from the hammock.

"You just need practice."

"You sleep in it."

"I will." She yawned and rolled onto her side so she could watch the red glow of the open stove as Chief shoved another chunk of wood in.

"Beans hot soon."

"For breakfast?"

"You cook mush?"

Somehow she'd awakened thinking of bacon and eggs again. "There's no milk."

"Brown sugar and butter are good."

"Oh. Beans it is, I guess." She sat up and swung her legs over the edge of the bed. "Where's Othello?"

"Out." At a scratch on the door accompanied by a whine, Chief cracked open the door. "In."

Othello sniffed her stocking-clad feet and plunked down beside her so she could scratch a place behind his floppy ear. The thump of his hind leg on the floor was the most normal sound she'd heard so far that morning.

"It is morning, isn't it?"

"Yes. Sun coming up."

"Will we be able to travel today?"

"I'll ride out and see how deep the drifts. Cattle need grazing."

"How, when there is deep snow?"

"Blizzard wind blows some patches clear. The buffalo will show the cattle how to dig down."

One of the horses snorted. It sounded like it was right behind her.

He gave the beans a good stir. "Eat first, then scout."

Cassie pulled her boots on, left them unlaced, and crossed to the table to pull out her trunk.

"What do you need?"

"My other boots. These take too long to lace."

Micah grabbed the leather handle on the side of the trunk and pulled it out, the metal on wood screeching in resentment. When the trunk cleared the table, Cassie flipped it open and dug down on the right side. Years earlier her father had taught her how to organize her equipment, so she always packed everything the same way. That made it easy to find something in a hurry. She pulled a pair of short boots out, repacking carefully as she put things back. Sitting on the bed, she shucked her fancy boots and pulled on the others. Unlike her heroine, Annie Oakley, Cassie had flouted convention and resorted to wearing pants instead of long skirts. She tucked her pants into the boots, only to hear Chief clicking at her.

"Now what?"

"Pants in boots means snow in boots."

"Oh." That made good sense. She pulled her pant legs over the boots and tucked her show boots into the lid of the trunk, where she had sewn straps to hold them in place.

While it was not as cold as the night before, one wouldn't call it warm, so she shrugged into her wool jacket too. No wonder Chief had a vest with the fur still on the leather. At first she'd thought it odd but no longer. It was helping keep him warm.

She was hungry enough that the not-quite-hot beans tasted good. And were filling. The men ate and left, leaving her to clean up. With no hot water and no creek, she set the bowls down for Othello to lick clean, then filled them with snow and set them on the stove for the snow to melt. That would sort of clean them. Taking a brush out of the drawer by the head of the bed, which she'd claimed for her own, she unbraided her hair, brushed the tangles out, and quickly braided it again. She used one of the bowls to dip out some warming water and then washed her face with a washcloth.

If they were going to leave, she needed to let the fire die down, but if they were going to stay . . . She stepped outside to inquire. The men were mounted and driving the herd out of their shelter. She unhooked Wind Dancer from the tie line, swung aboard bareback, and set him at a walk following their tracks. The sun had edged over the horizon, and the light shafting off the white drifts made her squint. Had she ever seen snow this pristine? She stopped her horse just to look around. It was iridescent, like millions of sparkling diamonds.

The buffalo had gathered in an open spot, and snow was flying up from beneath their digging hooves. Mounds of frosted white covered their backs, and the Longhorns looked small beside them. She'd read that buffalo hair was so dense that the snow didn't melt but acted more like insulation. These sure knew what to do. The cattle mingled with the buffalo and profited from the digging already done.

Wishing she had wrapped a scarf around her neck, she hunkered down into the collar of her coat and tightened her wide-brimmed felt hat down to shield her eyes. Was that smoke she saw off to the west? Perhaps a ranch house? Maybe they could stop there and—and what? Visit? Hope for an invitation to stay? How would they know where the road went with all this snow? She turned to look north. There were no black clouds bearing down on them, only a huge bowl of sky that changed hues as the sun rose higher.

She leaned forward and patted Wind Dancer's neck. The one good thing about riding bareback was that all parts of her in contact with her horse were warm. Othello came leaping through the snow to stand at her right foot and bark, once, twice, looking over his shoulder as if asking her to come play.

"I couldn't throw you a stick, you silly hound, even if I had one. All sticks are sacred to the stove." He barked again and went leaping off, snow flying as he did.

She rode forward into a patch of grass that had been pawed free of the snow. When Wind Dancer put his head down to graze, she let him, as if she had any control without a bridle and bit. Riding with only a halter probably wasn't the brightest idea this morning, even though she often rode him like this. But those rides had been around the show grounds or in a corral or field. Not on the open snow-covered range.

Chief rode up. "Snow is too deep. Won't leave today."

"That's what I thought."

"Need to bring out the other horses," he said.

"Me?"

"Yes. You know how to hunt?"

"I suppose I can shoot anything I can see, but I've never actually hunted, other than birds." And she didn't like the idea one bit. She wondered what kind of shot he was. In the scenes in the show, all the participants shot blanks and aimed over each other's heads or off to the side so that no one was injured. "The ammunition is in the wooden box." She hoped they had enough ammunition. She never dreamed that they would have to hunt for food. Back at the wagon she untied the rest of the horses and led them back to graze the places the buffalo and cattle had cleared. Amazing how they knew what to do, in spite of years of pulling hay out of a rack on the walls of the railroad cars or having hay tossed into the pens when they stayed in one place for more than a day or two.

Had the bank already claimed all the railroad cars, the tents, and all the other gear that made up the Wild West Show? Would they sell it off to another show? *If only . . .* There were those two little words again. How she wished she'd had the money to take over the show. But all her money was gone now. The thought burned her stomach. How long had Jason been lying to her, saying the show was fine, not to bother her pretty head about such man things? She clamped her teeth against the furious words that threatened to erupt. And to think she had a legal interest in the show and he'd never told her. Forgot about it! Of course! Was he truly a shyster or was he a man caught in something he had no control over?

He had control at one time and must have made some stupid decisions. If only . . . *If only* never got her anywhere but more bogged down in memories. And memories did not put food on the table or a roof over her head, two things she'd taken for granted for years. How could she have been so gullible?

Ignoring the other side of her that tried to make excuses for her lack, she listened to the horses grazing. Opening her eyes, she let her gaze rove over the white terrain. The silence of the snow-covered prairie was broken by a snort from one of the grazing animals.

Her mind returned to the problem at hand. Had Jason told her in advance, maybe she could have found some investors. *Maybe* had no more value than *what if*.

That life is over! She made herself repeat it out loud. "That life is over." The words got lost in the magnitude of a prairie morning after a blizzard. All she knew for certain was that they would soon be heading south again, to the Black Hills of South Dakota. Were they still in North Dakota or moving into South Dakota? Unlike roads in other parts of the country, she'd not seen any signs pointing the way. Not that she could see any road at all, only a white expanse, and the blue of the sky intensifying as the sun rose on its course. She closed her eyes again and lay back on Wind Dancer's rump, letting the sun soak into her from above and her horse's body heat her from below. A shot echoed across the land, like the crack of a branch. Had Chief found his prey, or were there others out hunting too?

6

The snow remained too deep for travel the next day, and they settled into a new routine of sorts. Late in the afternoon Chief came in from tending the livestock.

"We'll plan on leaving tomorrow if the melting continues."

Cassie nodded. If they had meat other than the bacon, she'd be more than happy. "Where's Micah?"

"Skinning the rabbits. You know how to fry rabbit?"

Cassie shrugged, figuring she could learn if someone would teach her. After all, she now knew how to cut up bacon to cook with the beans.

"You ever fried rabbit?"

"Chief, you know I've never cooked in my life. I always ate in the cook tent or with my parents. But my mother rarely cooked either." She kept her tone as emotionless as she could. No matter how testy his question made her feel, it wasn't his fault she couldn't cook a meal or even wash dishes. "But I learn fast, so tell me what to do."

"Heat iron skillet, add some bacon grease. Rabbits have little fat. Put flour in bowl and roll the meat in it. Put meat in hot pan."

"Where did the rabbits come from?"

"The snares I set. You learn to do that too. Indian squaws can—"

"So can white women, I am sure." She dug in the box and, after setting another pot aside, lifted out the black frying pan. She thought about Miz Mac, who had told tales of having her own home and the chores she took for granted. There had been no place to teach Cassie how to cook, but she had taught her how to wash and take care of her own clothes. Her own mother made sure her daughter knew how to do her personal toilet, even though she had been raised with a maid to help her. Her father taught her how to take care of her horse and guns.

"Put more wood in stove first."

Cassie nodded and did as he told her.

Micah let Othello in ahead of him and, after closing the door against the dropping cold, laid the carcass on the table.

Cassie stared at the naked meat. How would that ever fit in the frying pan?

"You want I should cut it up?" Micah asked.

"Please." *And flour and fry it. I don't even want to touch it.* But she found a cup and dug into the flour sack and dumped the white powder into the wooden bowl she'd found in the cupboard. She kept her eyes on the frying pan that had started to sizzle, flinching with every scrape of the knife. When Micah slammed the ridge of the knife with the palm of his hand, she glanced over at the thud and winced when she saw the backbone break in two. *Please, Lord, keep me from throwing up or fainting.* Never in her life had she prayed something like that, but then, never in her life had she been in such a situation.

When she recognized the silence, she also realized she had her eyes closed. She opened them as she turned toward Micah. "I will do this." His gentle voice made her blink back tears. She, who only cried on the anniversary of her parents' death, was about to break that tradition.

"Thank you." She made a beeline for the door, jerked it open, and thudded down the steps to stand panting in the snow. Ice pellets struck her face and lodged in her hair. *Deep breaths,* she ordered herself. *Take deep breaths.* She inhaled through her mouth and then her nose. The cold air burned her nose, so she breathed again through her mouth, but she no longer felt woozy. After one more deep breath, she turned and climbed the stairs. At least she could chop wood, and when they got a new ax she would be better at that too. But right now, cooking was most important.

The warmth wrapped around her like a blessing, and a delicious aroma now emanated from the pan on the stove. Micah set a lid on the frying pan and gave the beans a stir with the wooden spoon.

"Do you know how to do everything?" Her voice still felt a bit wobbly. "How come you know how to cook too?"

"When my mother died, someone had to take over."

She stared at him. He'd never mentioned anything of his life before the Wild West Show. He'd shown up half grown, as if nothing had happened before.

"I helped the cooks in the kitchen sometimes too."

"I see." She glanced over to see Chief leaning against the wall, eyes closed and one hand on Othello's head. She hadn't noticed before that the lines in his face were so deep or so many. The lamp highlighted the white hairs that grayed his dark hair. He was an old man. Why had she never noticed that before? What if something happened to him on this journey? She looked back at Micah. "Thank you."

The question in his eyes said he didn't understand, but then she didn't really either. "How do you know when it's done?"

"When you get tired of waiting?" He shook his head and, with a slight smile, continued since she didn't react. "All depends on how hot the fire. Watch so it doesn't burn." He lifted the iron skillet and pulled the bean pot forward to the hotter part of the stove and then set the frying pan in the back.

"What about the coffee?" She watched him, learning to wait for his response. Had he been making a joke with his comment about getting tired of waiting? Micah making a joke? The thought was intriguing.

"It will have to wait—no room."

"Sure smells good."

"Yeah, but you always have to start with raw meat."

Raw meat. One man wanted her to cook it, the other wanted her to shoot it. While they both tried to help her, she knew she was the only one who could overcome her trepidation. Or was it outright fear?

That night after they had all turned in, she lay in the darkness thinking of all the changes she was being subjected to. All thanks to dear Uncle Jason. She felt like spitting out his name. What perfidy. His name and the thought of his hightailing it for the train left a bitter taste in her mouth. What would her father do in this instance? Or more appropriately, what would her mother do? After all, she had fallen in love with a Wild West performer and left her high-class life behind, knowing she would never see her family again. From the stories she told, her father had forbidden her to see the brash young American. No matter that he owned a touring company that had a reputation for superior entertainment and management.

Down in the bottom of her trunk she had a picture of the two dashing young newlyweds, her father so dark and handsome, her mother so fair and regal she could be called a snow queen. They had met when the show played in Oslo, Norway.

"I fell in love instantly," she had told her daughter, one of the many times Cassie pleaded for a story of her life in Norway. "When your father rode into the arena on that magnificent black horse of his, I coveted his horse first, and then he doffed his wide-brimmed white hat and smiled at me. I am sure my heart fluttered right out of my chest and united with his—right in that moment."

"And then what happened?"

"And then he asked my father if he might call on me."

"And he did."

"And he did. When the show was about to leave Norway, I packed my trunk and met him at the wharf, much to the amazement of everyone, including me. I had always obeyed my father, just as you must obey yours. And now it is time for you to go to sleep, my sweet." She leaned over and kissed her daughter's rounded cheek. "Let's say your prayers, and then your father will come in to kiss you too."

Cassie found herself speaking those prayers in her mind, both the Norwegian one and her own, blessing everyone and everything she could think of to prolong the time with her father. His mustache always tickled her face when he kissed her, and he always smelled like cherrywood from his pipe smoke and the out-of-doors.

We were supposed to make this trip together, all of us, with wagonloads of household fixings, blooded horses, and thriving cattle. The only thing that remained from their dreams was the Gypsy Wagon—and their little girl all grown up—without them. Cassie lay still, listening to the wind pleading entry into the snug wagon. The ice pellets rattled on the roof like someone was throwing gravel. She heard Chief get up and go out to check on the animals but fell asleep before he returned. Her last thought made her blink. What if they had to stay right there and not get any closer to the valley?

7

The snow left as quickly as it arrived.

"So we continue on today?" Cassie asked Chief when he returned from checking on the livestock.

He nodded. "But we hunt first." He'd gone hunting the evening before but returned with empty hands. "You come with me."

Cassie stared at him. "B-but I've not had time to practice."

"You'll have to learn."

She stared at him, searching for excuses. "You didn't find anything when you went hunting. Shouldn't we just go on?"

"Deer are over there." He pointed toward a thicket off to the east.

"How do you know?"

"Deer sign." He held her gaze, his dark eyes serious.

"Oh. What about taking Micah?"

"He is not used to guns. You are a better shot."

She almost asked why he didn't shoot the deer himself, but something stopped her. She nodded instead. "Now?"

"Before sun gets higher."

"Take the horses?"

He nodded and headed back outside.

Cassie pulled two rifles out of her gun bags, dumped shells into her pocket, and once on the steps, closed the door behind her. Here she thought they would be on their way again immediately. Riding one horse and leading Wind Dancer, Chief stopped for her to mount. She handed him a rifle and ammunition and shoved her own rifle into the scabbard. Why did he insist she come along?

He set off and she followed. It was hard to believe they'd been snowed in for two days. The melting snow had left a soft layer of soil that had immediately turned to mud. Leaves still clung to the aspens and oaks in the wooded area ahead. Passing through sagebrush released an aroma that smelled clean and fresh, with a bite to it. Chief signaled a stop and dismounted, motioning her to do the same. She tied Wind Dancer to the sagebrush, where he dropped his head to graze.

"Aim for heart, right behind shoulder," Chief whispered. He loaded his rifle, so she did the same.

Keeping up with him took every bit of concentration she had. If she looked away, he seemed to disappear into the landscape. At one point, when she lost him, she hunkered down to wait until he returned, which he did within minutes. "I can't keep up."

He nodded. She could tell he wanted to say something, but he only turned to forge ahead. When he dropped to the ground, she settled in next to him, belly flat to the grass-cushioned earth. At least they weren't in a mud puddle.

"Deer break there." He pointed to the south end of the thicket. "Be ready."

She studied the distance as if she were in a competition. How could she shoot a living animal? Birds were bad enough, but a deer was big and alive and beautiful.

Turning to ask Chief a question, she discovered he had disappeared again. Why couldn't he tell her what he was doing? She heard brush crackling, and then one deer with horns broke from its cover, bounding over the prairie. Moving the rifle, she sighted and pulled the trigger. The deer kept on bounding away, disappearing into a draw.

"I missed." Disappointment kept her on the ground. What had she done wrong?

Not bothering to keep hidden now, Chief strolled back to join her, shaking his head.

"Sorry. I—"

"Moving target is harder."

"But I've shot moving targets before. Pigeons move, they fly."

"Fly straight. Deer are different. Best to shoot when standing still, but he ran."

"Why didn't you shoot?" She waited, keeping a close watch on his face. One eye watered and he blinked. "Your eyes?" She'd have missed his nod had she not been staring at him. "How bad?" He shrugged. "You could see the deer?" A nod. "But not through the sights?" Another nod. He stared out at the horizon, refusing to look at her again.

"And Micah?"

"Slow."

She closed her eyes against the knowledge and levered the shell out of the chamber, then picked up the empty shell and put it in her pocket. If having food to eat depended on her, then she'd better do some practicing, not just talk about it. She stood and stared across the plains. Surely there were other things to eat besides deer, things easier to hunt or more plentiful.

"I will check snares on way back."

"Snares?"

"That we use to trap rabbits. Been doing that."

Cassie felt her stomach roll. Soft, fluffy, cute bunnies. Her father had taken her out on the prairie once and shown her where a family of rabbits lived. They'd watched the young chase each other and tumble around together. She'd had a stuffed rabbit to sleep with for years. How could she bear to kill one, although she had appreciated the fried rabbit the night before. Somehow, after it was cooked, it was different. Then it was meat, not a furry bunny. She mounted Wind Dancer, and they rode back toward the wagon.

She knew Chief stopped a couple of times but made sure she didn't look his way. Back at the wagon, Micah had the team hitched and the livestock rounded up. "Ready. Where's Chief?"

"Checking his snares."

"Oh."

"You drive. He needs to teach me to hunt."

Micah nodded and tied his mount to the rear of the wagon. "Chief."

Chief rode up with several dead rabbits tied to his saddle. "Keep the skins to make clothes. I will clean them, and then we leave."

Had she dared, Cassie would have climbed up into the wagon and locked the door. Hunting to shoot a deer, frying fresh rabbit meat, heading south to only Chief knew where and wasn't telling. This was getting to be far more to handle than she had ever dreamed. When she'd decided—or rather was forced—to leave the show, she'd not given provisions much thought, if any. Taking what they needed from the cook tent had been bad enough. Now she was expected to shoot such beautiful creatures as those deer bounding out of hiding. Or a rabbit. Or who knew what else. Perhaps there were game birds out there too. Surely that wouldn't be any different than shooting clay pigeons or live ones in a match. Except she had to find them first.

Back on the trail she leaned forward and patted her horse's neck.

"I don't know, Dancer, this heading south to find the valley might not be the smartest thing I've done in my life." Dancer shook his head. "Is that agreement or disagreement? I know. All you want to do is head out, the faster the better." She heaved a sigh and, looking up, saw an eagle floating above her. "Oh, look," she breathed, wishing someone was near to share her delight. Her father had loved eagles above all birds. He'd said there was an eagle nest on a cliff at the far end of his valley, and one day he would take her there to see it.

Tears blurred her vision and made her nose run. There she was on the trip her father had always promised her, but he wasn't there. The tears were getting to be a habit— a bad habit. "That's enough," she ordered herself. "You know he'd be here if he could. And you know he's in heaven with Mor."

Dancer tugged at the bit and danced sideways. She mopped her eyes with the sleeve of her coat and looked for the eagle again. A verse floated through her mind, like the eagle caught in the updraft. What was it—eagle's wings. Where was it? In her Bible, but where? Maybe if she'd spent more time reading her Bible lately, she'd remember things like that. Isaiah. Tonight, she promised herself. *Tonight I will find that verse.*

Chief rode up beside her. "Supper will be fried or roasted rabbit."

"What will you do with the skins?"

"When I have enough, I sew you vest, so you keep warm like me."

"Thank you."

"Now, keep your eyes open for game trails. You get deer next time."

Game trail? What was a game trail? Cassie had a feeling that she was in for all kinds of learning experiences she'd not expected. She checked that the safety was on her rifle and followed the caravan as it turned south on what was called a road in this part of the country and a trail in other places.

She dropped back to ride by the cattle, since Micah was driving the wagon. George grumbled as he walked, his huge head bobbing with every step. The snow had finally melted off his and the other buffalos' backs, and if no one watched, they would veer off and start grazing. At least the ground was damp enough that the dust stayed put rather than choking the wranglers, as it had on the first day. She now knew why cowboys wore bandannas—more to cover their faces than to keep their necks warm or for decoration.

She'd never planned on being a cowboy . . . er, cowgirl.

They stopped at a creek to drink and refill the water barrel on the side of the wagon. The cattle immediately lowered their heads to graze. Chief beckoned her off to one side and pointed at a narrow path filing through the rocks and down to the water.

"Game trail. See?" He pointed to some dark pellets along the path. "Deer sign."

Cassie nodded. So that was what she was to look for.

"When deer lie down to sleep, they flatten the grass. Leave sign."

"Okay."

"Dusk and daylight they come to drink."

"What about game birds?"

"Roost in trees sometimes." He raised his arm and waved at Micah. "Head on out."

Back on her horse, Cassie stretched her neck, leaning her head from side to side. While she'd learned to be wary of her feet going to sleep if riding too long, the rest of her body was already complaining. Stopping more often would be good for all of them. But she knew Chief was hurrying them along in case the weather turned nasty again. He'd said it would take two weeks to get there, but they'd already lost two days due to the blizzard.

Othello yipped at one of the Longhorns that thought to choose its own way, drawing her attention back to her charges. If allowed, the animals would slow down more and more, snatching grass as they passed and then stopping altogether. When her own stomach rumbled, she felt even more sympathy for the critters.

The sun was well beyond high noon when they stopped at another creek. This time she grabbed the tin dipper off the barrel and filled it at the creek, following Chief's instructions to always drink upstream from the animals. She tied Wind Dancer to a wagon wheel and let down the steps so she could enter. Even cold beans sounded good to her about now. She dug some hard biscuits out of the box, sliced off some cheese, and took the food outside for the men.

"Do you want some cold beans?"

They both shook their heads. "This is enough," Micah said.

Cassie sat down on the steps and tipped her hat back so the sun could reach her face while she ate her biscuit and cheese. She knew this wasn't proper in society, but she liked the feeling of the sun on her face and the wind in her hair. And there was no one now to remind her about acting like a lady.

"I am going ahead, look for place to stop." Chief took a long drink from his canteen.

"Shouldn't we be joining up with the road from Medora to Deadwood pretty soon?"

Chief shrugged.

"What about stopping at a ranch to see if we can purchase some grain for the horses? Maybe some meat?"

He shrugged again. "Got rabbit."

"Right." If words were gold, these two certainly hoarded theirs.

Back on the road, she watched the landscape, buttes and draws and twisted oak, willows and cottonwoods following the waterways. She caught herself dozing in the saddle and jerked awake. Othello was walking head down, looking as worn as she felt.

"Othello!"

He looked over his shoulder and turned to watch her. "You want up?" Since he often rode behind her in the shows, this was nothing new. She patted Dancer's rump. "Come on. Up!" The dog dropped behind her, gathered his haunches, and leaped, landing on the horse's rump and nearly pushing Cassie off. She settled herself back in the saddle, and he stuck his head under her arm. "Good job, big O. We have to do some practicing if we are to keep in tune. There's no one to cheer us on out here." He whined, making her think he agreed. Often it seemed both Othello and Wind Dancer could read her mind. The three of them made quite a team.

She half turned in the saddle so she could give his ears and neck a good rubbing.

At that moment Micah yelled something, and she grabbed her saddle horn. "Now what?"

Chief rode up to the wagon and the wagon stopped. The cattle immediately set to grazing, and Othello whimpered in his throat. "All right, you can get down." She raised her arm, and the dog jumped to the ground, trotting up to the wagon, as if wanting the news. Should she leave the animals alone and go up there or keep an eye on the cattle in case something spooked them?

Chief dismounted, and Micah climbed down from the wagon seat.

That did it. Cassie's curiosity got the better of her, and she rode on up to see what was happening.

The team was already grazing, angling the wagon toward the edge of the road. She could see Micah's hat above the brush, but Chief had disappeared. Dismounting, she flipped the reins over the nearest juniper bush and followed the game trail down a slope into a gully with a stand of cottonwood saplings. "Micah, where are you?"

"Over here."

She followed the sound of his voice. "Is Othello with you?"

"Yes."

She pushed through some more close shrubs and stopped,

her hand going to her mouth. An Indian woman lay on her side, eyes closed, her lower right leg jutting at an impossible angle. A dog sat beside her, glaring at the intruders and growling whenever Othello moved toward them.

"How did you find her?"

"The dog." Micah squatted down, making soothing noises and half singing in a way she had heard him tame animals before. "Her leg is broken."

"Is she alive?" Cassie stepped closer, her heart thudding in her throat.

"Yes. You can see her breathing."

"But she's not responding?"

"No."

The dog licked the woman's cheek and whined, then pawed at her shoulder, all the while keeping an eye on the intruders.

"How did you know to follow him?"

"He ran out to me, barked, and ran back. Three times before I stopped."

"She is off reservation, whoever she is." Chief hunkered down beside Micah. "Can you calm dog so we can see how she is?"

"I'm trying." Micah took up his singsong again.

The dog nudged the woman under the arm. When she made a sound, he licked her face again.

"I'll go get a blanket, and we can move her." Cassie headed back toward the wagon. What had happened to the woman? Who was she? So many questions, how they could help her being foremost. She deliberately ignored a voice inside that asked why they should help her. They had enough problems of their own.

8

Brother, we need to talk."

Ransom Engstrom looked up from the ledger he'd been working on since supper. He nodded to the chair by the worn oak desk, but his younger-by-four-years brother, Lucas, chose to pace instead. Ransom heaved a sigh and closed the leather-bound ledger, giving his brother his full attention. Now was not a good time, since he'd just added to the red total. The Bar E Ranch was not doing well. He had a good idea what his brother was going to say.

Lucas stopped in front of the window, hands rammed into his rear pockets. Turning, he shrugged. "You know what I'm going to say?"

Ransom nodded.

"Then we need to talk Mor into being realistic. We've given this ranch all we have, and yet we go further and further into debt. Pa must be turning over in his grave, if he can see what is happening."

Ransom raised his hands in the gesture of surrender. He knew when Lucas referred to their mother as *Mor* that he was in a serious frame of mind.

"But if we talked with Mor together?"

"It still wouldn't do any good." Mavis Engstrom stood in the doorway, obviously having heard what her youngest son was saying. "We are not selling this land, and that is final. Our calf crop was good, and we'll have plenty of steers to send to market next fall. We just have to hang on."

Ransom wondered at the tenacity visible in his mother's face and locked in on her words. He'd always felt there was something she wasn't telling them, but being pushy with their mother was about as useless as a candle in a blizzard. She knew what the ledger made obvious. Their outstanding tab at the general store in town would make anyone choke, and yet JD continued to give them credit. They were fairly well set for the winter, but they would need seed in the spring. He had set aside what he hoped was enough oats to reseed the fields, but the harvest had been mediocre at best. Saving the seed cut into the feed for the winter.

"Say something!" Lucas scrubbed his hands over his head. While Ransom wore his hair longer and tied back by a thong, Lucas kept his short, so it curled around the lobes of his ears. Both men had the tall, solid body that came from both of their parents, but Lucas still wore a more boyish look. His mother teased him at times about his baby face, but the female population found him exceedingly attractive.

Ransom looked up from studying the ledger cover. What could he say? He looked to his mother, still standing in the doorway. The tension between the two people most important to him in all the world was nearly visible, a braided cord quivering at the stress.

"We have to cut costs somehow." Ransom shook his head. "Or bring in more cash. That's the bottom line."

"We could sell some of the steers as feeders." Mavis entered the room and crossed to the stone fireplace to add more wood. "The temperature is dropping."

Lucas returned to stare out the window, his back and shoulders rigid. "We'll lose money on them that way."

"But we'll have some cash now." Her gentle voice persisted. "I'm sure Jay Slatfield would buy maybe ten of them. That should cover the bill at the general store."

"But what about the bank loan?" They'd been forced to take out a loan to cover seed costs the year before, and the harvest had not been sufficient to cover it all. In reality it covered only a small partial payment.

"We could . . ." Ransom stopped in frustration. "We could work the mine."

"If we could cut some trees and get them sawed into timbers to shore up the walls and ceiling." Lucas leveled a glare at his mother. "Cash is crucial for anything we want to do."

"One of us could . . ." Ransom paused again, knowing Lucas would have a ready argument. "Go work for the Triple S."

"As if they need more help in the winter, and when spring comes, we need to be working our own place. We could bring Jesse home from school." The third son in the family dreamed of becoming a doctor and was in his third year of college in Denver.

"We send him hardly any money as it is." Mavis shook her head. "He's making it on his own. There's no need to deprive him of his dream."

But what about my dream? Ransom refrained from mentioning what he knew to be an impossibility. At least one of the brothers was off doing what he'd aimed for. As the oldest, Ransom felt responsible for preserving the ranch, and it took every bit of his time and energy. Not that he would call Lucas a slacker. He just had a different way of looking for solutions. Shutting the door on his own dreams had become a habit.

"This isn't solving anything. How would you like a cup of coffee?" their mother said. "The cinnamon rolls are about to come out of the oven."

"Where's Gretchen?" Ransom asked. Their only sister rode her horse into town every day so she could attend school. "Shouldn't she be home by now?"

"She asked if she could stop off at Jenna's for a bit. She promised to be home before dark."

"Then she better be getting a move on. It's her turn to milk tonight." Lucas flopped down in the cowhide easy chair, the frame of which was made of cottonwood branches. Their father had made most of the furniture in the house, using the raw materials of their land.

"I'll do the milking." Mavis left the room, heading for the kitchen that filled the house with the fragrance of baking bread and cinnamon.

Ransom glared at his brother. "Seems to me Gretchen has taken your turn at milking more than once. We'll call tonight payback time." He knew Lucas hated to milk the cows, but since they had only one to milk now, it shouldn't be so terrible.

"She hates me."

"Who?"

"Bess. She delights in kicking the bucket when I'm milking."

"Oh, for . . ." Ransom shook his head. "Put the kickers on her, then."

"I'll pitch out the hay, and you milk." Morning and evening when the snow got too deep, they loaded a sledge with hay from the barn and took it out to the pasture where the cattle grazed. As the winter progressed, they'd erect rail fences around the haystacks and let the stock help themselves.

"The cattle don't need hay now. The pasture is clear again."

"I knew that." Lucas shot his brother a half grin.

"We will not let Ma do the milking. Remember our agreement?"

Lucas nodded. For some reason, their mother had fainted one day in the barn, and in spite of her protests, the men of the family decreed that she was not to do the milking any longer. That was when the boys and Gretchen took the job over completely. While Mavis had never had an episode like that again, Ransom, especially, was taking no chances.

The fragrance of just-out-of-the-oven cinnamon rolls preceded their mor as she entered the room again. Lucas jumped to take the tray from her and set it on the table in front of the sofa, which matched the easy chairs. Comfort had been a primary concern of their father, and while the hides looked worn from years of use, the padding had been refreshed, along with the springs. Sitting down on the sofa was a sure trip to slumberland for a tired cowboy. While Lucas joined their mother on the sofa, Ransom judiciously took his favorite easy chair, the one made with the spotted hide of Thor, his father's first bull, a Longhorn whose horns hung above the fireplace in tribute.

With a roll in one hand and a cup of steaming coffee in the other, Ransom propped his feet on the matching footstool and enjoyed both the coffee and the roll. He let his mind wander as he stared into the cheery fire. He'd always believed the story that God brought them to this land, just like he believed the stories of the Israelites conquering the Promised Land. If God brought them there, then He must have a plan for them to continue raising beef cattle and producing as much of their own staples as possible. He led them to this land that also had a once-producing gold mine on it, not that much gold had been taken out, but there was always the possibility more could be found. He glanced up at the glass-encased nugget on the mantel. Selling that would bring in some cash, but again, his mother was adamant that it not be sold. Why was that? What memories did it hold for her? And how could they live on memories? One good year would turn off the drain. Two would put them back in control.

"Ransom."

He pondered the toe of his boot that needed patching, another of those things his father had done with ease, leaving a legacy to his sons of self-sufficiency. If only he were still alive . . . He jerked his mind back to the present. Had someone spoken to him?

"Ransom!" The tone said the call had indeed come before.

He looked from his mother, who rolled her eyes, to his brother, who looked plain put out. "Yes?"

"Every time you go off like that, I want to tackle you and bring you back." Lucas slapped his hand on his knee. Their cow dog, Benny, leaped from his mat by the fire, standing at attention, not sure which way to run.

Ransom patted his knee, and Benny came over to lay his muzzle on Ransom's thigh and gaze up at him with adoring eyes. Since the day Mother brought him home from town in a basket, the dog had belonged to Ransom. He worked well for all the family, but his human of choice was the quiet man sitting in the easy chair. Ransom stroked the fluffy mottled gray-and-tan fur and the perky ears. With one blue-gray eye and one dark, Benny had always seemed a bit off-kilter, but his short tail wagged in spite of its diminutive size.

At a sound only his ears could hear, the dog sprinted for the front door. Mavis let him out. "Gretchen's home."

"How do you know?" Lucas asked.

"Because Benny would have been barking his head off if he didn't know who it was." She returned to the sofa. "More coffee, either of you?" She refilled their cups and passed the platter. "At least you don't have to milk now, Lucas."

"Good. Think I'll go hunting, then. Saw elk signs out in the west pasture, so they are down for the winter."

"It's early."

"That's so."

Ransom knew that meant a hard winter in store for them all. It was a good thing they had plenty of hay. One year when the snow was really deep, he'd found elk grazing along with the cattle on the hay. From then on, he'd tried to put up extra, just in case.

Lucas set his cup down on the tray. "If I get one, I could probably sell half to the Hill City Hotel. We still have that side of venison that we smoked, don't we?"

"Much of it. And a couple of turkeys. I canned those three geese."

Ransom watched his brother leave the room. Why was a

place always more peaceful when Lucas left? His just being in the room seemed to stir it up somehow.

Gretchen burst through the door like a charging bull was after her.

"Did you put your horse up, little sister?"

Gretchen glared at her oldest brother. "What do you think I am? Stupid?"

"Not in the least," Mavis answered. "He's just being careful. Did you have a good visit?" She held out the platter. "Would you like coffee or milk?"

"How about coffee with milk." The twelve-year-old girl unwrapped her muffler and hooked her knit hat and muffler on the coat-tree, followed by her coat. While pants were not allowed at school, she wore them under her skirt when the weather turned cold and removed them before class started. Besides, they made riding back and forth far easier. She flipped her long wheat-colored braids over her shoulders, the cold making her fair cheeks glow red.

"Thank you." Taking cup and roll to stand with her back to the fireplace, she turned to Ransom. "Did you know that Emerson bought a Rambler automobile?" Emerson Hansel owned the blacksmith shop in town. "He brought Cindy to school in it today. That was the noisiest thing I've ever heard. Even worse than Johnson's steam engine."

"Couldn't be that bad. They say that in the East, folks are driving all over. We don't have enough roads yet to make one of those things practical out here."

"Have you thought of buying one?"

"Not really. I'd rather use horses any day. Tolerating that steam engine for harvest is bad enough." Ransom smiled at his little sister, now the baby of the family since another daughter had died before she'd turned two. His mother was no stranger to sorrow, having lost two babies, a five-year-old son, and her husband. In spite of her faith, life had certainly not been kind to her.

But you'd never know it by the serene look on her face. Interesting that her stubborn will didn't show.

"Are you in a deep-thinking mood again?" Gretchen asked as she crossed her legs and sat down on the floor to pet Benny. She drained her cup and let the dog have the last lick of her roll, then glanced sheepishly at her mother. Feeding the dog was not allowed in the living room. They didn't have a real parlor, just a large general room with cedar-lined walls and a stone fireplace as its centerpiece. Ransom's desk sat in one corner, with an oak ladder-back chair sporting cushions Mavis had made for it. In another sat a rocking chair with a table that always held books and often newspapers. A wool afghan lay folded over the back in rich black-and-gray stripes that Mavis both spun the yarn for and knitted one winter. Gretchen loved drawing the chair near to the fire and curling up with a book off the shelf above the desk.

"I better get to milking."

"Supper will be ready in an hour."

"Do you want the milk left in pans in the well house or brought in?"

"Strain it into the pans so we can skim the cream."

"Bess is not giving much anymore."

"I know. But Rosy is due to calf in November. All will be well."

Ransom watched Gretchen head down the hall. She'd begun to flare up when he called her *little sister*. He would leave the teasing to Lucas. After all, he was good at it, and they all expected it from him. But that didn't mean they had to like it.

He moved back to his chair at the desk, taking a kerosene lamp with him. Staring at the columns did not change the numbers. On the back of an envelope, he figured out how much ten feeders would be worth. While it would help, would the money be enough to make any difference? Of course, JD, short for Jason Daniel McKittrick, owner of the general store in Argus, might think so. There wouldn't be much left to give to the bank. Or should he divide it in half? He rested his head in the palm of one hand while he juggled numbers in his mind.

His mother came back into the room sometime later. "You better get your coat on. Lucas got an elk and needs the team and wagon to haul it back."

"All right. We'll dress it out in the barn. Perhaps we can sell the hide too." While Ransom hadn't heard two rifle shots close together, he knew his mother must have heard the pre-arranged signal.

"Good thing it turned cold. I could take it in to the hotel tomorrow. They have a refrigerator there to age it in," Mavis said, leaning against the doorframe.

"Talk to Slatfield about the calves on your way back, would you, please? We'll round them up tomorrow. I'm keeping all the heifers."

"I figured as much." She laid a hand on his shoulder. "Don't waste your time worrying on our financial situation. God has a plan."

"I surely do hope so." He shrugged into his wool coat and

tucked his thick scarf down into the neck. "Better put supper on the back burner. This will take awhile."

Lucas already had the elk gutted by the time Ransom had hitched up the wagon and driven it out to the field. They would leave the entrails out for the coyotes to clean up. It took all the combined muscle they had to drag the carcass up into the wagon.

"I shoulda cut the head off first," Lucas said, heaving breaths separating his words.

"This must be about the biggest we've seen. Look at that rack."

"Been around awhile. That's for sure. Think we should sell the whole thing. I got one. I can get another."

"It's up to Mor, I guess." Ransom stepped up the wheel and settled on the board seat. "See you at the barn."

The moon was floating above, casting dark shadows and glittering the frost-coated grass and bushes. This was the kind of night he used to love riding in. He'd head out at dusk and ride up in the hills. Then he'd come home in the moonlight.

Lucas had the double doors slid open and lanterns hanging on two posts with the pulley ready when his brother drove up to the barn. Ransom backed the wagon inside so that after they slit the skin around the hamstrings on the rear legs of the elk and inserted a bar between bone and tendon, they could tie ropes on the ends and use the pulley to hoist the carcass in the air. Once it was up, he pulled the wagon back outside and unhitched the team. Then he joined Lucas in skinning the animal.

"Pa would sure be proud of this one. You going to keep the antlers?"

"I thought to. I'll hang 'em up over the barn door and let them age before I do something else with them."

"You're not going to cut them up, are you?"

"No. Probably cut up the one that's hanging on the barn wall now." Lucas had a customer back east who bought all the buttons made of various kinds of horn that they could produce. While it didn't bring in a large sum of money, every little bit helped.

"Are you going to the barn dance on Saturday night?" Lucas asked as they folded the hide, hair to the inside, into a square packet and tied it closed with a thong made from other hides.

"No."

"Why not? I'm sure Miss Suzanne will be watching for you."

Ransom shook his head.

"Mor and Gretchen are going."

"I said no." His glare silenced even his persistent brother. They draped sheeting around the carcass and tied it in several places, then hoisted it higher. Each taking a lantern and blowing it out, they hung them on nails by the door where they could be found easily and closed up the barn, dropping the bars into the racks so the building was secure from prowling scavengers, like the coyotes they could already hear fighting over the scraps in the field. At least they'd not heard any wolves yet this fall.

Why not go to the dance? Ransom asked himself. But he knew the answer. Miss Lissa from the Johnson spread had flirted with him more than once, but trying to talk with a young woman like that was just too difficult. At least the animals didn't mind his silence.

9

*M*r. Chamberlain said he'd take another elk if you can shoot one," Mavis said as she came into the house the next afternoon. "I guess the hotel guests like to brag that they've eaten elk meat." As the head cook at the Hill City hotel, Mr. Chamberlain catered to a lot of travelers.

Mavis grinned at Lucas, who was shaking his head. "Wonderful, isn't it?"

Lucas nodded. "I'll head out again, then."

Ransom dropped his load of firewood in the box by the kitchen stove. "The elk probably will still be spooked tonight and not return."

"Could be, but maybe they have short memories." Lucas turned to his mother. "Is Gretchen coming straight home from school today?"

"I believe so. She should be here any minute. Why?"

"She wanted to go hunting with me. It's about time she got a deer at least."

"You know she is a girl, and hunting is not a requirement to be a lady. She'd do better to work on her bread-making efforts."

"I know, but she asked me. Asked you too, didn't she, Ransom?"

Ransom nodded. He had a feeling that his little sister was trying to fill her missing brother's shoes, although Jesse had never been one for hunting and fishing. He always said he wanted to make both people and animals healthy, not dead.

"If the elk don't come out tonight, maybe we can ride back up in the hills tomorrow and find them. I saw several spike bucks. They're far better eating than that old bull."

Ransom turned to his mother. "You want to come along with us tomorrow? You've not been out riding for months."

"Come to think of it, that sounds marvelous. Let's do it, even if Lucas gets one tonight. The aspen must be at their peak color right about now. I'd like another elk hide too. Been thinking of sewing gloves. Although deerskin would be better."

"Who's going to tan them?" Lucas shook his head. "Ah, Mor, you know I don't like tanning hides."

"Well, sometimes I don't like making breakfast either but . . ."

Ransom rolled his lips together to keep from laughing out loud at the look on his brother's face. "You could chew them like the squaws used to do."

"Eww. Ick." Gretchen came in on Ransom's words and shut the door behind her. "It stinks bad enough when you do it the modern way. But to chew one—ick!"

"Old Indians say that was the best way. Made the softest

hides for pants and shirts. Be glad you don't have to chew elk and buffalo. 'Course they were used for the tepees and blankets and didn't need to be too soft."

"Remember that rabbit-skin vest I had for so many years? I'd like one again." Gretchen lifted the lid of the kettle on the stove and sniffed. "Sure smells good."

"If we're not back from hunting in time tomorrow, you make the supper when you get home, before milking."

Gretchen made a face but nodded. "I could skip school and go along."

"You could, but you won't. Sorry."

Ransom felt sorry for his sister. He remembered the days when he'd missed out on things at the ranch because of school. "We can go again on Saturday." He returned the smile shot his way from his mother.

"But Saturday is the barn dance." Lucas glanced from his brother to his mother.

"We can be back in time for that." Mavis handed the plates to her younger son. "Put these on the table. And Gretchen, go wash your hands. Coffee or milk?"

"Milk," she shot over her shoulder as she trotted down the hall.

Lucas set the plates down on the table and headed for the back door, grabbing his coat and hat as he passed the pegs on the wall by the door. "I'll be back soon. Tell Gretchen next time." The screen door slammed behind him.

Ransom shook his head. Covering the screen door with oiled cloth was another one of the jobs that needed doing before winter set in. He ambled over to the cabinet and dug the silverware out of the drawer. Somewhere along the years, the line between men's work and women's work had blurred, and they all pitched in to finish whatever task needed to be done. With all of them gathered in the kitchen, setting the table together felt like part of the natural order of things.

It hadn't been that way when their pa was alive. Ivar took it for granted that he would be served by his wife and daughter. He demanded the respect of his sons, and if he had ever been able to laugh, something had stolen that through the years. While they had all been sad when he died ten years earlier, they had recovered quickly. Especially when Mor teased them or made them laugh. They'd been careful before then to make jokes away from their father's sight and hearing.

Ransom had learned in the years since that laughter did indeed make the load lighter.

But at the same time, Pa had been an excellent rancher, fair to his hands, and well respected in town. There was no one more honest than Ivar Engstrom, nor more respected. Ransom had always felt God must be like his earthly father, stern and unbending, always ready to correct and steer his sons on the path of life. But they'd finally met the God of love after Ivar went on to his heavenly reward.

Ransom brought in several more armloads of wood before he brushed the bark and wood bits off his coat and gloves. Several fingers had worn through his leather gloves. Like his shoes that needed fixing. Pa's motto: If it is worn, fix it before it breaks. Days like today, Ransom wondered how his father ever managed to do all he did.

"Thank you, son," his mother said. "Ever since you took over the woodboxes, I've never run out of wood."

"You are welcome." He knew Lucas had always hated

filling the woodboxes, and since it was a mindless chore, Ransom had taken it over. "You know, I've been thinking. We should take some of that elk hide, cut a rectangle about so big"—he spread his arms to show the size—"sew handles on the two shorter sides and use it for hauling in wood. One could carry a lot more at a time that way. Fact is, two would balance the carrier."

Mavis nodded. He could see her already figuring how to do it.

"Wonder why we didn't think of such a simple thing years ago?"

"Do we have an elk hide lying around somewhere?"

"The one from Lucas's first hunt isn't tanned yet." She narrowed her eyes and chewed on her bottom lip, a sure sign she was deep in thought. "Maybe we could use canvas. We could add leather handles."

"Do that for a practice run. Then we can adjust for the leather one to make it just right." He held up his gloves. "Is there any deer hide to fix these? And I need elk to repair my boot."

"There's plenty of scraps in the sewing room. Leave your gloves with me, but you're going to need your father's lasts to fix your boot. I think they are out in the barn in that pile of stuff on the back wall."

Ransom thought about where the iron foot-shaped forms might be. It could take some time to find them. He cocked his head. "Two shots. Sure enough. Lucas did it again. He has more luck."

"Thank you, Lord, for bringing the elk to us."

Ransom nodded as he shrugged into his gear. Shame they didn't come down before dusk.

By the time the two men returned to the house, an elk once again hanging in the barn, Gretchen was getting ready for bed. "Mor said to tell you your supper is in the warming oven."

"Where is she?"

"In her sewing room. Can't you hear the machine?"

The men hung up their outerwear and crossed to the kitchen sink to wash the blood off their hands.

"Your chin too." Ransom touched his chin to show his brother where to wash. "Good thing Mor sold this one too. Keep this up and we could whittle that account at the store down without using the calf money."

"But I thought Slatfield wants the feeders."

"Yep, deliver them next week." Ransom pulled both full plates out of the warming oven and set them on the table. "Coffee's hot."

They ate their meal without much discussion, using fresh bread to sop up the gravy. Gretchen, in her nightdress and robe, dipped water out of the reservoir to wash with. "There's gingerbread in the pantry. You want applesauce or cream on it?"

"How about both?" Lucas leaned back in his chair. "Full belly, full day's work, and now I'm ready for a full night's sleep. How about you ride with me into town tomorrow, Gretchen?"

"How will I get home again?"

"Ride with the Hendersons." The Hendersons, their neighbors to the east, had enough kids to have a school all their own. The oldest son who was still in school drove the wagon for all of them to ride in. Gretchen said she'd rather ride her horse to town most of the time, but she agreed to ride in with Lucas.

"You better be ready to leave early. If I show up tardy, that teacher will make me stay after school 'to make up your time,' " she said, parroting an older woman's voice.

"I will." Lucas tugged on her braid.

"Ouch." She glared at him and headed for her bedroom.

Ransom and his mother rode out the next morning after Lucas and Gretchen drove off to town. In the cool air their breath fogged as they rode the horses up into the timber. The elk trail was easy to follow, the biggest danger being dead branches that could sweep them off the horses if they weren't careful. Ransom smiled at his mother's obvious delight in being on horseback. She'd always enjoyed riding and had taken part in roundups and calf brandings, especially since her husband had died. While he was alive, Ivar had insisted she wear a full riding costume and use only a sidesaddle. After he was gone, she donned pants for the outside work, finding them far more practical, but for propriety's sake she never wore them to town.

They crested a ridge and paused at the bowl of glowing aspens below them. The sun turning the trees to brass and gold brought on sighs of delight.

"God is sure lavish with His paintbrush," Mavis said. "Thank you for suggesting this."

"You are welcome. Is your gun loaded?"

"Of course."

"Looks like the elk have used this area to bed down during

99

the day. If they're around and smell us, they'll be off before we can get a shot in."

They nudged their horses to start down the slope, weaving their way among the boulders. Ransom let his horse have his head so that he could use his hands to clear aside the branches and hopefully see the elk. While bedded down, the animals appeared like brown rocks or bushes, until they moved. When his horse stepped into a clearing, the earth erupted. Like huge waves the elk herd drove straight up the hills, their haunches flashing the light hair on their hindquarters. With no heads visible, Ransom sat disgusted. Had he been on foot he might have gotten a shot.

"What a glorious sight." His mother sat with her hands crossed on the saddle horn, shaking her head in delight. Glancing at her son, she chuckled at the disgusted look on his face. "I've only seen that one other time, years ago. Some things you never forget."

Ransom nodded and smiled back at her. "It is indeed a glorious sight, but dropping one would have made it perfect. They'll run for miles now."

"That's okay. Let's ride to the top of the next ridge and check out the deer hollow."

"Be prepared to do some walking, then. Or . . ." He narrowed his eyes in thought. "I know. Let me get around that thicket, and then you ride in. Some might take the game trail, where I'll be waiting. Or you want to do the shooting?"

"No, thanks. You go on ahead."

He nudged his horse up the trail and, checking the wind direction, rode on around the area. He should have told her to give him half an hour. Ransom left his horse higher on the ridge and made his way down to take up a shooting position off one of the larger tracks. *Okay, Mor, anytime now.* The silence that had greeted him slipped away, overcome by the sounds of the forest. A dove called off to the right. Something small scratched in the leaves. How could he be so lucky as to not have a crow announce the presence of a stranger? The wind sighed in the tops of the pine trees. He inhaled a deep breath of forest perfume, redolent of pine, rotting leaves, and fall.

Holding his rifle at the ready, he listened. Was that his mother's horse snapping twigs and moving rocks?

Two bucks broke through the brush, heading right toward him. He sighted and fired. One down. Tracking the other, he shot again. Two down. He waited to see if they would move. Three does rushed past his hiding place, but he ignored them and made his way to the closest buck. Clean shot, right in the heart. He slit the animal's throat to let it bleed out and went back down to the first one. As he was bending down to slit the throat, he heard his mother's voice.

"Did you get one?" she called.

"No, I got two."

"I'll be there in a few minutes. Congratulations."

Ransom counted the points: one had six and the other four. Good-sized mule deer and in excellent condition. This had been a good year for the animals, plenty of feed, and they'd seen twin fawns with many of the does. They liked the apples that fell from the trees not far from the ranch house. His father had planted them when he first settled the land.

"Lucas will be happy with those sets of antlers," he said when his mother rode in.

"You did well. I thought it maybe took two shots to down one." Mavis dismounted and pulled her knife from its sheath. "I'll start on this one."

Between the two of them, they soon had the deer gutted and slung across their horses' rumps, behind the saddles. They tied them in place and then mounted to head home.

"Well, you think the hotel might like one? And we'll keep the other? I want both hides."

"Either that or JD might like one. He's not done much hunting since his accident." They rode back to the ranch and hung both deer up with the pulley. Skinning a deer was like skinning a rabbit. Cut the skin around the rear legs and pull it down and off the front legs. Mavis folded one hide while Ransom finished the other.

"I guess we'll have dinner at the house after all," she said. "It's not much after noon. Thanks for asking me to go along. I needed some time out in the woods for a change." She patted his shoulder. "And with you." She paused at the door. "I'll take care of the horses."

Ransom finished by wrapping clean sheeting around the carcasses. He gathered up that used on the first elk and dumped it in a tub of water to soak before picking up the bucket that held the hearts and livers and making his way to the house. Fried liver sounded right good for dinner.

"I wish Gretchen had taken her horse in after all," Ransom said after finishing his last bit of liver sometime later. "Now I'll have to go get her."

"I thought she was coming home with the Hendersons."

"They make too many stops dropping off other kids."

"I'm surprised Lucas isn't back yet."

"Maybe he stopped to swap tales at the store. Prob'ly some of the old-timers chewin' the fat there."

"Most likely." She refilled their coffee cups and sat back down. "I finished that wood carrier last night. It's in the woodbox. See how it goes." She propped her elbows on the table and sipped from her coffee cup. "When I make the ones out of leather, I'll use rivets at the stress points."

"Prob'ly last a hundred years or so."

"Well, it never pays to build something flimsy, you know."

Ransom recognized the quote from his father. When Ivar Engstrom built something, it was built to last. *Flimsy* was near to a swearword for him. "Liver and onions for supper?"

"One of your pa's favorites. This seems to be a remembering kind of day."

He watched her face. Whatever she was thinking on was definitely a good one. Ransom left her at the table and, grabbing the new carrier off the edge of the box, headed for the woodpile. That was another thing to be done before winter set in—stack this pile of split wood and start working on the tree that needed to be cut to shorter lengths for the cookstove. The longer lengths would be stacked for use in the fireplace and when needed would be piled on the porch near the door. The roof's overhang would keep the wood dry and handy. If only he could keep the mice from nesting there. He'd seen a pack rat scurrying away down the porch. Who knew what they'd find in its nest when they got down to it. One year they'd found two shiny buttons and a thimble that Mor had accused someone of misplacing. They'd torn the house apart looking for it.

He set the log carrier down, and it flopped open. Stacking the wood on it, about twice the amount he could carry in his arms, he grabbed the handles and hauled the load inside.

"Works, eh?"

"Yep. A real muscle builder, that one." He dumped it into the box and continued on to do the same with the wood for the fireplace. Outside, after he'd stacked kitchen wood for about an hour, he loaded up again and carried it in. "You need to make one for the front porch too. This is right handy."

"You better head on over to get Gretchen. School's about out."

"And no Lucas. Surely he didn't stop off somewhere."

"He better not have." The look in his mother's eyes said there would be misery to pay if he did. After her husband died, she swore there would never be a drop of liquor in her house again. Or in anyone, if they wanted to stay.

What else could have kept him? Ransom went out to the corral and whistled for Gray Bar, his favorite mount. He tied the horse in the opening of the barn after a struggle to get him near the door. Gray Bar did not like the smell of blood, so Ransom never took this horse hunting.

He was tightening the cinch to go to town to get Gretchen when he heard a dog bark. He'd wondered where Benny was, but the dog often went visiting if a female from miles around came in heat. Most likely some other ranch or even a family in town would have puppies in a couple of months.

He heard something in the distance and could see the Henderson wagon drawing near. He took off the saddle and let Gray Bar back in the field with the other horses. No trip to town necessary.

Gretchen yelled at him when the wagon drew near enough. "Guess what happened at school today!"

Ransom's stomach clenched. Now what?

Gretchen and the others groaned. "Two boys got in a fight, and we all had to make up time."

A sigh released Ransom's tight muscles. "You better get a move on."

10

North Dakota

*C*assie ran back to the gully with a blanket in her arms.
Micah met her, shaking his head.

"Is she still alive?"

"Barely."

Cassie handed him the blanket and knelt by the woman,
ignoring the growls of the dog, warning her away. She felt
the woman's forehead. No fever. Instead, she was very cold.
"How long do you think she's been here?"

"At least a day. If the snow was still here, she'd be dead
by now." Chief and Micah spread the blanket between them
and laid it on the ground. "You hold her leg while we lift."

"But the dog . . ."

"Shoot if it attacks."

Cassie gulped. She couldn't shoot a dog. But she couldn't

let it rip a hole in one of the men either. Should she run back to the wagon and get her pistol? "Please, dog, we're just trying to help her. You brought us here. Now let us help."

The dog continued to growl, but it sat down just beyond the blanket, watching the woman, then glancing at the men.

Cassie studied the leg. At least there were no bones poking through the skin. She touched the swollen lower leg, but the woman didn't respond. Perhaps her being unconscious was a good thing. "Roll one side of the blanket and lay it next to her. We can scoot her over easier than lifting her." Micah did as she suggested.

Chief knelt beside Cassie and ran his hands over the leg. "We will set it now."

"Set it?"

He nodded. "Before she wake up."

If she wakes up. Cassie's mind finished his statement.

"Let me get some wrappings. What can we use for a splint?" She'd watched the doctor who'd accompanied the Wild West Show care for those who got injured and sometimes helped him, so she had a smattering of medical knowledge. Broken bones happened often to rodeo riders. But then there wasn't this lag time between the break and the setting. What could they do?

Chief thought for a moment. "Micah, pull one board off storage box under wagon."

Micah and Cassie both climbed up the side of the gully and ran to the wagon. While Micah got the board, Cassie rushed to drop the steps and tripped going up. *Saved by the door*, she thought as she pushed into the wagon and pulled open a cupboard that held the bedsheets and some other linens. Good thing that *Uncle* Jason liked the finer things of life. She threw one sheet on her bed and, with the other in her arms, hustled back to the woman. Chief took out his knife and cut the edges so she could rip the sheets into usable widths. When Micah returned with a board—one that wasn't essential for the integrity of the storage box, he assured her—she wrapped some of the strips around it quickly.

"Ready?" Chief looked at Cassie and at Micah, and both nodded. Cassie chewed on her bottom lip. What if they made it worse? What if they killed her while trying to help her? *God, please.* She had no time to continue praying or thinking.

Cassie instructed the chief to kneel by the woman's leg while Cassie knelt by her foot and Micah by her head. "Micah, put your hands on her shoulders and hold her steady."

"You've done this before?" he asked.

"I've helped the doctor."

"Good." Micah swallowed hard.

"Chief, get a good grip on her thigh."

Chief grasped the woman's thigh while Cassie gripped her ankle with both hands.

"I'm going to pull hard but not jerk." Cassie felt sweat break out on her forehead and neck. "Ready?"

Both men nodded.

"One, two, three."

Cassie pulled, the woman jerked, and the leg gave a muffled snap. Chief probed the shin again and nodded. The leg lay straight and the woman was still breathing. Laying the padded board along the outside of the swollen leg, Cassie began wrapping the board to the leg. Since their splint was longer than the leg, she wrapped the two together so that the board ended at the sole of the woman's foot with the other end nearly to her waist. When she tied the final knot, she nodded and the two men carefully moved their patient to the blanket.

Cassie glanced at Micah and saw that his face had gone white. She hoped hers had not done the same as she wiped the sweat away with the back of her hand. "We'll put her on my bed. I'll go get it ready. You bring her as gently as you can." She slipped on the gravel going up the gully wall but grabbed a bush for balance and kept on moving. Hearing the dog growling again, she ran faster. They didn't need another injury to go along with this one. In the wagon she pulled off the blankets and smoothed out the sheet on the bed. They'd use the clean one over her and add the quilt on top of that. They had to get her warmed up. People could die from exposure to the cold, let alone an injury this severe.

A yelp from outside and an expletive she didn't understand brought her to the doorway. Chief had his back to her, hands gripping two of the blanket corners, thus supporting the woman's shoulders and head as they started up the steps. Micah carried the woman's feet, trying to keep the blanket firm enough to keep the splint from putting more pressure on the woman's body. Slowly Chief found his footing and backed into the wagon, glancing over his shoulder as he did so. When Micah was in the now crowded wagon, they eased their patient onto the bunk bed.

A suffocating odor made Cassie gag and head for the open door. Staring out at the sage- and juniper-covered land and sucking clean air, she tried to figure out what to do. They had to clean the Indian woman up. But how to get her clothing off and bathe her in the cramped space of the bunk bed? All without vomiting from the stench. The cotton skirt would be the easiest part. Could she ask the men to help her? It certainly wouldn't be proper and might scare the woman to death if she awakened while they were undressing her.

She stepped back in at hearing some lids clatter.

"We pull off the road and stay here tonight." Chief nodded to Micah, who slipped out the door and climbed up on the wagon seat. He backed the wagon and then clucked the team ahead.

Wind Dancer. Without a thought Cassie jumped out the door and landed running. Her horse, still tied to the same bush, nickered when he saw her. Othello trotted beside her. "Where's the other dog?" Cassie asked, as if Othello could answer.

She untied the reins and led Wind Dancer back to the wagon, which had now been pulled off the road onto a level space, and tied him up at the wheel. A growl from under the wagon answered her question.

Inside the wagon Chief had the fire going and a pot of water on to heat.

"Has she responded?"

He shook his head.

"I'm going to clean her up. If I need help removing her clothes . . ." Her voice trailed off.

"Cut them off."

"Oh."

He handed her his knife. "I will round up cattle."

Cassie swallowed against the lump that had taken up residence in her throat. Vomiting was not to be tolerated. She watched Chief leave the room and turned her attention to the woman. "Who are you?" she whispered, laying the back of her hand against the woman's forehead. Her dark hair lay twisted in two braids. Cassie gently probed the woman's head and found a lump the size of a duck egg on the back. Wishing she could see if there was any blood, she dipped a cloth in water and applied it to the spongy lump. The cloth showed dirt but no blood. Was this head injury the reason she was sleeping on instead of screaming out the pain when they set the bone and then moved her?

Before the water was too hot, Cassie used the soap from her trunk and washed the woman's face and her hands. Her skirt was badly torn, so that made it easier to rip and remove. Several scrapes had scabbed over on her legs. By the time Cassie was finished, she and the room were hot from the heat of the stove, and she had a second kettle of water heating. She collapsed onto a chair, wiping the sweat that was starting to drip into her eyes and stared at her charge.

Chief entered the wagon and pulled the rabbits out of one of the pans. "Cook outside. Cattle are grazing while Micah guards."

"Good. Would you please open the hatch to air it out in here?" At his nod, she picked up the sparse mound of clothing and dumped it outside to be scrubbed later. The woman slept on. Was there a difference between being unconscious and regular sleeping? Cassie watched the woman breathe. Her lungs seemed to be working all right. Was this normal for a head wound and a broken leg?

If only she could ask Doc her questions. If he were there, he would tell her what to do. That thought took her right back to the Wild West Show. Even as a little girl she had been fascinated by medical things, dogging the doctor when he took care of the troupe. He finally started letting her help with simple things like bringing water for a patient to drink or sweeping the tent floor or rolling bandages. When she progressed to holding a patient's hand, the smiles as they thanked her were her reward. After nursing her father once when he was sick, she was called on to sit with the wounded or injured even more. While her mother had figured this interest kept her out of trouble, Doc had come to depend on her for simple nursing care of his patients. But nothing like this.

She had to get the wet sheet out from under the woman and a dry one in place. Finally she rolled the wet sheet up from the other side of her patient, laid the dry one in place, and heaved a sigh. She couldn't roll her over alone.

Stepping out the door, she called Chief and asked him to help. She covered the woman with a blanket, and the two of them rolled her over onto the dry sheet, pulled out the wet one, and tugged the dry one under her. Cassie cracked her head on the bunk above her and stepped back to rub the sore spot.

"Thank you. I hope we don't have to do that again." When the woman lay clean and dry under the sheet and quilt, Cassie felt weariness roll over her in waves. What if the woman died and they had done all this for nothing? She sank onto the lone chair and propped her elbows up on the fold-down table. The breeze blowing into the wagon was turning her sweat to cold. She pushed the hatch cover up enough to free the board propping it open, and darkness took over the wagon.

When she finally stepped outside, the sun was setting, flinging banners of orange and vermilion against the clouds, setting them afire. All the horses but the one Micah was riding were grazing with the cattle and buffalo. The scene brought her a sense of peace, filling her heart and soul. The breeze bore the tang of sagebrush and juniper, blowing away the stench from inside the wagon.

The woman, if only they knew her name, would have nothing to wear unless her clothes were scrubbed and boiled. The chances of her needing clothing by the morning were so slim that Cassie decided to heat the water for washing the clothes over the campfire after supper. It wasn't like she had a lot to wash. She would hang them in the wagon to dry. Having made that decision, she wandered over to the fire, where Chief had the rabbits sizzling on sticks over the flames.

"My, but that smells good." She pulled in a deep breath. "It'll probably bring coyotes from miles away. We better watch the dogs tonight."

"That one hasn't left his spot since we stopped wagon."

"Are he and Othello doing all right together?"

"Not together," the chief said. "Othello off with Micah."

"Oh. Did anyone give it something to eat?"

"Get bones from supper."

"I see. If she lives, she has her dog to thank." Cassie cupped her elbows in her hands. "What do you know about her?"

"She is Lakota Sioux."

Cassie refrained from asking him how he knew. "She's not very old, I think."

"More than you."

"We need to make her drink."

"Drip warm water into mouth."

"Of course." Cassie turned back to the wagon. She should have thought of that. The clouds were turning dark purple and gray, the air colder. The spectacle was over for another day. Time to light a lamp and see if she could manage to get a little water into their guest. She moseyed back and climbed the steps. *Please, Lord, keep her alive and make her well again.*

The three of them took turns during the night, spooning liquid into their patient and the men checking on the herd. While it took Cassie several tries at first, now the woman opened her mouth when the spoon touched her lips. The men were already rounding up the cattle in the morning when Cassie tried again. This time the woman's eyelashes fluttered.

"Hey, Indian woman, are you getting stronger?" When there was no response, Cassie spooned a couple more times before she stopped. Broth would be better, but what did they have to cook to make it? Between them and the dogs, they'd eaten all the rabbit. She should have kept out enough to boil into broth. How was she supposed to think of everything? Now, not only did she have to think about the cattle, but food for all of them, including two dogs and a severely wounded Indian woman. Knowing for certain where they were going might help make things easier, but perhaps not. For a person who was usually so decisive, she found herself flapping like a flag in the wind.

"You riding with her?" Chief asked later as they were ready to leave.

"I guess so. What if she wakes up and tries to get up?"

Chief didn't answer. Just nodded and, slamming the steps

in place, climbed up on the wagon seat. The jerk when they started moving was announcement enough that they were under way.

A moan came from the woman in the bed. Cassie immediately moved back to her side and soothed a hand over the brown cheek. "You are all right. You are safe now." The eyelids fluttered, and with a sigh, the woman relaxed again. She had warmed up through the night, but she wasn't overly warm. Cassie slid her fingers under the woman's head to feel the lump. It had definitely shrunk. The rocking of the wagon made spooning water impossible. So what could she do?

Her gaze fell on the skirt hanging on the line above the stove. After making sure it was dry, Cassie retrieved her sewing kit from the drawer where she had stashed it and sat down in the square of light from the small window in the door. After several attempts, she was finally able to thread the needle. She knew she'd never win any sewing contests, but she could make the skirt wearable again.

Stitch by stitch she sewed the cut and ripped pieces back together. When finished, she held the skirt up and turned it this way and that. Satisfied, she folded it and laid it at the bottom of the bed. Cassie turned her attention to the woman's shirt, which had at one time been white or a light color. Now, stained gray was the only description possible. It was a shame she didn't have any bluing to soak it in. Nor had she brought flatirons for ironing.

The wagon lurched to a stop and Cassie could hear the steps going down before Chief opened the door. "How is she?"

"She moaned and I thought she might be waking up,

but . . ." Cassie pointed to the bunk and shrugged. "I've been mending her clothes."

Chief grunted. "Watering here."

"Good. You want something to eat?"

He shook his head, giving her a feeling of relief. What did she have to offer the men? They'd dunked the rock-hard biscuits in their coffee for breakfast.

"Come out. Walk around."

Wind Dancer nickered as soon as he saw her. What she wouldn't give to be riding him in the glorious sunshine instead of being cooped up inside the dim wagon. She stretched her arms above her head and bent from side to side. If she didn't work through some of her routines fairly soon, she'd be too stiff and out of practice to make it through even one repetition. But what was the sense in practicing? If those days were really behind her . . . The thought made her blink. Her throat caught on a swallow, and she coughed to clear it.

"We will go hunting tonight."

She nodded. Hopefully it would be too dark to actually shoot at another deer. As Othello was her nose in the wilds here, was she supposed to be Chief's eyes? Micah rode up and leaned over to talk more easily. "How is she?"

"Same."

"Must be rough, riding in the wagon."

Did he mean for Cassie or the Indian woman?

"Would you rather guard the stock?" he asked.

She shook her head. She wanted to be near when the woman opened her eyes.

"Ready?" Chief swung up onto the wagon seat. Cassie climbed inside so Micah could lock the steps in place. And with another jerk they were off.

She rapped on the small door behind where Chief sat. When he opened it, she hollered, "Is her dog still with us?"

"Beside the wagon."

"Good." She wasn't sure why she was so concerned about the dog, but she wanted the woman to have something of her own when she woke up. Something familiar. Sewing now on the woman's vest, which had some beading along the front edge, she studied her patient. The two front pieces of the vest were soft leather, while the back was cotton. She'd cut the back to pull it off the woman. What was she going to do when this chore was finished?

The rocking of the wagon answered her question. She fell asleep and nearly fell off the chair. A nap in the hammock sounded better than on the floor, so she climbed up in it and instantly fell asleep.

Something woke her. She lay there and listened. The wagon was still moving. She heard Micah say something to Chief, but what had awakened her? The mumble came again. She slid out of the hammock and knelt beside the bed. Sure enough, the woman was making sounds. Not English, that was for sure, and since Cassie didn't know any Indian words, if the woman said something discernable, Cassie would be no help. She rapped on the small door again and told Chief what had happened.

"You come drive and I will listen." He stopped the wagon, and they changed places. Cassie hupped the team and they continued south another hour or so. Off in the distance she saw smoke rising. Maybe it was a ranch and they could buy some supplies. She opened the little door.

"Ranch ahead."

"Trade places."

She stopped the team and climbed down to lower the steps. She'd heard about western ranch hospitality. Would they be welcomed as she'd heard if they went there, or were they taking a chance? Chance of what, she wasn't sure, but . . .

11

"So do we go visit that ranch and see if they will sell us some supplies?" Cassie looked from one stoic face to the other. Micah shrugged and Chief seemed to be thinking on it. She sipped from her coffee cup. What if they could buy eggs and butter, grain for the horses, meat other than rabbit? Surely they would be coming to a town where they could buy a real ax—or maybe two. She thought of the roll of money Jason had handed her. She had no idea how many fifties it contained but that's what was on top. If it were all fifties, they would buy two axes for sure.

"Might be better for one to go, not take the wagon and animals down there."

Cassie tried to understand if he was warning her about something. Better to ask than be caught dumb. "Why not all of us?"

Chief nodded to the wagon. "People might think Gypsies. Don't like Gypsies. Not Indians either."

"Why?" She knew he didn't like a lot of questions, but she needed to understand.

"Gypsies steal. They think Indians do too."

"So people think all Gypsies are thieves? And Indians?"

He nodded.

Cassie heaved a sigh. "So I should go."

"Not by yourself."

She almost asked why but hesitated. *Think like Chief would think.* The silence stretched. "I'd take a gun." She looked at Micah, who was doing the same thing as Chief, studying his clasped hands, arms resting on his thighs.

Chief shook his head. "Take Micah with you."

Cassie rolled her eyes. "Oh, all right. But let's get going."

Within minutes he'd saddled the horses and was waiting for her. As they headed west, she looked for the chimney smoke again. Nothing. They loped under the entrance arch and down a trail with two tracks for wagon wheels.

Maybe they'd be able to buy a loaf of bread, cookies, ham, or some other meat. She'd not realized how the thought of seeing a woman's smiling face had branded itself on her mind, but the picture of a woman in her kitchen wouldn't leave her.

They'd been riding for more than half an hour when they finally crested a hill and saw ranch buildings laid out in a shallow valley. There was no visible smoke, although cattle were grazing on the valley floor. Haystacks waited to winter feed, and three horses in a corral whinnied when they saw them coming. They reined in the horses at the hitching rail in front of a long, low log house. Micah shrugged when she looked at him.

She dismounted, climbed the three steps to the porch, and knocked at the door. Nothing. No answer, no sound from inside. She knocked again, the sound thudding around her.

Disappointment doused her like cold water. There would be no fresh food, no grain for the horses, and no friendly voice. She left the porch and remounted without saying a word. After they'd loped beyond the hill she turned to Micah. "Sorry."

"It's not your fault."

"We'll find a town soon." Knowing that she'd not given the trip south any thought, let alone planning, made her wonder about her sanity. But then, she'd been pushed into this, ordered actually. If her father were running the trip, the important things of life, like food and a comfortable place to sleep and feed for the animals, would have been taken care of. Jason let her down. That was it, pure and simple. Some family friend he'd turned out to be. All he had worried about was getting himself on the next train before the men arrived to confiscate everything. And now they were traveling south through land that was so sparsely populated that they'd not seen a single traveler other than the injured Indian woman. She couldn't think of a name bad enough to call him. Sparks of anger made her tighten her jaw.

Wind Dancer tossed his head, then shook it.

"Sorry, fella." She forced her hands to relax on the reins and her legs against his sides to do the same. When they arrived back at the wagon, Chief was rounding up the livestock and the horses were already hitched to the wagon.

After letting Wind Dancer loose, she returned to her vigil in the wagon. What a waste of precious time. She picked up the vest to finish stitching it back together.

That evening no one mentioned the waste of time the ride to the ranch had been, and Cassie kept to her duties without comment. Spooning water into their patient didn't seem to be helping, but other than keeping her clean and dry, she didn't know what to do. With the men sleeping under the wagon again, Cassie enjoyed her hammock.

The next evening when Chief called a halt for the day, he stuck his head in the wagon.

"She seems to be waking up," Cassie told him.

Chief stared from the woman to Cassie.

"She's restless and muttering again."

The woman had been unconscious for two days. Three days if they included the day they found her. Since that brief time when Chief had sat with her, she'd said nothing.

"Any words?"

Cassie shrugged. "If there are, I don't understand the language."

Chief nodded and let down the steps for Cassie to come out.

An hour later she gave the bean pot a stir. They'd cooked beans again and then added the latest rabbit after it sizzled over the fire. Snaring only one wasn't much to feed three people, let alone four. And two dogs. Cassie had skimmed the juice off the mixture and spooned that into the woman's mouth. She got at least a little nourishment. So far she'd not spit anything out. But the woman was wasting away before their eyes. What if she never really woke up? But surely the sounds she was making indicated a recovery—of sorts.

The thought made Cassie fight back tears. Even though she had no idea who the woman was or what had happened to her, she'd come to care for her. She'd tried talking to her, but there was no response. Not to singing either. The muttering had stopped again too. "What if we bring her dog in here?"

"Indians don't make pets of dogs like white man. When hungry, dog is good."

Cassie closed her eyes. Yes, she'd heard that the Indians ate dog, but one would have to be starving to do that. But people often ate horse meat too. She shook her head. She'd better watch out for her two best friends when they got to the Pine Ridge Reservation, where Chief had lived before he joined the Wild West Show. "I'm going to bring him in."

"Won't come."

"I can try." She swung the door open and, once on the ground, looked for the dog. There he was, right under the wagon under the bunk bed. She returned to fetch a biscuit dipped in bacon fat. Surely no dog would be able to resist that treat.

She held it out. "Come on. You can have it." He reached out, nostrils quivering. She backed up. He followed a couple of steps, nose quivering all the while. She backed up again. He lunged, jaws snapping. She fell back on her rear and yelped. He grabbed the biscuit and retreated back under the wagon, growling while he devoured it. Cassie checked her hand. He'd not even left a scratch, but she was still shaking.

Chief stood on the steps, his sober face fighting a smile.

"Go ahead and laugh. At least I tried." She picked herself up and dusted the back of her pants. "You can be sure I won't try that again."

"Told you."

"You told me he wouldn't come. Well, he came all right. Where's Othello?"

"With Micah and cattle." Chief sat down on the step. "Need to go hunting."

Cassie groaned. While she understood the need for more

meat, the thought of killing for it made her stomach do flip-flops. "I guess. But who will stay with her?"

"She safe here. I bring up horses."

Cassie stepped back into the wagon to get the rifles. If a deer came close enough, maybe Chief would be able to shoot it. As she started to leave, she looked over at their patient. Her eyes were open, and she was looking around. "Welcome back."

The gaze wandered over to Cassie and stopped.

The two women studied each other without moving.

"Hello," Cassie whispered, as if she might frighten the woman with any louder noise.

The woman nodded—barely.

"I am Cassie." She pointed to herself.

"I Runs Like a Deer."

The words were so soft and scratchy that Cassie could hardly understand them. "Runs Like a Deer?"

A nod.

"And you speak English?"

"Some." She touched the board at her side.

"You have a broken leg."

"Broken?"

Cassie nodded. "We set your leg and put a splint on it. Sorry the board is so big. That's all we had."

The woman stared at her, making Cassie wonder if she understood.

"Splint?"

"To keep the break from getting worse."

The woman asked something, but Cassie didn't understand her, so she shrugged.

"Can walk?"

"Not yet, but one day."

"One day?"

"Someday."

"Oh." Runs Like a Deer closed her eyes, slowly rolling her head from side to side.

Cassie couldn't figure out how to tell her where the break was. With the size of the board she probably thought her entire leg was smashed, instead of just her shinbone.

"Can I get you something to eat?"

"Ready?" Chief called from outside.

Cassie opened the door and stuck her head out. "She woke up. Her name is Runs Like a Deer, and she speaks some English."

Chief shook his head. "No more Runs Like a Deer."

"It might heal perfectly straight."

He shrugged and shook his head.

"I need to feed her something."

"Hunt first, before dark. She sleep."

Cassie heaved a sigh and fetched the rifles. He was right. Now they needed more meat than ever. She shoved her rifle into the scabbard and mounted Wind Dancer. "Let's go."

They rode quite a ways, with Chief watching the ground intently. When he stopped and slid to the ground, she rode up to him.

"See? Deer sign."

"So?"

"Fresh." He studied the tracks. "Go that way." He pointed down the hill. "Water running over there. Tie up your horse."

Cassie did as ordered and slid shells into her rifle, handing Chief some for his. But trying to mimic the way he moved without a sound sent a pebble bouncing before her. He shook his head, a frown making words unnecessary. He pointed to a rock behind a low shrub. "You wait there. Be ready to shoot." He pointed ahead. When she nodded, he left the trail they'd been following and swung off to the right. Since he'd explained his method of scaring up the deer for her to shoot, she understood what he wanted. But it still meant she would have to kill one of the beautiful animals. Or maim it. The thought made her choke.

"You have to hit it," she told herself. "This could be life or death." She positioned her rifle and made herself comfortable on the rock. Chief had disappeared. A hawk *screed* high overhead. She loved the sounds of the hawks and eagles flying so free.

Never had she been on the land this long before. She'd only taken short rides sometimes after a show, to see one of the local sites, but never this close to wild things.

A movement caught her attention. She raised the rifle just as a buck broke through the thicket. She tracked his front shoulder and fired. The deer dropped as if he'd hit a wall.

Cassie stood and made her way down to the fallen animal. She'd shot well. Her father would be proud, but the bloody hole in the beautiful hide made her throat choke.

Chief appeared at her side. "Good."

She turned away, drawing in deep breaths of clean air not yet tainted by the smell of blood.

"Now, cut his throat so he can bleed." He handed her his knife.

She shook her head, her hands, whispering, "No, no. I can't." Then she turned and retched into the brush.

Chief muttered. She could hear him doing something but kept herself from looking. She'd shot that beautiful creature. Surely that should be enough. But when she heard Chief grunt, she turned back and helped him hoist the carcass onto the rump of his horse and tie it to the back of the saddle. She carefully kept her focus away from the pile of entrails left behind.

"You okay?"

She nodded. Surely she would be able to get used to this. After all, they had to have meat, and in order for them to eat it, it had to be killed and dressed. She understood that fact of life, but it didn't mean she had to like it.

They rode back to camp without a word.

"The woman's awake," Micah said as he helped untie the deer. "Good shot."

"Cassie shot it."

"She did?" Micah stared at her, respect all over his face. "But . . ."

"I know. I said I wouldn't shoot animals, but I have to get used to a different kind of life out here." She unsaddled Wind Dancer and hobbled his front feet so he wouldn't be able to run off. Not that she thought he would, but he was learning all about a new life too. She stepped up into the wagon and saw that her patient was sleeping again.

Cassie laid the rifles on the folded-down table and dug out her cleaning supplies. All in hand, she sat outside on the steps and set to work using the cleaning rod to clean the inside of the barrel. After hers was wiped down, she decided to clean Chief's. Since he'd not fired it since the last cleaning, she simply wiped it down with a rag and wrapped them both in the cotton cloths she kept for that purpose and put them in the gun bag. It was dim in the wagon, so she lit the kerosene lamp and set it on the shelf, then set about lighting the stove. When the fire was devouring the kindling, she added several bigger pieces and, setting the lids back in place, picked up the pot of rabbit-and-bean stew and set it on the hottest section of the stove. She could hear a fire crackling outside too.

With all her banging around, surely the woman would be awake. She turned to the bunk to find dark eyes watching her. "Are you hungry?"

"Water."

"That we have." Cassie took a cup outside and filled it at the water barrel. "She's awake, Chief. Do you want to talk with her?"

"Later."

"What are you doing?" She walked over to the campfire to see thinly sliced venison draped on stick racks.

"Drying meat."

"How long will that take?"

"Till morning."

"You aren't going to sleep?"

"Micah will take turns." He pointed to the frying pan full of sizzling meat. "Liver."

"Oh. Good." She'd heard that Indians ate the livers of their kills raw. At least he was cooking it. Maybe he had already eaten his piece. The thought made her hurry back into the wagon.

After holding the cup of water for Runs Like a Deer, she stirred the pot and dished some stew into the cup. She blew on it and then, sitting on the edge of the bed, held out a spoonful. "Just a few bites so you don't get sick." Somewhere she had heard that bit of wisdom. But the woman drifted off to sleep before she could eat too much. So Cassie stirred the kettle again and took a bite to see how hot it was. The flavor made her smile. Rabbit was good with beans. After it was bubbling, she took the cast-iron pot outside and set it by the fire.

"Supper's ready."

The men each hung the last strips they had on the rack before taking the bowls as she filled them and sitting on the nearby rocks. Othello came over and sat beside her, his nose twitching at the food smells. The other dog eased out from under the wagon, well away from Othello. When Chief threw him a bone from the rabbit, he caught it and backed under the wagon again.

When she handed Othello a bone, he took it gently, his tail thumping his appreciation. Micah threw one under the wagon, and the Indian woman's dog snatched it up. Othello gave Micah a sad look.

"You hurt his feelings."

Micah and Chief both rolled their eyes, but Micah tossed the next bone to Othello.

When Cassie felt sufficiently full, she set her bowl down for Othello and stroked his back as he licked it clean. Chief called him and handed him one of the leg bones from the deer and threw another under the wagon.

"How far do you think we have come?"

Chief looked up at her. "Maybe eighty miles. In South Dakota now."

"How far do we have to go to reach Deadwood?" Any small town would provide some relief from the monotony of being on the trail day after day.

"Maybe hundred thirty, hundred forty."

"So we're not even halfway."

"Tomorrow we meet road from Medora heading to Deadwood. Faster then. Some towns."

"I'd like to buy an ax. That hatchet is not good."

"Sharpen it."

"I did. Many times."

Chief had taken up slicing the venison again and hanging it on the racks, pushing the already shrinking pieces closer together.

"How would we cut down logs for a house with that hatchet?"

He shrugged.

"You'd have thought Jason would have kept more supplies in his wagon."

"Why? Not need them. He had lots of men to do the work."

"True. He didn't much like to get his hands dirty."

"Lazy."

"Well, I don't think I'd say that." She stared into the fire, thinking back to the show. When they were setting up or taking down, Jason always managed to be somewhere else. Oftentimes sitting in his wagon, she surmised. Often drinking. A whiff of his breath gave him away the times she'd gone looking for him. She'd learned to not do that if she didn't want to be embarrassed. Things sure had changed after her father died.

Deciding not to spend her evening reliving sad times, she took the bowls down to the creek, scrubbed them with sand and water, and returned to the wagon. "Night."

"You feed her?"

"I will try again." She leaned over to pat Othello, who sat by the stairs waiting for his good-night attention. "You take care of things out here. That's your job." He leaned against her legs, rubbing his cheek on the pant leg and grinning up at her. "One of these days, boy, we'll have a house or a tent again. Some place bigger than this so you can come inside too." One more pat and she climbed the steps. The fire should be out by now, but she had left the kerosene lamp burning. What a waste of kerosene if Runs Like a Deer was still sleeping.

But she wasn't. She stared at Cassie from the dimness of the bed.

"Can I get you something?"

"Drink."

"I have a pitcher of water right here. Would you like a few more bites of stew?" Cassie poured water in the cup and held it for the woman. She raised her hand to say stop when she'd had enough.

"Too fast."

"Oh, I'm sorry. Want to try again?"

A knock at the door and Micah announced, "Here's the stewpot."

"Bring it in."

He opened the door, handed it to her, and closed the door again, as if afraid the women were not completely dressed.

Three or four spoonfuls and again the woman signaled enough.

"They are drying venison over the fire outside," Cassie said, hoping for some kind of conversation.

No answer. She hooked up the hammock and got ready for bed. At least she didn't have to wear all her clothes to bed at night like during the blizzard. What could she expect from the woman who was so terribly weak? That she would talk and tell her what had happened? That would be good, but Cassie felt pretty sure that wouldn't happen. Tomorrow Chief would have to come in and try to talk with her, if they spoke the same language. What could they do with her? Maybe there would be a doctor in one of the towns, and they could leave her with him until she healed. Acting the part of the Good Samaritan certainly had its drawbacks. How could she afford to feed one more mouth?

12

*D*isappointment dogged Cassie.

Why had she set store by visiting that ranch? Three days later and it was still bothering her. It wasn't the only one along the road, and Chief assured her they would come to a town fairly soon. Disappointment dragged together with regret and missing the show. At least there'd always been someone to talk to when she'd been with the troupe. Here, Othello carried on a better conversation than her three human companions did. Maybe it was being stuck in the wagon that was doing her in. Accomplishing anything in the wagon while they were traveling yielded bruises like the one on her thigh when the wagon hit a rut, which seemed to happen on a regular basis.

How their patient stood the pain the rough roads were

causing increased Cassie's respect for the woman tenfold. However, Runs Like a Deer was growing stronger daily. When they were stopped for the night, Micah brought a piece of wood that he had flattened into a smooth board that extended from her heel to her knee.

"Please wrap this."

Cassie nodded, running her fingers over the smooth surface. "How did you get it so smooth?"

"A rock."

"She'll need a crutch next."

"I'm working on that."

"Good. In the meantime she can lean on me to get around." Chief and Micah had used a blanket to carry the Indian woman outside once, but the board had been too long and did not allow her to sit down.

"Crutch will be done tonight."

"Thank you." She pulled out a drawer that held bedding and proceeded to rip the sheet into strips and then wrapped the board. Cassie showed it to her patient. "This should help." Starting at the woman's foot as the woman lay on the bottom bunk, Cassie untied and removed the ties that bound the long board to the leg. She lifted the board away and leaned it against the bed frame. The woman's leg seemed to be healing nice and straight, so she laid the new board in place and bound it to the leg, being careful not to wrap it too tight.

"You still have to be careful, but now at least you can sit up. Micah promised to make a crutch for you tonight. Then you can walk again, but don't put that foot on the ground." She wished she knew if her patient understood what she was saying. "Do you want to sit up?"

Runs Like a Deer nodded and propped herself on her elbows, nearly banging her head on the frame above her.

"Careful. Let me help you." Cassie grasped the bound leg and helped ease both legs over the edge of the bed. When the woman flinched as Cassie lowered her leg, she stopped. "Better not do that." She glanced around the small space, searching for something to help, but since every inch was filled with necessary supplies, she shook her head. *If we could get you to the chair* . . .

Runs Like a Deer looked in the direction Cassie had been looking.

"Chair."

"I was thinking the same thing, but I think we'd be better having Micah pick you up." She went to the door and called for him.

"Here" came his voice from the direction of the fire pit Chief had already constructed. Micah arrived at the wagon door immediately and nodded as Cassie explained what they wanted. "You want I should carry her outside?"

"No, I think not for this first venture. Let's just move her to the chair, and we can prop her foot on the wooden box."

Micah took the woman into his arms, and trying to turn his burden around, he bumped her into the bed frame.

Runs Like a Deer flinched and clung to his arm, her jaw tight, but she relaxed when he settled her on the chair and propped her leg on the box. "Thank you."

"Welcome." Micah grabbed the pillow off the bed and, raising her leg, arranged the pillow under it. "Better?"

She nodded and leaned back in the chair with a sigh.

Cassie studied her patient. She had found an old shirt of Jason's in a drawer and dressed Runs Like a Deer in that, plus an old skirt of her own. "Maybe we can change your clothes when you are stronger. I have your own clothing all clean and waiting."

"Thank you."

"Bring out the kettle and the frying pan," Chief called.

The kettle of beans had been soaking since the morning so were now ready to be cooked. He would be frying the last of the fresh deer meat, the remainder of it dried and hanging in bags from the ceiling. Cassie handed the kettle to Micah and dug the frying pan out of the storage box. She could feel the Indian woman watching her.

"Can I get you something?"

A shake of the head was her only answer.

What had she been thinking about during these long days in confinement, Cassie wondered. They still knew nothing about her. Where was she going? Or coming from?

While the men did the cooking outside, she decided to clean up the wagon. The broom was still in the same cupboard as when her father had lived in the wagon. Sweeping was a good place to start.

Who was out with the cattle if both of the men were in camp? She propped the broom and headed outside. With a sigh of relief she saw the animals not far from the camp, where the prairie grass looked to never have been grazed. Surely the ranchers around there still believed in the open range. They'd not seen any farms. Maybe this area was too desolate for farming. Not that she really understood the difference between ranching and farming. She clamped down on those kinds of thoughts. She was on her way to a valley that must be truly beautiful, since her father carried the memory with him all those years. Once they were there, they would raise cattle and horses, like her pa always talked about. Where she would get the money to do all this was one of those thoughts she kept stuffing back in a box in the far recesses of her mind and slamming the lid on it.

She sat down on the bed by Runs Like a Deer. "Can I ask you some questions?"

The woman looked at her.

"Do you understand what I am saying?" The nod in return made Cassie smile. "Good. I'm not sure how much English you speak." Watching the woman's face told her to slow down.

"Will you tell me if you don't understand?" Another nod. "Can you talk with Chief?" Cassie continued after this nod. "In English or Sioux?"

"Sioux more." She said something else, but Cassie had no idea what. This time it was her turn to shrug. "Let me go get Chief." Out the door she went again and down the steps, feeling like they had come a long way. She explained what they'd said. "Will you go talk with her, find out about her?"

"You will watch the fire?"

"Where's Micah?"

"Out with cattle."

"Okay." When he returned sometime later, she waited for him to tell her what he had learned, but instead, he sat staring into the fire.

"Well?" When he didn't answer, she gave the pot of beans a stir and glared into the fire. Why was it so hard to get these men to talk? All she wanted was simple answers, after all. Grabbing the coffeepot, she went over to the water barrel, and after swishing a small bit of water around in the pot and tossing it on the ground, she filled it and set it on two rocks positioned on the edge of the flames. "So what did you find out?"

"She's running away from a man who beat her."

"Oh." Cassie heaved a sigh. "Where is she going?"

"Rosebud is her reservation, but she doesn't want to go there."

"Her reservation?"

He nodded. "But farther than Pine Ridge."

"Can she do that?"

"All Indians are to be on reservations."

"Does she have family there?"

"Maybe. She walked from Montana, but Rosebud was her home. She fell and broke her leg."

"Is the man after her?"

"She thinks he might be dead."

"Was he sick or injured?"

He nodded.

"Which one?" When he stared at her, she wished she'd never asked. "She killed him?" Her question came out on a whisper.

He half shrugged. "She thought so, but when she went back, he was still alive. She dressed his head wound, got him into bed and left, after asking the neighbors to check on him. She doesn't think they did. He was mean to everyone."

Aching to know more of the story, Cassie stirred the beans. "I better help her back to bed."

"I did."

Cassie lifted the lid on the frying pan and turned the meat before covering it back up. With the coffee water heating, she returned to the wagon to fetch the coffee and some salt for the meat. Visions of the dining tent at the show flitted through her mind. There had always been a variety of food—real choices, not like now where you had two: eat it or don't. And she'd never had to cook a day in her life. Or hunt for the meat they needed, or carry water, or scrub dishes with sand in a cold creek. And there'd always been plenty of people around, most of whom she thought of as friends.

She paused on the step before heaving a sigh. Her mother had always said to be thankful for everything. That sounded much easier from a soft bed in her parents' tent than now. When traveling they had used the wagon, but once the show was set up for a few days, they moved into the spaciousness of a tent. Or did she say be thankful *in* everything? Either way, Cassie was having trouble with the whole idea. Yes, she believed Jesus Christ died for her sins. Yes, she believed God loved her. But if this whole fiasco was His idea of love . . .

Okay, she ordered herself. *Think of one thing to be thankful for. Right now. One thing.* A coyote howled off in the distance. Another answered. *God, thank you that I can hear. And see.* There. Two things. She pushed open the door to the darkness of the wagon. She should have come in and lighted a lamp for Runs Like a Deer, but the regular breathing from the woman on the bunk bed told her their patient was sound asleep. Moving around like that must have been mighty tiring.

The next morning, after helping Runs Like a Deer into her own clothing, Cassie left her sleeping in the wagon and climbed up on the seat beside Chief. She'd awakened in the middle of the night with a whole list of questions she wanted to ask him. If she could get him talking.

She chewed on the idea awhile before asking, "Would you please tell me how you met my father?"

"I heard he was asking for a guide to the Black Hills, so I went to him and said I could do that."

She'd not heard him string that many words together since they'd left the show. "When was that?"

He shrugged. "Long time ago."

"I know that, but when?"

"After the white man invaded our land to find gold."

"I see. What happened?"

"Your pa and a friend of his wanted to find land, go hunting, look for more gold, whatever. White man banned again, but it made no difference."

"Why did you become his guide, then?"

"He offered good money."

"I see. You lived on the reservation?"

A nod. "Pine Ridge."

"What was my father like? What did he like to do?"

"He played cards, was a good gambler, won a lot of money."

"He did?"

Chief turned to look at her. "He said something, he did it. No lying or cheating."

That made her feel warm inside. "He was good-looking, wasn't he?"

"Women liked him."

"Men too." She remembered that well. There were always lots of people wanting to talk with her father. "He loved to tell stories."

"He did."

"So you were his guide. Did you help him find his valley?"

"Yes. Him and Ivar Engstrom."

"Was he a good friend of my father?"

Another nod.

"Where did he meet up with Jason Lockwood?"

"In Rapid City. They talked long time, then said, 'Start a Wild West show.' "

Cassie rested her elbows on her thighs and propped her chin on her hands, staring out at the landscape. So her father was a gambler. Somehow that didn't surprise her, but his answer, while giving her something to ponder, raised more questions.

"And they asked you to join them?"

"Me and others from the reservation. I stayed."

When she asked another question, he grunted and shook his head. "Enough."

The next day they met up with the road coming from Medora and leading to Deadwood. They had to get off the road for a mule-drawn line of dray wagons to go by and wait for the billowing dust to settle, a sure sign there must be a town up ahead.

As they finally neared the town, the road grew busier. They encountered teams pulling buckboards, riders on horseback, and even one on a mule, everyone calling out greetings. They caught up with a wagonload of pigs, the stink announcing the cargo far sooner than sight.

Driving the wagon for a change, Cassie wrinkled her nose. She heard someone tell a boy that this was a Gypsy wagon. Couldn't they read the sides of the wagon that boasted of the Lockwood and Talbot Wild West Show? But then, perhaps they should have covered up the sign. What if there was a warrant out for her arrest for stealing this wagon? More things to worry about. At least they had money to buy supplies at a store here.

Chief rode up beside her. "We're taking the cattle around the town. Will wait on the other side."

"All right." She flicked the reins, wishing she were riding Wind Dancer instead of the wagon. But who else could do the shopping? Not that she was adept at that either. Some days just seemed a heap more trouble than they were worth.

When she saw a mercantile, she pulled past it and parked on the side street. No sense flaunting their wagon if she could help it. Stepping down, she tied the horses to a post and felt in her pocket for the roll of bills. Sugar was one of the things on her list. And more coffee. Real bread would taste mighty good for a change, if they had any to sell. She let down the steps and opened the door to tell Runs Like a Deer what was happening.

"It won't take me long," she said, shutting the door again. While the woman was awake, she lay in the bed as she'd asked her to do. If she got up when the wagon was rocking, who knew how badly that leg could be reinjured.

When Cassie stepped inside the mercantile, the wonderful fragrance of freshly baked bread greeted her, making her mouth water.

"How can I help you, miss?" The smile of the man behind the counter was missing one front tooth. The town probably wasn't big enough for a dentist.

She laid her list on the wooden counter that looked about ready for the cast-iron stove that warmed at least one end of the long room. What did they do? Chop wood on it?

He looked over her list. "I can get this together in a few minutes. You want to look around while you wait? We have fresh bread and eggs. Both just arrived today."

"I'll take a dozen eggs and a loaf of bread, then. Thank

you for telling me." She wandered the aisles, marveling at the assortment of goods they had. Boots and saddles, harnesses, metal pails and washtubs; there were spices behind him on the wall, and on the right side, bolts of fabric stood at attention along with other sewing notions. It was a good thing she had plenty of clothes, so she needn't spend money there. She stopped at a rack of sheepskin jackets lined with the wool on the inside and then walked on. Her wool coat would have to do for at least another year. Maybe Chief could trap enough rabbits for a vest.

When the man called out to tell her that her order was ready, she returned to the counter.

"See anything else that suits your fancy?"

"Plenty, but we need to be pushing on. You wouldn't know how long to Deadwood, would you?"

"You ridin' or drivin'?"

"Both." She almost mentioned they were trailing livestock too, but something warned her to keep quiet.

"Probably about five days, depending on how hard you push. That'll be ten dollars and fifty cents."

She wished she'd left the roll in the wagon but peeled off a fifty without exposing the roll and laid it on the counter.

"Sorry, miss. I can't make change for that. You'll have to go to the bank to get change. You have anything smaller?"

"I think so." She glanced down to find a ten and a one and held them out.

With a smile, he gave her the change. "You have someone to carry that sack of oats?"

"Ah no. Guess I'll have to do it myself."

"I'll take that out if you can manage the rest. Where you hitched?"

"Around the corner." She scooped up her packages and walked ahead of him, pushing open the door and holding it for him to get through.

"Mighty nice day, ain't it?" He slung the burlap sack of grain up on his shoulder and followed her around the corner. "Land o' mercy. That rig yours?"

She nodded and let the steps down to set her packages inside. "That goes under here." She motioned to the wooden box attached to the wagon, next to the water barrel, and lifted the lid. The grain went in with a *thunk*, and she closed the lid.

"Where'd you get a wagon like this?" He read the banner on the side. "Always wanted to see a Wild West show."

"Yeah, me too. Thanks for your help."

"Good luck on the rest of your trip."

"Thanks." She levered herself back up onto the seat. "Good day." As she drove back onto the main street, she could sense him watching her leave. She should have ridden Dancer in and led a pack horse. Would have caused a lot less interest both in the shopkeeper and the folks on the streets. Should have. Why was hindsight always right?

13

"hought you decided to stay in town," Chief called.

Cassie waved as she drove into the open area where the animals grazed or lay chewing their cuds and the men waited. Othello barked a greeting, his tail whipping, flews wide in a doggy grin of delight.

Cassie shook her head. "Getting all these supplies takes time." And money. She should have gone to the bank and changed that fifty. Whatever possessed Jason to carry bills of such size? She realized she knew the answer before she asked the question. How could she have missed it all this time? He liked to look big and successful, and that's what probably drove the show into bankruptcy. "Let's get a move on, then."

Since most of the cattle and George were lying down, it took some whistling and Othello's nipping at their heels to get them up and stretched and in forward motion. Cassie sat in the driver's seat of the wagon, waiting patiently. She should get down and go check on their patient, but she decided that could wait. Surely Chief would come and take over the reins, and if he did, she was going to ride horseback for a change, even if it wasn't on Wind Dancer. This sitting on a board seat was hard on the rear.

They'd driven a couple of miles before Chief finally rode up. "How is Runs Like a Deer doing?" she asked.

"Restless. Not like towns."

"So where is Pine Ridge Reservation?"

"South and east of Rapid City."

"And we go through Rapid City?"

He shrugged. "If you want, but the valley is south and west."

"There are other routes?" Sometimes—no, make that often—she wished that Chief, and Micah too, would be a little more forthcoming. A real conversation would be a pleasure. Like being hit with a board, she missed the show, the friendly chatter, and people helping one another, more like a family than a business. Within seconds fury lit a fire in her middle. If Jason Talbot had been handy, so help her, she would have used him for a target. His hat first and then—

She jerked herself back from such contemplations. He'd managed to destroy her entire life with his announcement that they weren't making enough money and were closing down. She tried to ignore the inner turmoil. Interesting how often this was stealing up on her and trying to slam her to the ground. She watched the horses pulling the wagon, the scenery, anything to get her mind off the past. She glanced to the side. Chief had left sometime during her backward skip in time. Now she couldn't even ask him to drive so she could ride. Anything sounded better than thinking those thoughts again.

But her mind refused to obey and brought up another point. What about the roll of bills he'd given her? Not that it would have gone far in paying all those people and keeping them and the animals fed. She felt it still in her pocket. After seeing the man at the store eyeing it, she realized what a stupid thing she had done by taking the entire roll into the store. Castigating herself ate up a couple more miles.

The sun was still high in the sky when Chief rode back to say he thought they should stop for the night. After being on the trail for the better part of two weeks, the livestock were growing weary and he thought it best to stop early. She followed his lead and drove the wagon off the road and into an area that already had a fire pit. Obviously other travelers had used this for a camping spot.

"River is right over there." Chief pointed toward the west. "I will get wood."

She watched him ride off, wishing it were her on the horse. She could drag wood in as well as anyone. Why didn't she tell him that? After all, who was in charge here? She was, supposedly. One more strike against her today. Instead, she climbed down and stretched before unhitching the team. Exchanging their bridles for halters with lead ropes, she led them over the little rise and saw the river about a hundred yards away. Micah already had the cattle and spare horses standing ankle- and knee-deep and drinking their fill. Wind Dancer lifted his head and nickered a greeting.

Knowing the team shouldn't drink much water yet, she pulled them back after a short time and, much to their dislike, led them back to the camp and tied them to the wagon wheels.

Opening the door to the wagon, she was surprised to see Runs Like a Deer waiting.

"You're using your crutch."

She nodded and patted the wood stick propping her up. "Come out."

"If you want, but I don't know how you'll manage the steps. You shouldn't put weight on that foot yet."

The woman eyed the steps, awkwardly sat down in the doorway, and using her good foot, she scooted down the first step. She sat for a moment and then slid down the second. With her crutch, she pulled herself upright and walk-hopped to a nearby rock. She sat down and took time to catch her breath.

Cassie realized how weak the woman was, but wasn't surprised, since she'd been in bed for nearly a week by now.

"Very good. How we'll get you back up, I don't know, but I guess Micah could carry you."

Chief dragged in several large branches with plenty of limbs and dropped them by the fire pit. Coiling his rope, he tied it back to the saddle and dismounted to remove the saddle and bridle and let the horse loose to join the others. The team nickered and stamped their feet, so he let them go too. They all dropped their heads to graze not far from the camp.

Cassie climbed into the wagon to get the matches and, while there, stuffed the roll of bills into a corner of her trunk under her clothes. Back outside she handed Chief the matches, as always, marveling at the ease with which he started fires.

"Don't need matches."

"I know, but you have to admit this is faster."

His grunt was a standard reply. "Make biscuits?"

"We don't need to. I brought fresh bread from the store."

"Good."

"I could make biscuits."

Cassie spun to stare at Runs Like a Deer. "How?" she blurted out.

"You bring the flour and all here, and I make them. Use the frying pan." The woman could speak far better than she'd led them to believe.

And here she'd been wondering if Runs Like a Deer understood her. Feeling more than a little disgruntled, Cassie shook her head and climbed back in the wagon to fetch the ingredients. Might as well let her make them. They could save the bread for breakfast and for sandwiches for the noon meal. She picked up flour, lard, salt—what else was needed? She'd seen the cooks at the Wild West Show make the biscuits using milk, but she didn't have milk, so water would have to do. A can of baking powder on the cupboard shelf caught her attention, and she grabbed that, along with a bowl and a spoon, before returning to the now crackling fire.

Watching Runs Like a Deer carefully, Cassie resolved to learn how to cook. No matter how few ingredients they had now, it wouldn't always be this way. Once they reached the valley and built a real house, things would be different. Not that she'd ever lived in a house of her own, but she knew how to dream.

She thought of one of the ranch houses they had seen during their travels. Built of logs with a rock fireplace and chimney, it fit into the trees nearby as if the spot were created just for it. From that moment she'd had a dream. Something new for her. A home of her own in her father's valley of dreams, as she'd come to call their destination. Of course she had dreamed before but always about being the best in the business, or just about improving what she was already doing.

But a home of her own—with curtains at the windows, a place to grow flowers like her mother had always dreamed of doing, a big kitchen stove with an oven to bake biscuits in. She had a lot to learn about cooking and gardening and anything else that needed doing, but she knew she learned quickly. The trick was having a good teacher.

Surely the Black Hills would be more beautiful than the land they'd been traveling through these past days. While she had to admit she had seen some signs of beauty, like the rusts, vermilions, and oranges in the leaves of some trees and the yellows and golds in others on these many miles, she'd also seen enough rocks and scrub trees and dust to last several lifetimes.

Runs Like a Deer stood up on her good leg, and holding out the cast-iron skillet, she handed it to Chief, who was squatting by the fire, feeding it larger wood chunks as he broke them off the branches. He set the pan on a rock beside him and continued feeding the fire.

"Do we use the dried venison tonight?"

"Soaking."

"I was wondering when you would set snares for rabbits again."

"Tonight." Chief flipped one of his braids that was hanging down toward the fire over his shoulder. "Prairie chickens roost in that tree by the river."

Cassie looked to where he pointed. "When?"

"Early dark."

"Will they come if I'm over there?"

"Not too near."

"Once they are up in the tree, you can get closer," Runs Like a Deer said, joining the conversation.

When the sun was behind the horizon but the sunset was still blazing above the hills on the other side of the river, Cassie went into the wagon for her long gun. Would she be close enough to use the shotgun? Since she wasn't sure, she brought out both and the ammunition.

"Shotgun is good."

"I just shoot them out of the tree?"

Chief nodded. "The birds are small, so we cook them on sticks."

Cassie returned her rifle to the storage box and strode off toward the river. When she got close enough to the tree, she hunkered down behind a rock and made herself comfortable. Othello left Micah with the cattle and came to her to get his ears rubbed before flopping down beside her.

She had just started to feel the evening cold when the whir of wings caught her attention. A bird flew in and settled itself next to the trunk of the tree. If she'd not been watching she would have missed it, because he disappeared when he quit moving. As she watched, two more appeared and then a flock flew in together. Reminding herself to mentally mark which branches had birds on them, she heard another rush go by. These were so close, she was sure she felt the air from their wings. She kept stroking Othello's ears so he wouldn't move and scare them away. Once the birds seemed to have settled down and the evening star appeared in the west, she crept forward. Othello bonded himself to her knee. While she heard the birds rustling, none flew away. If only she could see them better.

When she was within ten feet of the trunk, she lifted her shotgun and aimed at a bump she thought must be a prairie chicken. When she pulled the trigger, two birds bounced off some branches and fell to the ground. Afraid all the birds would fly away, she immediately blasted the tree again and reloaded, and within minutes she had what she thought must be ten. Othello sniffed one of the lifeless bodies and looked up at her for instructions.

"Bring them here." She should have brought a bag to put them in. She picked up a couple of them, wishing for at least something to tie their feet together.

"You done shooting?" Micah called from somewhere behind her.

"Yes."

He rode up, his horse snorting at the smell of blood. "I'll put them in the saddlebags."

She helped him stuff the limp bodies into the bags and tied the latigo so they wouldn't fall out.

"Good."

"Thank you. That was sure different than shooting in a match." Often in a match they'd shot clay pigeons, and when they'd used live birds, she had never picked them up. "I'll meet you back at camp."

"Be careful. Hard to see."

"I know." She and Othello trudged after the horse and rider, the gun over her shoulder. "Well, I can shoot them, but I sure don't know what to do next. Gut them, I suppose, huh, Othello?" *We need these for food, so there is no sense in feeling bad about shooting them. After all, God provided quail in the wilderness for the Israelites, and here He is doing the same for us.* That thought made her feel much better. Even so, she was glad she hadn't seen them up close and alive on the ground.

The dog stopped tracking something and came to walk right beside her, close enough so her hand could trail on his head. By the time they arrived at camp, Chief and Runs Like a Deer had half of the birds gutted, feathers removed, and the meat on spits over the fire.

"What are you doing?"

"Skinning them so don't have to pluck feathers." The woman tossed a piece of something over to her dog, still under the wagon, and then a piece to Othello. "Gizzards," Runs Like a Deer answered before Cassie could even ask.

Since there seemed to be nothing for her to do, Cassie returned to the wagon and brought out her cleaning supplies. Sitting down on the wagon steps, she cleaned her shotgun, all the while listening to Chief and the woman talk in their native language. Not that they said a lot, but she had no idea what was being said. That bothered her too. It looked like lately just about everything bothered her.

Cassie put her things away and stopped long enough to light the kerosene lamp. While the lamp was running low on fuel, she decided not to refill it at the moment. Instead, she looked around the tight space, trying to determine what she could put away so there would be more room to move around. Strange that she'd not bothered to do this earlier, but it wasn't like there had been any spare time. She began opening drawers and cupboards, realizing quickly that Jason had used only a few of the spaces or had removed things before he left. Some contained housekeeping things, some were empty, and some she had already used.

There was no food anywhere, other than what they had bought and brought. She used the lower drawers for clothing and the cupboards for foodstuffs, so they would be out of the way if any mice found their way inside. If she could get her trunk emptied, they could tie it to the back of the wagon.

She lost track of time as she moved some things and sorted others. One drawer was stuffed with papers and envelopes, letters, and what looked to be bills. She heaved a sigh. If all of these were unpaid, no wonder the show went belly-up. She pulled the drawer out of the wall and set it on the table so she could see better. The farther down in the drawer she dug, the farther back she went in time.

Micah knocked on the doorframe. "Supper's ready."

"Thanks. I'll be right there. It sure smells good."

When Cassie finally went outside, Runs Like a Deer handed her a full plate, with steam rising off of it. "Thank you. These fresh biscuits look so good."

Cassie sat down on a low rock near the campfire. Chief and Micah were already chewing the meat off the bird bones.

Micah raised the carcass he'd been eating. "Really good. Start in."

"Thanks, I will." The first bite made her close her eyes in bliss. Good did not begin to cover it. "And I thought chicken was good. This is delicious. Why have we not done this before?"

"Didn't see any birds roosting like that. Some sleep on the ground, harder to find." Chief slid a bird off a stick and onto the Indian woman's plate, then handed it to her.

"Well, I hope we find plenty more such trees."

"Different than shooting deer?"

Cassie knew he was teasing her, so she just nodded and kept on eating. It was different, a lot different. She'd shot birds for years, and while she'd never eaten pigeons, maybe someone had. Shame to waste all the meat if pigeons were as good as these. She cleaned up the juices on her plate with her biscuit. Now this was some supper.

"Will we have birds like this at Pa's valley?"

"Lots of deer and elk."

Cassie groaned. "That's not what I asked." She tossed the bones to Othello, scrubbed her tin plate, and went back inside. The lamp was nearly empty. She blew that one out and shook the lantern. Plenty of kerosene in that one, so she lit it and went back to her sorting, making sure she opened every envelope and read every piece of paper.

She opened one envelope and found a five-dollar bill in it. Who had left it there? Surely this wasn't far enough back to be her father. What a gift! First God gave them quail and now cash. This was easy to be thankful for. Besides, if there was one envelope with money in it, there just might be another.

After adjusting the wick in the lantern so she could have more light and tucking what she now called *the money envelope* under the drawer for safekeeping, she dug in again. Now it seemed more like a treasure hunt than a duty. Unpaid bills went in a pile for trash, receipts in the same pile. This envelope was heavy. She opened it. A gold piece. She just found a gold piece! *Thank you, Lord.* She held the coin up to the light. *A gold piece.*

"I'll bet Jason never looked in here, or that would be gone for sure." She rubbed it on her pants to bring up the shine and then tucked it into her pocket for now. "Back to digging."

Someone was laughing outside. Was that Micah? What was going on out there? She debated stopping what she was doing, but the lure was too great.

Supply lists for the show, letters regarding booking shows. Did Jason not keep a record of expenses and receipts? She stopped and glanced around the wagon. A row of small cupboards surrounded the interior of the wagon right under the ceiling. She had never gone through those either.

"You want coffee?" Micah asked from the doorway.

"No, thank you. I want to see what's in this drawer."

"More bird ready."

"Save it for the morning." She was nearing the bottom of the drawer. She pulled out the final handful of papers and found another envelope, this one with her father's handwriting on it. Out came what looked to be a legal document with the word *DEED* printed at the top. She leaned closer to the lantern so she could read the faded ink. If only there were someone she could ask about this. She read the paper, not understanding the numbers but realizing this was the deed to the valley.

Her father's valley, his valley of dreams. He owned it. He didn't just dream of it. Four hundred acres in a valley near Hill City, South Dakota.

Was this truly the legal deed? Would Chief know anything about this? Four hundred acres. How much land was that? A lot for a ranch or a little?

Deed in hand, she opened the door and stepped down. Othello greeted her with his usual delight. The dog under the wagon growled, as was also his usual response. Trying to appear nonchalant when she was about to burst with good news took some doing.

"Chief, do you remember my father signing a deed to land in his valley?"

The man turned to her, the dancing fire reflecting off his lined face. "I don't know. Maybe."

"Well, he did, because here it is." She held up the paper. "We—I own the valley." She paused. "How big is four hundred acres?"

Chief shook his head. "I do not know. Come, Runs Like a Deer. I help you into wagon before you fall into fire sound asleep."

Cassie went ahead of them, needing to clean up her mess before they could turn out the light. She might not know how big four hundred acres was, but she understood one thing clearly. Her father had indeed set his dream into motion. What a shame he never went back.

14

I told you I'm not going, and that's final!"

"All right, if you insist." Mavis tucked the dish towel around the loaves of bread she'd baked for the party. "It's not like we have dances all the time. I just thought we could all go together and have a good time."

Gretchen stared at her oldest brother. "You said you'd teach me to dance at the next dance. I've been looking forward to that." Tears trembled on her lashes as she spun around and pelted down the hall to her bedroom. "Then I'm not going either," she threw over her shoulder.

Mavis heaved a sigh.

The reproachful look she sent Ransom made him feel about two inches tall. He glared at his mother, glared down the hall after his sister, and slammed the palm of his hand against the

doorframe. "All right, I'll go, just to keep peace in the family."
Guilt forced his feet down the hall lined by cedar boards cut
on the diagonal, another example of his pa's fine woodwork.
He rapped on Gretchen's bedroom door.

"Go away."

"I'm here to say I'll go. And yes, I will teach you to dance."
He waited for an answer. When none came, he rapped again.
"You better be getting ready."

"I will."

When she opened her door, her tear-stained face made
his heart clench.

"You sure?"

He nodded. "I'm sure." But inside he felt the old familiar
churning. He liked to dance, but it was talking with his dance
partners that spoiled the evening. And even though all the
young ladies knew he didn't enjoy chatting while he danced,
for some reason, they couldn't just dance and not expect conversation. When he tried to pay attention to their chattering,
his feet ignored the prescribed steps and went their own way.
He'd stepped on more than one pair of toes that way, much
to both his own dismay and that of his partners.

He made his way to his room, stopping by the reservoir in
the kitchen to get a pitcher of hot water to wash with. He'd
much rather be staying home in the quiet house and studying the old maps that showed the sites of the local mines,
especially the two located on their own ranch. He'd already
marked what trees to fell and had sharpened up the crosscut
saw so he and Lucas could saw the trees into six-by-six timbers for shoring up the mine.

Why he was so convinced there was more gold ore in that
hill, he wasn't sure, but it was as if a voice from the past kept

whispering in his ear. He'd not mentioned this to anyone. They'd all think his brain had gotten addled the last time a horse he was breaking threw him. He'd heard that someone had located a vein fairly recently, but he didn't know if that was true or just hearsay.

The others were all ready and waiting for him, Lucas tapping his foot.

"We'd better ride rather than take the wagon," he said with a glare. "Now that we're so late in leaving."

Gretchen tugged on his arm, staring up at him, pleading with her eyes for them not to argue.

"The team is all hitched. We'll make it in plenty of time." Ransom lifted his sheepskin jacket from the coat-tree by the door.

"I'm going to ride."

"Suit yourself." Settling his hat on his head with undue precision, he turned to his mother. "Is that basket all that you have?"

"Yes, other than those quilts and hides in case it gets cold."

Ransom swooped up the quilts and shut the door behind them as they trooped out onto the front porch. "Did you bank the stove?"

"And the fireplace." Mavis set her basket in the rear of the wagon behind the seat and waited while Gretchen climbed up, using the wagon spokes for steps, and then followed her daughter. "What a glorious night."

Ransom found his place on the wagon seat and took a moment to study the sky. The moon was just cresting the horizon, all brassy gold and shimmery. "A harvest moon for certain."

"Jenna said the harvest moon is a good time to go sparkin'." Gretchen glanced up at her brother's face. "You think so?"

"I think that Jenna is getting too big for her britches. She's too young, and so are you, to be filling your heads with such talk."

"Ransom, I am twelve, goin' on thirteen. Other girls learned to dance years ago. I'm way behind."

"That's 'cause you have more sense."

"How does sense have anything to do with dancing?" Mavis asked.

"Well, dancing has to do with boys and . . ." Ransom knew he was getting in over his head, but since he was the oldest, he felt a certain responsibility for his little sister. And she was too young to be thinking about boys. "Just trust me on this."

Mavis chuckled first and then burst out laughing. "Oh, Ransom, you are so far behind the times. Not too long ago, and in fact in some places it still happens, girls were getting married at fourteen and having babies."

"While still children themselves."

The clatter of iron shoes on the rocks told them Lucas had almost caught up with them. He slowed to a trot beside the wagon. "I'm going on ahead."

"Tell Alvira that I'm on the way. I'm supposed to help with the punch tonight."

"I will. Sure you don't want to ride up behind me, Gretchen?"

"No thanks. I'll get horsehair all over my skirt."

Ransom flinched. Gretchen loved to ride almost as much as she loved to read, although it was probably a toss-up, depending on the season.

He'd better keep an eye on her. Admitting that his baby sister was turning into a real beauty with her wide-set blue eyes, the color almost turquoise, turned-up nose, and heart-shaped face took some serious talking with himself. While she usually kept her hair in braids, when it was down, it fell in deep waves to her waist. One of these days she'd probably decide to fuss with her hair; and fussing with her hair would only lead to all the other things girls did, not that he'd had a whole lot of experience with those of the feminine sex.

Ransom flicked his reins to bring the team to a trot. Lucas was right. They were running late. And they would say it was his fault. Why couldn't they just have left him at home in peace? He could have taught Gretchen to dance at home. But he was the first to admit it was hard to learn to dance without music. He glanced at his little sister.

She must have felt his gaze because she looked up at him with a smile that near to broke his heart. "I'm glad you came," she said.

"Me too." Mavis wrapped an arm around her daughter. "You warm enough?"

Gretchen nodded. "I'm hungry."

Mavis reached over the board that made up the seat back. "I just happen to have some cookies. We should have had a bite before we left. They won't be serving food until the musicians take a break."

"Why do they wait so long?"

"I have no idea. And I also have no idea why the musicians need so many breaks. Playing an instrument doesn't look all that wearing to me."

When they arrived at the granary in town, Ransom helped the womenfolk down before driving the team over to the long line of wagons and horses. A few buggies with a single horse broke up the line. He removed the bridles and slipped halters with lead lines in place to tie them before heading back to the granary, which was empty again, since all the gunnysacks of wheat had been loaded on the train and hauled off to Minneapolis.

The music invited him in. Couples were spinning around the room, feet stomping out the rhythm, laughter making the rafters ring. He stepped inside and leaned against the wall, his gaze traveling around the room to see who all was present. He knew everyone and nodded to those who called a greeting or waved as they danced by. Lucas waved and nodded toward the group of young women gathered off to the side.

As if he didn't know they were there. And waiting. Ready to pounce.

After heaving a sigh that followed his frustration at being coerced into something he did not want to do, Ransom made his way over to the circle and tapped one of the girls on the shoulder. "Care to dance, Miss Lissa?" The other girls giggled and batted their eyelashes at him, but he ignored the flirting and smiled only at the young woman he'd chosen. Besides being attractive, with her dark hair in curls down her back and a dimple in her cheek, she managed to dance without the chatter of the others.

She smiled and nodded, slipping her hand in his as they moved onto the floor. They'd made only one circuit of the room before the final chords of the song. Everyone clapped, some folks patting their chests at the exertion.

"You want to wait for the next one?" he asked.

"Fine with me. How've you been?"

"Good."

"Getting ready for winter?"

He nodded. Why couldn't he think of anything to say?

"I saw Lucas in town the other day."

"Lucas likes to go to town." Grateful that the music had started up again, he took her hand and they joined one of the squares of four couples. The caller announced the name of the song, and they all followed his directions as he called out the patterns.

"Swing your partner, do-si-do."

Since they'd all been square dancing since grade school and some even earlier, they knew the steps, exchanging partners as called. At least with a square dance one didn't need to talk to either the partner or the other dancers in the square. At the end of the dance, he walked his partner back to the group, thanked her, smiled, and headed for the punch table. When they announced that the next dance would be a waltz, he looked around for Gretchen. This was the dance he had promised to teach her. She was purposely threading her way through the crowd to get to his side.

"Hey, Gretchen, I saw you in that square. You did real well."

She grinned up at him and slid her hand in his. "Remember when I used to stand on your feet and you would swing me around the kitchen? We could do that again."

"And mash my toes. You've grown a bit since then, you know."

"I know."

"Okay, just follow me. I'll guide you with my hand at your back. Just don't look at your feet."

"But how will I know what they are doing?"

"Like I said, just follow me."

The music floated across the floor, encouraging couples to enjoy a slow dance so they could catch their breath.

"Now think like this: step, slide, together." He took her hand in his, with his other at her back. "I won't let you slip or fall."

"Okay." Her jaw tightened.

"Relax. Like when you're riding. Go with me like you do with your horse."

"But I'm on his back."

He guided her more firmly than he would anyone else, and within a couple of steps, her feet were following his. "See? What did I tell you? Now, I'm going to turn us around, easy and free."

Her eyes took on a sparkle that made him smile. "I'm really dancing a waltz."

He glanced up to see their mother smiling at them, nodding in time to the music. Next thing he knew, she was waltzing by in the arms of Jay Slatfield, one of the local ranchers, a widower who'd been trying to get her attention for the last few months. He had purchased their feeder steers. Jay's wife had died several years earlier, and one of his daughters had stayed home to take care of the house while two of the sons helped run the ranch. Jay had aged a lot since his wife's death and only recently started taking part in church and community events again. While he was slightly taller than Mavis, he somehow looked kind of shrunk.

"Ma is having fun," Gretchen said, looking up at her brother. "But I don't particularly care for Mr. Slatfield."

"Why not?"

"He thinks he owns the whole county."

"Is that so?" Gretchen had indeed given him something to think about. Slatfield seemed to have plenty of money for ranching, that was for sure. As the music drew to a close, Ransom bowed to Gretchen and led her off the dance floor.

"Thank you," he said.

"Can we do it again?"

"Most assuredly." *Then I don't have to ask another one of that gaggle of young ladies.* He figured he knew what a rabbit felt like when zeroed in on by a hawk. If only he could find a woman who didn't require conversation and courting and . . . He wasn't sure what else at this point. All of his friends were married, at least all the ones near his age. Sometimes he felt like an old man compared to Lucas, who flirted with every female and made them go all twittery. He shook his head.

"What's bothering you, son?" His mother held out her arms and indicated they should dance.

He shook his head again and led her out for a schottische, a patterned circle dance that left little time for talking. Folks of all ages took to the floor, including mothers who were teaching their sons social graces, fathers paired with their daughters, white-haired couples, and even some women partnering together. Ransom remembered when his mother had taught him this dance. He'd had three left feet and was sweating like a racehorse by the time the music ended. Now he enjoyed this dance about the best. Other than the waltz.

Lucas was dancing with one of the neighbor girls, who was laughing at something he'd said. Gretchen, partnered with Mr. Stenerson, a gentle old soul who had trouble hearing anything softer than a trumpet, danced by. He could tell she was counting the beat for the steps so she wouldn't make a mistake. He raised his arm for his mother to duck under and grasped her other hand again. At the end he bowed to her and caught a soft look in her eyes. His coming was a good thing, if for no other reason than to please his mother, who asked for so little from any of them.

After the second set, following the break for supper, he was walking over to talk with one of the neighbors when

Miss Suzanne stepped in front of him with her most winsome smile, a smile she was known for, since she'd begun practicing it long before she became old enough to truly flirt.

"Good evening, Ransom. I thought it was about time you and I shared a dance."

What could he say without being stupendously rude? "Of course."

She put a pretty pout on her lips. "I was beginning to think you were ignoring me, dancing with all the other girls like you have." *And not me* screamed as if she'd shouted it.

"You were dancing."

"But I wanted to dance with you."

He held out his arms. "We're dancing now."

"I was hoping for a waltz."

"A polka will have to do. My next waltz is taken." He put his hand on her waist and clasped the other, counted the beats, and joined the revolving dancers. If he had to dance with her, this one was a good choice. The faster they danced, the less she could talk. Even so, she somehow managed to chat away about every topic under the sun. He swung her on the corners and double-timed until he was near to panting. As was she.

When the music stopped, she nearly collapsed against his chest. "That was the fastest polka—" she sucked in a decidedly unladylike breath—"I've ever danced."

He didn't say *Me too* but he sure thought it. He steered her back to her friends. "Thank you, Miss Suzanne. You're a fine dancer."

Before she could answer, he turned and headed across the room. He saw Gretchen making her way toward him. It must have been time for another waltz.

"I thought you didn't like her," she said, looking up at him.

"I like her fine. It's her nonstop talking that I can't abide."

Gretchen giggled into her spread fingers. "I think she wanted this dance, not that one."

He held out his arms as the musicians floated into a waltz, and Gretchen stepped into them.

"Jenna said you are one of the most handsome men here."

Ransom rolled his eyes. "She must be in need of glasses."

Gretchen looked up at him. "I agreed with her. Lucas is second."

He swung her around to make her stop talking. Silly girls.

He thought of his former partner. How could he tell her she about wore his ears off? He'd been careful not to dance with any one of the young women more than once, since doing so would start the gossip going.

"You did very well," he told her at the end of the dance.

"Thank you. How come dancing makes me hungry?"

"I have no idea, but there are still some cakes and cookies left from the feed."

"None of Ma's," she said.

"Her baked goods always go right away." He walked with her to the table where Mavis and the other women were claiming their bowls and pans, packing up to leave. Mavis handed Gretchen a couple of cookies and, at Ransom's nod, gave him some too.

"We should have just left everything out for a few more minutes—not that there's much left."

"I agree." The woman next to her took the lid off her tin and set the cookies back out to be immediately consumed. "Shame there's not any coffee left."

"Nor cider." Mavis stripped off the tablecloth and folded it before stashing it in her basket.

"I'm riding Betsy—with her ma's permission—home," Lucas said, stopping for a moment. "Don't lock the door."

Mavis snorted and shook her head. "One of these days we might have to find that old key, but you're safe for now." She handed her basket to Ransom. "You got everything, Gretchen?"

"I didn't bring anything."

"Coat? Scarf? Hat?"

"I'd like to ride along with you," Jay Slatfield said as he stopped next to Mavis. "After all, we go out the same road."

"Now, why would you want to do that? We brought the wagon, so we'll be slower."

"Makes no nevermind."

Ransom headed out for the wagon to bridle up the horses again. For some reason he was glad his mother was showing Jay no interest. He never had liked change, and if she allowed Jay to court her, it would indeed bring about massive changes.

15

*C*assie stared at the deed on the table.

After reading it yet again, she placed all the other papers she'd decided to save back into the drawer. She would sort them all again in the daylight.

Jason had said the wagon was hers. It had belonged to her father personally and was not the property of the show. And Wind Dancer was hers, a gift from her father. But did he know about the deed in the drawer? She doubted it, or surely he would have said something. He always just referred to the valley as her father's dream. Had there possibly been a slightly derogatory tone at times? She thought back. Strange how all these things were coming to her mind now.

She glanced around at all the cupboards and drawers. Where to keep it. She needed a safe place. Opening her trunk, she dug out her mother's Bible, slid the envelope in between the pages, and put it all back in place. What had her mother known about the valley? Had she ever heard them discussing it? She thought back. Her mother referred to it as *his dream valley*. That's what it was. After looking at the date on the deed, she'd realized he had paid for the land before he went into the Wild West show business. What had happened to that land in all these years since? Did someone else build a ranch on it? He'd always said the soil was so rich that the grass would be belly deep on the cattle.

Taking the paper out of her mother's Bible, she read it again. Yes, the deed had been recorded at the county seat in Rapid City, although the seal was difficult to read. She studied her father's signature. What had he been thinking then? Did he know he was going to start a traveling show, a Wild West Show, as it came to be called. Had he dreamed they would one day form a trio called the Dashing Lockwoods? Had he met Jason Talbot yet? Oh, so many questions she wanted to ask. She hoped Chief would have some of the answers. If she could get him talking.

A knock on the door brought her attention back to the present. "Yes?"

"You want Runs Like a Deer to sleep in here tonight?" Chief asked.

"Of course. Micah might have to help her back in."

"He's on first watch. She could sleep out here."

"No." Cassie removed some papers from the bunk and opened the door. "Your bed is ready for you." She stepped down and stood aside to let the Indian woman approach. "Here, use me as a brace." With Chief on one side and Cassie on the other, they helped the woman up the steps so she could sit on the bed. Cassie heaved a breath of relief. "Did that hurt, jarring your leg like that?"

"Some." Runs Like a Deer lifted her splinted leg up onto the bed. But when she struggled to pull up the quilt, Cassie stepped in to help.

"You need anything else?" She thought for a moment the woman might smile, but instead she closed her eyes, signaling sleep. Cassie pulled her hammock out and attached it to the hooks before retrieving her bedding from the cupboard she kept it in. After removing her boots she blew out the lamp and, wrapping her quilt around herself, snuggled into the hammock. One of these days she was going to start wearing a nightdress to bed again. One of these days she was going to do all manner of things—take a bath, wash her hair, scrub her clothes. A soft snore greeted her from the other bed, so she didn't bother to say good-night.

Othello's barking woke her up. While sometimes he barked at wild animals passing through, this was his deep warning bark. She rolled out of her hammock as quietly as she could and drew a pistol from the holster she kept hung on a peg at the end of the bed.

"What do you want?" Chief called, loud enough for Cassie to hear.

"Whatever money you got." The man's voice sounded slightly muffled. Was he masked?

"No money."

"I heard about a wad of bills. Now, just don't go movin' around. Stay where you are."

Who knew she had a roll of bills? The storekeeper, of course. He must have been bragging about it to someone else.

"Hey, there in the wagon. I got your Injun friend covered here, and if that money don't come out, I might have to shoot a hand or somethin'."

173

Should she bluff or not? Shoot or not? The thought of actually wounding a human being made her stomach twist. "I can't see in here. I have to light a lamp."

"You're stallin'. Now, I'm gonna count to three. Might just start with this here big dog."

Not Othello. "Wait a minute." She tried to make her voice sound like an order, but it squeaked on the end in spite of her.

"About a minute's all I got."

"I told you I can't see in here. I have to light a lamp." She dug for the matches, dropping them on the floor. *Calm down.* Hands shaking, she found a match and struck it, then lifted the chimney to light the wick. "Okay, I'm lighting the lamp. Surely you can see that there is light in here now."

She heard a gun cock. Go out the door with guns blazing or toss out the money? *Come on, Cassie, you starred in a Wild West show, not an Old West town.*

"Okay, you got light. Now don't go throwin' the money. You give it to the Injun here, and he can bring it over to me, nice an' gentlelike."

Cassie opened her trunk, dug down for the roll, and holding the money tightly, slammed the lid shut. How could she prove who did this? Surely there was a sheriff around here somewhere. This was all the money they had. "Are you all right, Chief?"

"Ya."

"Tell Othello to back off."

"Did."

"One . . ."

"I'm coming." She unwrapped her rifle.

"No guns."

She laid her revolver and the rifle on the table.

"Two . . . and make sure that fifty is still on the roll."

"I'm putting it in a bag so it doesn't fly all over the place." *Has to be the store clerk or someone he told about my visit there. Why did I ever take that roll of money into the store anyway? A bag. Find a bag.* She snatched one off the hook on the wall. The roll of money caught on the edge of the bag and several bills peeled off. The fifty and ten and then a dollar bill. She flipped through the rest. They were all dollar bills. Jason just needed to feel important. She almost laughed aloud. Shame to lose what they had, but it was not nearly as sad as it might have been. She'd been thinking they had far more money than they did. She stuffed it all in the bag.

"All of it." Impatience colored his voice.

"Here it is." Cassie opened the door and stepped onto the stairs. She didn't recognize the big man, who had a bandanna across his face.

"Nice an' easy. If you drop it, you come pick it up."

She tossed it to him, and he caught it with one hand.

"You got anything else?"

"No, and now how will we eat?"

"I'm sure you'll figger out somethin'. Girl with all your skills." He nodded toward the wagon so bright in the moonlight. "I should come search that wagon."

"Still won't find anything." *Please, Lord, keep Micah away.* She couldn't see Chief around the corner of the wagon, but she kept sending thoughts his way to stay still.

No one's life or health were worth that roll of money, or any money, for that matter. *Please stay where you are, both of you.*

"Much obliged, miss." He touched the tip of his gun to his hat, spun around, and tore out of the camp.

Cassie vaulted back into the wagon, grabbed her rifle and shells, and leaped out the stairs. She took three steps while loading and raised the stock to her shoulder. The moonlight showed a man riding away. She squeezed the trigger, shoved in another shell, and fired again. Was that a yelp she heard? If so, he might be injured, but he kept on going. She knew if she'd aimed lower she might have killed him. But she was right before. No money was worth a killing.

She lowered her rifle and clamped her teeth, shaking her head. He got away. The dirty rotten excuse for a man got away with all the cash they had. And it was all her own fault for taking that roll of bills to town.

She tamped down the fury, but it smoldered very much alive in her middle. His horse had a white star and a blaze down its nose. While he'd worn a bandanna over his face, he couldn't hide his height. Was it worth going back to town and confronting the sheriff there, if there even was one? They had to keep a watch on the cattle, but did they need one on the camp too? When would they get any sleep?

"Going to relieve Micah now."

"Good. Sorry, Chief."

Chief grunted and swung aboard his horse.

Cassie climbed back in the wagon, put her guns away, and closed up the cupboards. "Some bad people around." Runs Like a Deer spoke softly so as not to startle her wagon mate.

"Guess that's always the case. He didn't get as much as he thought."

"How did he know you had money?"

"From the supplies I bought at the store."

"Hmm."

"Good night." Cassie wrapped herself back up and slid

into her hammock. Morning would be there before they knew it. They'd have to make a decision then. Go back to town or continue on.

She woke with one thought—she had to get their money back. *But what if the authorities are looking for me regarding the show?* The thought intruded, but she ignored it. Feeding and taking care of her friends until they could set up in her father's valley was the most important thing.

"I'm sorry," she said as they gathered around the fire for a breakfast of scrambled eggs with venison, slices of the bread from the store, and hot coffee.

Chief and Micah looked at each other and then back at her. "Not your fault," Chief said.

Cassie decided not to waste the time arguing. "I am riding back to town to get it back."

Chief shook his head. Micah stared at his hands. Runs Like a Deer copied Chief.

"Look, we will soon need supplies again. We need the money." Why did she feel like she was arguing with posts? "Is there enough grazing here for another day and night?"

This time Chief nodded. "Slow us down."

"I'm aware of that." She finished eating and went to the fire to refill her coffee cup. "I'll be back as soon as I can."

"You want Micah to go with you?"

She thought a moment, then shook her head. "I'll ride your horse, Chief, so no one is tempted to steal Wind Dancer."

She was on the road in minutes.

This time when she rode into town she looked first for a sheriff's office, then a doctor's. She stopped in front of a stone building with a sheriff's sign hanging over the door. Sucking in a breath of confidence, she dismounted and flipped the reins over a hitching rail off to the side. Pulling open the heavy door, she made herself stand straight as she entered.

A clean-shaven man with a receding hairline looked up from the papers spread on his desk. "Can I help you?" The badge on his chest pocket announced his position.

"I hope so. I need to report a robbery."

"I see." He stood and picked up a chair to set in front of his desk. Motioning for her to sit, he walked back around the desk and pulled a piece of paper out of a drawer. "First, I'm Sheriff Timmons. And your name is?"

"Cassie Lockwood."

"You don't live around here."

"No, we are on our way to Rapid City."

He laid down his pencil and folded his hands on the desk. "Why don't you tell me what happened." He frowned. "Lockwood. Why does that sound familiar?"

"Have you ever been to a Wild West show?"

He nodded. "Some years ago."

"My father was part owner of a show that traveled the train routes west. We played in Fargo and Dickinson, in Omaha, but never in South Dakota."

He squinted to think better. "More recent than that." His eyes widened. "You drove a fancy wagon into town. Yesterday, wasn't it?"

She nodded. "Bought supplies at your general store." She huffed a breath. "That's where I made my mistake."

"Shopping at our store was a mistake? I have a hard time believing that. Old Otto has a great reputation, best store in the region."

"Well, if Old Otto has a loose tongue, he caused the robbery."

Sheriff Timmons leaned back in his chair, hands locked behind his head. "You better tell me the rest of your story. What was your mistake?"

"I had a roll of bills and, like a fool, brought the whole thing in with me. To pay my bill, I handed him a fifty, and he said he couldn't change that. I needed to go to a bank. So I found a ten and a dollar under the fifty and gave him that." She watched the man's eyes, his eyebrows drawn together.

"Okay. And?"

"I returned to my group, and we drove on a few more miles before we camped. In the middle of the night, a very tall masked man rode into our campsite, and at gunpoint he threatened to shoot my friend, and my dog too, if I didn't give him the roll of bills."

"And you complied?"

"I did. One doesn't argue with a gun like that. I put the money in a bag and gave it to him. He threatened to search the wagon but decided to take what he had and leave. I ran back inside, grabbed my rifle, and shot after him. I heard a holler, so I may have wounded him but not enough to slow him down. We discussed just going on, but Sheriff, that was all the money we had, and we have a long ways to go yet. So I rode back, and here I am."

"You say you shot at him?"

"Yes, but I didn't shoot to kill."

"In the moonlight? At a man riding away on a horse?"

"Yes."

"And you learned to shoot where?"

"From my father. Sheriff, I am a world-class shooter, but

I don't usually aim at people." Why did she get the feeling he was not quite believing her? "I am also a trick rider. My father taught me that too." She paused. "I aimed high."

"Would you recognize this man?"

"He was pretty tall, he talked rough, and he had a dark horse with a star and a narrow blaze down to a white nose."

"That's more a description of the horse than the man." He stood. "Was he taller than me?"

"I think so."

"*You think so* is hardly an accurate description."

"You could check with the doctor and see if a man came in with an injury."

"I could and I will." He wrote some things on his paper. "You have no address, then?"

She shook her head. "All I want is my money back."

"You have others traveling with you?"

"I do."

He tapped his pencil against his chin and then shoved his chair back. "You wait here, and I'll go check with the doctor."

"Now?"

"Yes, now."

"I'd like to come along."

"You don't trust me?"

"I'd like to ask him some questions is all."

Sheriff Timmons shrugged and pushed back his chair. "You're welcome to go shop in the store until I get back."

She stared at him. What kind of an offer was that? She started to answer and caught a glint in his eyes. He was teasing. "No thanks. You see, I don't have any cash."

He ushered her out ahead of him and locked the door as he went. Pointing across the street, he said, "Right over there."

Three steps and she quit trying to match her steps to his. He too was a big man. He pushed open the gate of an unpainted picket fence and took the two steps to knock on the front door before pushing it open and ushering her in. The room would have been the parlor if the house were being used for its original purpose, but while chairs lined the wall, a desk blocked the hallway. A desk with no one there.

"Doc, you here?"

"Coming."

A thin man with wire-rimmed glasses and graying hair pushed aside the curtain. "What can I do for you, Sheriff?"

"You treat anyone for a bullet wound late last night or early this morning?"

"That I did. Why?"

"Where?"

"Well, right here."

"No. I mean, where was the wound?"

"On his upper right arm."

"Did he say how he got it?"

"Said someone accidentally shot him."

Cassie rolled her eyes. Her shot had been no accident.

Who is he? Give me a name. Why she wanted a name so badly she wasn't sure, but they obviously knew who her thief was.

She glanced at a clock on the desk. Ten o'clock already. She was wasting an entire day.

"Did he pay you?"

With my money? Cassie had a hard time keeping her words to herself.

"He did. That was the amazing part. You know, with that passel of kids Big Alfred has, he never has any cash money."

"I can't picture him holding anybody up, though. Not Big

181

Alfred." The Sheriff turned to Cassie. "He must have been some desperate."

"You know who he is?"

"Well, I'm fairly sure. Just having a hard time believing he would do something like this."

"Desperate times call for desperate measures." The doctor looked from Cassie to the sheriff. "What happened?"

"A man on a horse robbed us last night of all the money we had. We're camped south of town. I purchased some supplies at your general store yesterday. He knew that I had money."

Doc looked to the sheriff, who shrugged. "You going to bring him in?"

"What choice do I have?" Timmons turned to Cassie. "I'll ride out and get him. You can wait at the office."

"Please make him bring my money with him."

"I'll do my best."

"Will it take you long?"

"No, he lives just a mile or so out. His kids walk to school."

She followed him out the door, pausing to toss a thank-you to the doctor over her shoulder.

"On second thought, why don't you wait over at the hotel in the dining room, have a cup of coffee."

"You forget, Sheriff. I don't have any money."

"Tell 'em to put it on my tab."

Cassie stared at the man's back as he strode to his office. He who had started out so brusque was now offering to buy her coffee. What did he expect from her? She shook her head and did as he said.

When she told the young woman waiting on her table what the sheriff said, the girl nodded. "That's Sheriff Timmons all right. Tries to be hard on the outside, and he can be tough, let me tell you, but then the inside is soft as goose down. He really cares about the people in this town. We've never had a man like him in the office before."

"He was barely civil when we started out."

"That's him. Be right back."

Cassie looked around at the comfortable dining room. Red-and-white-checked tablecloths and curtains at the windows, boards with brands burned into them on the walls, a few framed pictures, one of a stern couple, looked to be a wedding picture. Gaslights in sconces on the walls, a stone fireplace with a merry crackling fire.

The serving girl returned, setting a cup of coffee and a piece of apple pie in front of her. "Forgot to ask if you want cream."

Cream, what a treat. And pie. "But I can't take this pie. I mean . . ."

"Don't you worry none. That's what he would order for you. Trust me, apple pie is the way to that man's heart for sure."

Cassie gathered her courage together. "Is he married?"

"Nope. But not 'cause all the girls and women around here aren't trying. Says he's waiting for the perfect woman." She leaned closer and dropped her voice. "Just between you and me and the lamppost, he's gonna look a long time."

Cassie swallowed the rest of her questions and took a bite of the pie. Cinnamon and apples and a crust to float up to heaven on.

"Cook does good with pies. She's known all over the region for her pies and her chicken and dumplings. Her brisket ain't bad neither. Why, hon, you act like you had no pie for a long time."

"If you only knew."

"Gotta go."

Cassie watched her greet a couple who just came in the door and, with a smile, show them to a table. Maybe this wasn't such a bad town after all, now that she was getting to know it a bit.

She was making her second cup of coffee last as long as possible when the sheriff walked in with a tall man wearing a sling on his arm. Surely she'd not injured him that badly.

Sheriff Timmons pulled out a chair and motioned for Alfred to do the same. The man stared down at the table, not meeting Cassie's scrutiny.

The young woman brought the coffeepot and two more cups. "Pie will be right up."

"Did you try Odell's apple pie?"

"Thank you." She nodded toward the serving girl. "She insisted. I've not had pie since we left Dickinson."

"That's Sally serving us." He grinned at her when she put the pie in front of them. "Thanks for the pie and for taking good care of our guest here."

"You're welcome. Holler if you need more."

Timmons looked at Cassie. "You want another piece?"

"No, thanks. Coffee is just fine." As was sitting on a chair, at a table, with good food and unlimited coffee. He had no idea how fortunate he was. She turned her attention to the man across the table.

When he looked up at her, she saw the most woeful eyes she'd ever seen.

"I took your money, miss, and I want you to know I would never have shot your dog or the Injun."

"You sure sounded like you would have."

"I'm sorry." He dug in his pocket and laid the fifty-dollar bill and the ten on the table. "This is all that's left. I bought some food for my family and paid the doctor with the rest."

"Do you know how much there was in the roll?" Timmons asked Cassie.

She shook her head. "I'm sure not a lot—the rest was all ones."

Alfred nodded.

"It was Otto's loose lips, all right. Whatever possessed you to do this, Alfred?"

"I just thought to get some food in our house. Thought they'd go on down the road and not miss it. Thought with their fancy wagon and all that they had plenty. I never stole nothing before in my life, and I won't again." He looked at Cassie and then pushed the money toward her. "I can't say when I can pay the rest, but . . ."

Cassie heaved a sigh. "Look, I did a stupid thing too, so you don't need to worry about paying me back. I'll take this, and we'll be on our way. You sure put on a good act last night."

"It's easy to be big behind a bandanna." Timmons pushed his empty plate away. "I'd say she's being mighty good to you." He turned to Cassie. "You're sure you don't want to press charges?"

"I'm sure. We need to get to my father's valley before the snow comes. This way we can still put some miles on today." She rose and pushed back her chair at the same time. "Thank you, Sheriff."

He smiled at her. "If you ever come back this way, let me know."

Back on her horse, Cassie replayed that smile. His whole face had changed. His voice had changed. What on earth had happened back there?

16

*S*unday morning found the Engstrom family back in the wagon heading for town and church. Ransom hupped the horses, and they picked up a trot, making him wish they had a buggy with springs. He'd been dreaming of one for the last couple of years. He glanced over at his mother. Somewhere during the night, she'd lost her smile. Lucas didn't come home last night after the dance.

"He's all right, Ma. Remember, you said you don't worry about us. You let God do that."

"I know. But it's easier to say when everyone is home under our roof and not lying out on the ground somewhere, freezing, with broken bones."

"Lucas is fine. He'll probably meet us at church." If only he had some idea that his brother would indeed do that.

187

Worship on Sunday wasn't Lucas's favorite way to spend a morning. Ransom reminded himself he had forgotten to check the bunkhouse and to see if Lucas's horse was in the pasture. Sometimes if his brother had stopped for a nip or two, he slept in the bunkhouse so as not to be on the receiving end of the glares from his mother. Mavis Engstrom hated liquor with a passion that left no doubt as to her feelings. Ransom knew it was because his father had stopped at the tavern far too often. Ivar not only drank frequently at the saloon but kept a bottle spirited away for *emergencies*. Only the emergencies became a daily occurrence.

"Ma, can Jenna come home with us if her mother says it's all right?" Gretchen asked, interrupting his musings.

"Maybe not today," Ransom answered in his mother's place.

Gretchen glared at him, glanced up at her mother's somber face, and didn't ask again.

Right now Ransom was in no mood for church either. Most certainly the message would be about loving your brother or about forgiveness, neither one of which he was in the mood for right now. Lucas knew better. It wasn't like he hung around with the scum of the area, but he liked to play cards at times, and euchre or hearts or whist at home wasn't the same as at a gaming table with the liquor flowing, the cigars plentiful, and the money real.

Thankfully the sermon wasn't on either of those topics, but it did manage to step on his toes more than once. Trusting that God would indeed live up to His word reminded Ransom how often he plowed ahead on his own without seeking guidance from above. After church he greeted people, all the while trying to surreptitiously look for his brother.

Lucas had not made it.

"May Gretchen come home with me?" Jenna asked, the two girls dancing in place. "Ma said we could make fudge." Jenna and Gretchen had been best friends since before they started grade school. The Henderson ranch abutted the Engstrom spread on the east with the public road carved out between them. Adeline and Joseph, known as Joe, had a large family with six children still at home and two grown and gone. The families exchanged labor and machinery when needed, and the oldest boy at home drove a wagon to school in the fall and spring and a sledge, complete with an enclosed compartment with a stove, in the winter, picking up other children along the way. Gretchen more often rode her horse to school, always in a hurry to get there and get home.

Mavis smiled at her daughter. "I don't see why not. Ransom will come and pick you up so you can be home before dark."

"Can you ask Lucas to milk for me? I've milked that cow all week while he was off delivering the cattle."

"Don't worry." Ransom tugged on her single braid. "We'll take care of her."

"Thank you." The two girls spun away, chattering like they'd not seen each other for a week or more instead of just one day.

Ransom watched his little sister switch between becoming a young lady and remaining a little girl. Did all girls grow up like this? He waited while his mother finished her conversation with one of the women and then touched her arm. "I'll get the horses." She nodded and said good-bye to her friend. He knew it would take her several more minutes to make her way to the door, what with all those greeting her. His mother had friends everywhere, including a couple who now lived in the state of Washington that she wrote to on a regular basis.

"How are you doing, Ransom?" Reverend Brandenburg asked as they shook hands.

"Good." He wanted to add something about his tender toes that the sermon had stepped all over, but that didn't seem a polite thing to do.

"We have a family here in town that needs some repairs to their roof. Is there any chance I can count on you and Lucas to help us out?"

"When?"

"The sooner the better. Before the weather changes." He paused. "Tomorrow?"

Ransom kept a smile on his mouth and consternation from his eyes. He needed to be out felling his own trees and riding the fence line to make sure all was ready for winter. He hated to obligate Lucas to anything without talking about it first. He heaved a mental sigh. "I know I can be there, but I'll have to ask Lucas."

"That will be good. I have a couple of others coming. That roof should have been shingled years ago."

Ransom nodded. Lots of things should have been done years earlier, but if there was no money to buy the supplies, well, what else could you do? "The shingles will be there?"

"I've ordered them from the lumberyard."

Ransom didn't even ask who it was that was getting the new roof or who was paying for it. He knew. The wife and children were faithful church members, but the mister hung out at the saloon more often than not. "See you tomorrow, then." He set his hat on his head and headed toward their wagon.

"What was that all about?" Mavis asked as he helped her up onto the wagon seat.

"Putting a roof on the Beckwith house tomorrow. He wants both me and Lucas."

"I see. No one said anything about providing dinner for the roofing crew." Mavis waved at someone else.

Ransom stopped the team when he heard a familiar "Yoo-hoo," called by Mrs. Brandenburg on her way to intercept them.

She stopped by the wheel. "Mavis, could you possibly send some food for dinner along with your men tomorrow? I was meaning to ask you but somehow the time got away from me."

"What about a cake and a loaf of bread—oh, and some sliced ham for sandwiches? How many are we feeding?"

"Oh, five or six, I'd guess. The more there, the sooner they'll be done." She looked up at Ransom. "Thank you for agreeing to help. I hope Lucas will too."

"Yes, ma'am." *Me too. If I don't knock him senseless.*

As soon as they said their good-byes, he clucked the horses into a trot and headed out of town.

"That's the place," Mavis said, pointing to a weathered house off to the side of the road. One window was still boarded up after being broken so long ago no one could remember when. The porch needed a new post to hold it up before the broken one gave up the ghost. The first bad snowstorm could cause serious damage to a house already so decrepit. He knew what his mother was thinking. The only time she ever swore, she made booze into two words.

"What are you planning to do this afternoon?"

"Think I'll go through that old pile of lumber and see if there's something that can be turned into a post for that porch. We can't shingle it the way it is."

Mavis reached over and patted his knee. "You're a good man, Ransom Engstrom."

The smell of baking chicken greeted them when they drove up to the house. As usual, Mavis had set Sunday dinner to cooking before they left for church. Ransom let her off at the gate and took care of the team. He saw Lucas's horse in the pasture and felt a relief that told him he'd been worried about his brother too. Why did he, or their mother, bother? Lucas would do what Lucas would do. Back at the house, he inhaled the chicken aroma and hung up his hat and coat.

"Is Lucas here?" he asked.

"Not that I know of."

The simmering began in his belly. "His horse is home."

Ransom strode down the hall and checked his brother's bedroom. No one there, but the shirt his brother had worn the night before was hanging over the back of the chair. Where could he be? Back in the kitchen, he asked that of his mother.

"Try the bunkhouse, I guess. But please stoke the fireplace first and bring in some more wood. I want to get dinner on the table."

Ransom did as asked, taking the carriers his mother had sewn out to the woodpile. That was another thing he'd planned to do tomorrow—stack the wood under the shed roof they had built to keep the wood dry. He would stack it along the house wall on the front porch too, for when the snow got deep. With the fire starting to eat the logs, he grabbed his hat and coat and stuffed his arms into the sleeves.

Lucas was not in the bunkhouse. No one had trekked through the dust on the floor for weeks. One time he had found his brother there, the smell of whiskey overwhelming and Lucas passed out on a bunk, one booted foot still on the floor. It looked like he barely made it to the bed. Disgust had dueled with compassion—and won. He'd never told his mother.

Ransom stood on the porch, cupping his hands around his mouth and calling his brother's name.

"Down here" came from the barn, muffled by the closed door.

Ransom strode down to the barn and slid the door open to multiple screechings. The track on that needed oiling too. So many jobs to do before winter hit. How had his father ever kept up on all the little things that made this such a successful ranch? Success that had deteriorated in the last years, the years that Ransom was in charge. The thought ate at him whenever he let it get a foothold. The smell of blood hit him full force. He stepped inside, where a lantern hung on the post by the block and tackle for skinning game, beef, or pork. A headless elk hung from the crossbeams, still steaming in the cold.

"Ma was worried about you."

"Sorry. Harry and I had a bet on who would get an elk first. I won, but not by much." He wiped his nose with the back of his hand. The Hudson spread lay in the next valley, so the young people had known each other all of their lives. Betsy was the middle daughter of three, and Harry the elder of the two boys.

"You didn't come home."

"I know. We decided to go out early, so it didn't make sense to ride all the way out here. He got one too."

"Where'd you get them?"

"In that meadow up behind their place. The elk sure had a good year. Look at all the fat on this one." Lucas picked up the sheeting he'd brought down. "Help me wrap it. I got the liver and such in that bucket. I thought we should smoke these hindquarters, maybe the back strap too."

"Not sell this one?"

"Nope." Together they wrapped and tied the sheeting around the carcass, and Lucas picked up the pail. "I didn't spend the night in town, if that's what was worrying you."

Ransom shut the door behind them and they headed for the house. "Did you keep the guts to clean out for sausage?"

"Nah, it's too far to carry them. I'll keep the next one out here."

"Did you take a wagon out?"

"Nope. Led the horses back. Kept the hides, though. Harry gave us his and drove me home."

The elk was plenty of proof that Lucas wasn't making up tales to cover his carousing, but Ransom still felt like giving his younger brother a clout on the chin.

"It's your turn to milk tonight. Gretchen went home with Jenna."

After dinner Ransom spent an hour sorting through the stack of lumber in the lean-to against the barn. He finally found one piece seven feet or so long. It still had the bark on, but that would have to do. He loaded the pole and his tools into the bed of the wagon and then put in the ladder too, in case it was needed. Back at the house, he took his place at the desk in the big room with the fire blazing in the fireplace. He could hear his mother and Lucas talking in the kitchen. The dog at his feet thumped a foot on the floor while scratching behind his ear with the other.

Pulling a couple of plain pieces of paper forward, Ransom drew out the dimensions for the supports needed out in the mine. They should be able to get six-by-sixes side by side on many of the trees he was considering. Or they could slice them down the middle and leave the bark. Rot wouldn't set, dry as that hole was. He dug out the maps of the mine where he and Lucas used to play cowboys and Indians on a summer's day. When they'd found that little nugget, glinting gold in the lamplight, they were sure there had to be more back in there somewhere. Their father had caught them, whaled them good, and made them promise not to go back into those mines before he first replaced the beams that needed it. Ransom had marked on the map where they found the cave-in. Was that why no one continued digging in that direction?

"I brought you some coffee." Mavis set a cup and saucer on the cleared space on the desk. "Are you still dreaming about finding more gold in that old mine?"

"Thanks. I just feel a pull to try again. When Pa and Lockwood mined it, they found quite a bit of color. How do we know it's been mined out?"

"Your pa said so—that's why. Had there been any indication of more after they cleaned out that pocket, he'd have kept on."

"But what about beyond that cave-in?"

"That put the fear of God in those two men, let me tell you. Lockwood left not much later."

"You ever hear from him?"

"No. I think I heard that he died a few years ago."

Ransom tapped the end of his pencil on the edge of the map. "I'm thinking of cutting timbers to shore up the part that collapsed." When his mother didn't answer, he looked up at her. Unable to read the expression on her face, he started to ask what was bothering her and for some reason stopped. For years he'd felt there was more to the story of his pa and Lockwood, but his mother had always changed the subject when he asked.

"You better saddle up and fetch Gretchen. It'll be dark in an hour or so."

"All right." He folded his maps and put away the papers he'd been working with, leaving the desk cleared as he always did. "You want to come with me?"

"No, thanks. I need to bake the cake for tomorrow and get a basket ready. But one of these days . . ."

They drove out of the yard before full daylight the next morning. Lucas had thrown in a basket with the cleaned liver, heart, and tongue, and in addition to the dinner basket for the workers, Mavis had included a basket for the family with a pint of rhubarb-and-strawberry jam, several quarts of canned beans, and a bag of dried ones, plus a meaty ham bone for soup.

"You be careful now," she said as she waved good-bye.

"We probably should have brought a can of milk for the little ones," Ransom said, hunkering into his sheepskin jacket against the chill. Frost glazed the weeds and grasses along the road.

"It would be butter before we got to town."

The miles passed with no other comments between them.

Ransom glanced at his brother. This silence was not like him. "You okay?"

Lucas nodded. "This wasn't the way I planned to spend my day."

"Me neither. We got plenty to do around the ranch to get ready for winter."

Houses had sprouted up alongside the road the nearer they drew to town. A dog barked at them but was kept out of the road by a picket fence. They heard the school bell calling the kids in to begin their day. Gretchen had taken the shortcut trail to town, so they hadn't seen her.

Ransom turned the wagon in to the road that led by the soon-to-be reroofed house and stopped even with it. The two brothers stared at the weathered gray building, and Lucas heaved a sigh.

"Well, let's get at it. No sense waiting on the others." A stack of split shingles waited beside the house. While Lucas tied up the horses, Ransom climbed down, picked up the baskets of food for the family, and strode to what could hardly be called a porch. He placed his feet carefully so as not to go through the flooring and knocked at the door. When it opened, he handed the woman the baskets. "These are from Ma, Mrs. Beckwith. Figured you could use some extras."

"Thank you, Mr. Engstrom." A small child with a runny nose and bare feet peeked out from behind her skirt.

"Well, we better get started. Thought we'd put a new post in for the porch first thing."

"That is most kind of you." Her soft voice still wore a bit of her southern beginnings.

The two brothers got the post measured and cut to fit and then tried to figure how to slide it into place beside the broken one.

"We need something to prop that roof beam up a couple of inches so we can fit it."

Lucas looked around. "Nothing around here."

"Can we jack up the old post?"

"With what? Shoulda brought some more lumber along."

"Now you say so." Ransom felt like saying more, but what he was thinking was not kind.

"Here, let's take the nails out of the bottom of this. I'll lift it and you slide a couple of those shingles under it."

Ransom stared at his brother and gave a slow nod. "Pull the nails out if you can find them. I'll get the shingles."

"This thing is so rotten we can prob'ly just kick it loose."

"And have the whole porch down on our heads."

Ransom could hear Lucas digging into the post with the claw of his hammer. If he had any sense, he'd have known to bring some extra supplies, just in case. He snapped the tie around the bundle of shakes and picked up a handful. Standing upright, he saw a little child watching him through a window that shone in the sunlight. They might be poor, but the missus did her best to care for her family. The names he called the father of this household were best kept inside.

"Think I got 'em all." Lucas laid the nails on the floor where they wouldn't step on them. While they were a bit bent, they could be straightened and used again. "You ready?"

Ransom nodded and, with Lucas holding the old post, gave it a kick. Sure enough, they just might be able to do this.

Lucas grinned at him. "Told you so." He wrapped his gloved hands around the base of the post, and bending his knees, he put all his strength into the job. The roof frame shrieked and screamed.

Ransom glanced up to check if it was safe.

"Hurry up!"

He shoved the narrow edge of the shingle under the post. "Okay, relax."

"We need another?"

"Think so."

They repeated the process, and this time every nail in the roof screeched in agony. Ransom shoved the second shingle into place.

"Do we need a third?"

"Let's try to slide that new one in. We shoulda peeled it first."

"We'll let the kids do that." Together they set the new post next to the old one and, with one of them at the top and the other on the bottom, eased the post into place, using hammer blows to finish the job.

"Well, how about that?" Lucas grinned at his brother and extended his hand. "Good job."

After a shake they straightened the nails, using a flat rock in the yard, nailed the new post securely, and gave the old post a shove. It toppled right out into the yard, and when it hit the ground, it split in half, the jagged rotten ends mute testimony to the short lifespan it had remaining.

"Fine job there, you two," Pastor Brandenburg said from the street. "I was wondering how we would safely roof that porch."

"Thanks. We're putting the new shingles right over the old ones, right?"

"Seems that would be best."

"Who else is coming?"

"Well, two more, I'm hoping, but we'd best get started. Glad to see you brought a ladder."

"Let's get a couple bundles up there, although we can nail the first rows on from the ladder." Ransom shoved the handle of his hammer into the belt of his pants, grabbed a bundle out of the square, and climbed the ladder. "You hand them to Lucas on the ladder, and Lucas can hand them up to me."

"Good idea. One thing for sure, they never taught us about roofing at the seminary." Within a few minutes all three had taken off their jackets and hung them over the wagon. They were about done getting the shingles up on the roof when two more church members strolled in, carrying another ladder.

"You want us to take the other side?" Sig, the barber in town, asked.

"Good. We can all carry half the stack around to the other side."

"Scaffolding would have been a good idea," Ransom said to his brother. "At least for these first rows."

"Oh well. We should be done before dark anyways. How this shanty can hold all those kids is beyond me."

Ransom nodded, real grateful at the moment for the spacious log house they lived in.

The ring of hammers on nails took up a rhythm, leaving not a lot of time for talking. Soon Mrs. Beckwith came out with a coffeepot and cups. "I made coffee."

"Thank you."

After a short break, the men went at it again, now with Ransom and Lucas up on the roof. Sig called for something from the other side, and Lucas walked across the roof to answer.

A screech of wood sounded, and before anyone had time to blink, he'd fallen through the roof up to his armpits. When the last of the broken pieces of shingles and debris clattered to the floor, Lucas let out a groan that could be heard clear to the store two blocks away.

17

ucas, are you all right?"

"I think so. I can't believe I fell through like this—
the wood was so rotten."

Ransom could hear the children screaming in the house and
their mother trying to calm them. "You think we should pull
you up or pull you down?" He stared at his brother, propped
on his elbows. "You bleeding anywhere?"

Pastor Brandenburg charged around the house and climbed
up the ladder but remained standing on the second to the top
rung. "Thank God you're not terribly hurt."

Ransom studied the remainder of his side of the roof.
"We're going to need to replace more than we thought."

"Forget the roof, brother. Help me get out of here."

"Can you lever yourself up?" the pastor asked.

"Or if you raised your arms above your head, could you
slide through?"

"How about letting me off the roof, Pastor, and I'll go inside to see what I can find." Ransom didn't dare look the man in the face, because he was fighting so hard to keep himself from laughing.

"Oh, of course."

"Will you hurry up, Ransom? My shoulders are killing me."

"Hang on to your hat. I'm not the one who fell through the roof." His snort might have given him away if Lucas wasn't heading toward a temper blowout. Ransom made his way down the ladder and into the house, where his brother's legs were dangling through the shattered roof. He smiled at the children and walked around to view the problem from all sides. Lucas's jacket was bunched up under his arms. If they could scoot the table over, perhaps he could help push him back up or pull him through.

"Can we move your table over here?"

"A'course." The woman motioned the children out of the way, and she and Ransom moved the table directly under the hanging feet.

"I think we should pull you through," he called up to his brother. "I'll be on the table and can help lower you."

"Can't you push me up? If I stand on your shoulders, could I push myself back up to the roof?"

"We can try it, but I have the table in place right now."

"Well, move it."

Ransom half shrugged, and he and the missus moved the table over. He grabbed his brother's booted feet and bent over to place them on his shoulders. "Okay, I'm going to stand up now."

"I'm ready."

As Ransom stood, Lucas bent his knees, then pushed hard

enough to make Ransom stumble. "Sorry. I'm braced better now." They tried it again.

"Okay, I'm standing."

"Hurry up. You're heavy."

"Throw me a rope."

Ransom gritted his teeth, feeling like he was being driven down into the floor. He heard the rope scrabble on the roof and felt his brother putting more pressure on one foot than the other. "Hurry up." Ransom knew it sounded more like a groan than an order.

"Got it. I'm tying it around my chest."

Ransom felt every shift of weight like nails driven into his shoulders.

"All right, Pastor, you two pull, and I'll see if I can lever myself out."

"Lord, give me strength." Ransom staggered under the load as Lucas shifted his weight again. The roof squealed and squalled. Pieces of shingles and rotten roofing rained down into the house. But Lucas's feet disappeared through the hole, letting the blue sky show through. Ransom braced his arms on the tabletop and fought to catch his breath. When he could talk, he forced a smile for the children, nodded to the missus, and staggered outside to lean against the newly installed porch post. As attractive went, it failed miserably, but it held up the porch roof just fine. And at the moment—him.

After a few more deep inhales, Ransom walked around to the side of the house, where the men were staring up at the gaping hole.

"You got any more lumber, Pastor?"

"I'll have to go by the lumberyard. Maybe they'll donate some. We need to figure out what we need first."

"We'll need to pull the shingles off and see how far the rot goes. Best thing would be to pull it all off and start over."

"I know, but we can't afford that." Pastor Brandenburg scratched his chin.

"Who owns the house?"

"They do."

Ransom nodded. "I see." So where was the mister while they were working on his house? At the saloon already or passed out somewhere? How did the woman tolerate it? Or better yet, why did she put up with such goings-on?

Brandenburg leaned closer. "She's afraid, Ransom, and until she can find some backbone, things will most likely stay this way."

Ransom swallowed. Flashes of when he was a small boy and his father had been drinking made him sigh. "She needs to talk with my mother."

Brandenburg nodded. "I'll go see about some lumber. You two figure out how much we're going to have to rebuild."

"He fell between two rafters. I think those are good, so just get us a bunch of spacers, those one-by-threes. Take our wagon."

The pastor climbed up into the wagon seat. "Back as quick as I can."

Sig and the other man kept working on their side of the building, making sure they put their weight only on the rafters, while Ransom and Lucas climbed carefully back up on their side. Taking care to keep their weight on the rafters also, they used the claw of their hammers to pull away the rotted shingles around the hole.

"When they built this, they should have put the rafters closer together," Lucas said as they worked. He stuck the claw in another piece of one-by-four that crumbled. The hole grew bigger.

"Looks to be clear up to the roof peak." By the time they reached solid wood all around they had a five-foot section to the peak that continued for about two rafters either way. Shingles rained down on the yard, and a lot of debris fell into the house.

The pastor drove back up, stepped down, and tied up the horses. "They said to bring back whatever we don't use." He stared up at the cleaned-out hole. "I doubt we'll finish today. How about we have some dinner before we tackle that?" He wandered over to look at the other side of the building. "You men are doing a fine job. Come on down and let's eat." He returned to the wagon and pulled out a basket. "My wife sent over some dinner for us."

"Ma did too." Ransom and Lucas climbed down the ladder and stopped to stare up at their handiwork. "No way can we finish this today."

"Well, we'll have one side done and a good part of the other. Hope I can get some more men to finish it off tomorrow." He set his basket down on the tailgate of the wagon, and Ransom pulled his out from behind the seat.

After the pastor said grace, they dug into ham sandwiches, potato salad, and various other foods found in the baskets, topping it off with coffee brought out by Molly Beckwith, the woman of the house.

When the Engstrom brothers left for home, the sun was close to setting, and the roof was about three-quarters completed.

"Don't worry about it," Pastor assured them as they climbed into the wagon. "I'll find someone to finish this."

"Why can't that lazy lout of a husband of hers do at least

a part of the repairs on that house?" Lucas grumbled. "We keep bailing him out, he'll never do his part."

"I, for one, didn't want to hear him yelling at her today, so I was glad he wasn't there," Ransom said. "Do you think he beats her?"

"He sounds awful mean when he gets riled up. Maybe watching someone else do his work is easier on her and the kids than putting up with him."

Ransom kicked his boot against the footboard in front of them, then pulled off his boot and dumped a bunch of wood bits over the side, watching them join the roiling dust from the wheels. "Hope that's the last we see of that mess." He pulled his boot back on and stomped on the floorboards.

"I've been thinkin'," Lucas said.

"And?"

"You know, when Pa used to drink. What made him stop?"

Ransom wanted to say he didn't know, but if he let himself remember back, he did know. He'd not been able to fall asleep that night because his pa wasn't home, and he knew when the man had been out that late, he would come home liquored up. Drunk and loud and yelling. But that time . . .

"You know?"

Ransom nodded. "You were just a baby, and I must have been five or six. I heard him come home and hid behind the door to the kitchen. I could see through the crack between the door and the frame."

"Were you afraid?"

"Terrified. I'd get a whipping if I got caught, but something drew me there that night. Pa was banging around in the kitchen, and Ma just sat in her chair, watching him. When he stumbled over a suitcase, he swore a mile long and then asked where she

208

was going." Ransom rested his wrists on his knees, his feet braced against the footboard. With a sigh, he continued. "Ma said it wasn't for her, it was for him. If he ever drank and got drunk again, she would bar him from the ranch."

"How would she do that?"

"I don't know, but he gave the suitcase a kick and then went to stare out the window. It got so quiet I was sure they would hear me breathing. She pushed a paper across the table. 'It says in here that you will take the money that is waiting for you at the bank and leave town. You talked about going to California to the gold fields, and this is your chance.'"

" 'You can't do this, keep me away from the ranch,' " he said.

" 'Try me,' Ma said. 'I need a place to raise our boys, and I'd much rather they had a father here to help with that, but this is your last chance.'

"He sputtered and stomped back to the table, grabbed up that piece of paper, and read it through before laying it down on the table. 'You can't do this,' Pa said again."

"What did the letter say?"

"I have no idea. I've never seen it again."

"So what happened next?"

"Pa sat down at the table and stared at his hands. He sat there for the longest time. I think he was stone sober by then, the way he acted." Ransom could see his father sitting at that table, plain as if it had happened the night before. "Then he picked up that paper, folded it, and handed it to Ma. 'We'll never speak of this again,' he said. His voice was so soft, I could hardly hear him.

"Ma nodded and took the paper. 'I pray we never have to,' she answered. Then she asked him if he wanted a piece of pie. She fixed him the pie and poured him some coffee, and when she turned back to the stove, I heard her give a sigh that came clear from her toes. I could tell she was praying. I'm sure she had done a lot of praying over this."

"And he never drank again?"

"Not that I know of."

"And you really don't know what was on the paper?"

"Nope. But he changed after that. It was like a lot of the mean drained out of him that night."

"He was still mighty strict."

"Yes, he was. But he wasn't mean." Ransom clucked the horses to pick up the pace, and they turned into the lane to the ranch house at the same time as the moon rose over the eastern hills, bathing the valley in light and shadow as it rose higher in the sky.

"The elk are back."

Ransom gazed across the pasture to where the elk had mingled with the cattle, many of them grazing, some lying down. What a beautiful sight. His breath formed a white cloud in front of him. The moon was bright, but it shed no warmth to the dropping temperature. "Freeze tonight."

"Good thing for that hanging meat."

"It's only been up for a day."

"Let it go two or three more. There's that old apple tree that came down in that storm last spring. We can use some of that for smoking."

"Is it dry enough?"

"Parts are."

Ransom didn't say anything for a time, and then put it out. "Now you know why it bothers Ma so much when you stop at the saloon. Gambling and drinking are two things she just can't abide."

Lucas didn't answer.

"You think on it, and you think real good." He drove the wagon up to the corral fence by the barn and stopped. "Tell Ma we're here, and I'll be up in a few minutes."

"You tell her. I'll put away the team."

Ransom stepped down and headed for the house. *Please, Lord, let him pay attention.*

"Ransom!"

He turned and stared at his brother, who was beckoning him back to the barn. He looked to the house and back to his brother. "Coming," he called. "This better be important," he muttered on the way. "I'm hungry."

Lucas was hanging up the harness. He paused, heaved a sigh, and turned. "I never came home real drunk."

I'd rather you said you never got *real drunk, but this isn't my story.* He shrugged. "Seemed you were a couple of times. Remember when you fell over the coffee table and knocked yourself out?"

"I remember the falling part."

"And the time you fell asleep in the wagon in the barn?"

"Okay, I get the picture. At least I'm not mean when I've been drinking."

"No, you're the life of the party."

The team stomped and snorted, wanting to be let out.

"There's nothing wrong with a drink or two. Even the Bible says drink some wine."

"For your stomach is what Paul was referring to. It also says some stern stuff against drunkenness. Ma made me look all those passages up the time I came home with a couple under my belt."

"Why'd you quit?"

"Can't stand the hurt in her eyes. I know I'm a lot like Pa, but I sure didn't want to be like him in that respect." *Now if I could just get this ranch back to the successes of his day.* The thought sneaked in and bit. He watched Lucas check the sheeting wrapped around the elk carcass.

Finally Lucas nodded, his eyes narrowed, mouth straight. He nodded again and heaved a sigh. "I'll put the horses out. Be up to the house shortly."

"Okay." Ransom stared into the dark shadowed holes where his brother's eyes were. Could he? Would he do it? Time alone would tell. *Lord, it's in your hands. At least I hope he puts this in your hands.* He glanced up at the moon as he strode to the house, windows brightly lit, welcoming them home. How he loved this place. *Guess that's in your hands too—whether we can keep this or lose it. But I sure want to keep it.*

18

*L*et's head out after we eat."

Chief went for the team while Cassie tied his horse to a wagon wheel.

"Micah is with the cattle?" she asked Runs Like a Deer, who was stirring something that smelled good at the campfire.

She nodded and pointed to the steaming kettle. "Rabbit and wild turnip."

"What is wild turnip?"

"A root good for eating."

"Like potatoes?"

The Indian woman nodded and raised another plant. "Wild onion."

Cassie grinned at her. Sounded like they'd be eating better with Runs Like a Deer in charge.

213

That evening around the campfire, she told them all that had happened in town. "The people there were very nice to me—not what I thought it would be."

Micah flicked the prairie chicken bone he was gnawing on over to Othello. The other dog was sitting beside Othello, watching for his turn. He had come out from under the wagon when Runs Like a Deer came out. Now she hobbled around with her crutch under one arm, keeping the splinted leg off the ground. And taking care of the cooking.

"You got some money back?"

"Sixty dollars. I was going to cash the fifty at the bank, but then I decided I can do that in Belle Fourche. How many days until we get there?"

"Tomorrow night, if we press hard."

Cassie stared into the fire. Flames of red, white, and gold devoured the wood. Two spits of prairie chicken were still roasting on the rim of the fire pit, sending a mouthwatering fragrance to tease her nose. For a change she knew she could have more, but she was full. Memories of the fresh-baked pie made her close her eyes. Was there any chance that someday she could make a pie like that?

And what about Sheriff Timmons? Might she see him again sometime?

The next evening as they neared Belle Fourche, the road grew rutted from wagons hauling supplies into town and all the normal traffic of a town. Chief located a place for them to camp on the banks of a creek, and the morning after they set up, Cassie mounted Wind Dancer.

"I'm going to see what kind of place this is and maybe pick up some supplies."

"Big changes since I was here," Chief said.

"When was that?"

"When your father bought that valley."

Cassie studied the man. She had no idea how old he was, and he'd never talked about his people. It was like he stepped from behind a curtain and never looked back. "I found the deed in with a drawer full of papers."

"Good."

"Chief, are there some things I need to know that you're not telling me?" She watched him shrug and then his face turned inscrutable. One of these days she had to get him talking. "Anything else, anybody?" she asked Micah and Runs Like a Deer.

The three shook their heads, so she rode out of camp and down the road toward Belle Fourche. She knew they had supplies enough for at least a few more days. Cassie was constantly amazed at the way Runs Like a Deer was stretching things. They didn't need anything so desperately that they couldn't do without it. Other than news.

She didn't want to mention anything to Chief, but she was afraid to trust his memory to get them straight to the valley. After all, it had been many years since he'd been there. With the weather getting colder by the day, she didn't want to waste any time. Hopefully there would be a gathering place that was not a saloon. She rode into town looking for the general store first. If she couldn't find anyone else to ask about the valley, she would look for the sheriff.

What about a pastor? Surely there was a church. She could

feel folks studying her as they walked along the sides of the street. Wind Dancer always caught people's attention. She noticed two women who looked safe to ask. She rode up to them and stopped.

"Could you please tell me where the local church is?"

The younger one smiled at her. "You go two more blocks, turn right, and you'll see it. What a gorgeous horse you have."

"Thank you. His name is Wind Dancer." Cassie caught the frown levered her way by the older woman. What was wrong? Her pants were causing consternation—that's what. Of course. "Thanks for the information." She turned her horse and headed up the street. She'd worn pants for so long, she'd forgotten how those outside the show might view them.

The church wore the traditional white paint and sported a steeple with a bell in it and a cross on top. A hitching post off to the side of the front entry invited her to tie up her horse.

Dismounting, she stood looking around. Houses bordered a grassy elm-tree-studded area that seemed to belong to the church. She took the three steps and opened the door. The dim interior made her blink after the sunshine.

"Anyone here?"

"I'm back here. Come on in." The voice echoed from behind the altar, so she followed the side aisle and approached a door that opened as she reached it. The man standing in the doorway wore a smile as big as all outdoors, and his eyes matched in their warmth. "Come in, come in." He motioned her to join him and closed the door again. "Need to keep the heat in here or it would be too cold to work. My name is Reverend Obediah Hornsmith. And you are?"

"Cassie Lockwood."

"And what brings you to our fair town?" He moved to the small round stove, with a steaming pot of coffee on the top. "Coffee?"

"Please." Cassie took the seat he pointed her to and gazed around the room, admiring all the bookshelves and the desk. It bore the look of a pastor's study, according to the books she'd read. "What a comfortable place."

"Ah, my dear, thank you. I can already tell we are going to get on famously. I do hope you are moving here." He handed her a steaming cup and held out a plate of cookies. "My wife made these fresh this morning. Oh, have more than one. You wouldn't want to hurt her feelings."

"Thank you." Cassie sat back in her chair. Coffee, fresh cookies, a warm welcome. What a haven within these walls. "I've never been in a place quite like this."

"Oh, really?" He set his refilled cup on the desk and leaned against the wooden top, dislodging some papers as he made himself comfortable. "Oh, don't worry about that. I can always pick up papers, but I can't always entertain a stranger to town. How did you hear about us?"

"I stopped to ask two ladies who were walking toward the store. The younger one was nice and friendly and told me the way. The older one glared and sniffed."

"Why, what a pity. I apologize for her rude behavior."

"I think she didn't like that I'm wearing pants and was riding astride."

"Mercy. Now, how can I help you?"

"I am heading for a valley that is south of Rapid City and

east of Hill City. By a little town called Argus. At least when my father was there, it was not much of a settlement. Perhaps it grew. I don't know."

"So you've never been there?"

"No."

"I hate to be nosy, but what is there that draws you?"

She smiled at him, enjoying the way he put words together. Taking another bite of cookie, she closed her eyes in delight. "Please tell your wife that these cookies are the best I've ever tasted."

"Ah, these are her famous sour cream lemon cookies. She'll be pleased." He picked up his coffee cup and came over to sit in a chair that he pulled around to face hers. "There. Now we can chat in comfort. More coffee?"

She shook her head and, totally to her own surprise, told him the whole story, or at least what she knew of it.

"So you are indeed the famous Cassie Lockwood? I remember attending a Wild West show in Fargo a few years ago. An act there had a mother and father with their darling little girl on a pony. That had to have been you."

"Most likely. I don't know of any other show that had a headline act like that."

"And your mother and father have both since died?"

"Yes. And now the show is no more." Cassie sniffed. What was there about this man that made her want to tell him everything? "And then a couple nights ago we were robbed, all because I was so foolish as to take my roll of cash into a store and . . ." She sniffed again and was afraid she was about to cry. She couldn't believe it. Wiping under her eyes with her fingertips, she said, "What is the matter with me?"

"I'd say you are a young woman who has been thrown out of the life she knew and into one she has no idea how to manage. All the training she knows is no longer relevant."

"All I can think is that I want my mother. And my father, and they can't come back."

"No, they can't."

Cassie huddled into the comfort of the chair and then took the proffered handkerchief and wiped her eyes, blew her nose, and wiped her eyes again. "I've never missed them as much as right now." Her whisper fell gently in the silence. A piece of wood fell in the stove, snapping and popping.

"You do know that you are being held safe in God's mighty hands."

"I guess so. Mor always said that."

"I remember meeting your father after the show. He asked me what I planned to do with my life. I was a young man in search of a dream. He said something to me I've never forgotten: 'Never let your dreams die.'"

Cassie nodded. "He said that a lot. That is why I'm on my way to find his valley of dreams."

"How can I help you?"

"Just tell me how to get there, at least to Rapid City. The Indian chief I'm traveling with says he knows how to get there, but I want to make sure we're taking the most direct route possible."

"That I can do. I can also invite you to come home with me for dinner, and we will put together a basket for you to take to your people. Now, I don't know about Argus, but I have a pastor friend in Hill City, and he will be a help for you. I'll write him a letter and mail it in the hopes it gets there before you do. I'll send a note with you also, just in case. There is a fine group of Norwegians in Rapid City, and I'm sure they would be pleased to help you too."

Cassie shook her head. "I had no idea when I rode in here that—"

"That God would provide?"

"I guess so. I thought some general instructions would be sufficient."

"Glad to be of service. Let's go to my house, and I'll write those letters while Mrs. Hornsmith can have a chance to help you in her ways." He banked the stove and closed the lid on the tin of cookies. "Shame you didn't bring the others along. They might have enjoyed a good home-cooked meal for a change too."

Cassie preceded him out the door and through a side door to step out into the sunshine.

Why did it feel like a huge load had been lifted from her shoulders? Could it be that the worst of their trip was over?

The map in her pocket made Cassie feel far more confident about the rest of the trip. She signaled Wind Dancer to settle into his rocking-chair lope as they returned to the camp outside of Belle Fourche. Runs Like a Deer looked up from the rock she was sitting on with her splinted leg straight out in front of her and nodded a greeting.

"Where are the others?"

"Grazing cattle and horses."

"Good." Cassie dismounted and untied the basket Mrs. Hornsmith had sent with her. "I brought supper." She set the basket on a rock and took Wind Dancer to the wagon to strip off the tack. After finding him a patch of grass, she hobbled his front legs and left him to graze. Pastor Hornsmith had fed him a scoop of oats and hay back in town. *What a good man*, she thought, continuing her train of thought from the ride home. Both he and his wife, so friendly and caring. She patted her pocket, where not only the map resided but a letter to a pastor in Hill City and another to one in Rapid City. Back in camp she decided to go through more of the drawers and cupboards in the wagon, this time with a bucket of soapy water to clean as she went.

"What are you working on?" she asked Runs Like a Deer.

"Mittens for winter." She held up the rabbit skins Chief had been tanning. "Cold in Paha Sape, Lakota name for the Black Hills."

"Did you used to live there?"

She shook her head. "No, from Rosebud tribe south of here. Cold there too in winter."

"Do you want to go back?"

Another shake of her head.

Cassie wished she could get the woman talking about her past. She'd heard her and Chief talking in their language and wanted someone to translate, but they didn't offer and she didn't ask. Having someone to talk with was such a delight today. She'd not realized how much she missed the other performers from the show and their conversations when they would sit around after a meal and share stories of their lives. Sometimes on the trains they talked far into the night. Her father had been one of the better storytellers. While he had talked about his valley of dreams, he'd not talked a lot about his life before the Wild West Show, other than his childhood, touring, and then meeting his Norwegian princess. Her mother wasn't really a princess, but she was of the royal family. She had told stories of growing up in Norway and her love of riding as a girl.

She made Cassie dream of mountains, so when the show train traveled through the Rocky Mountains, both mother and daughter were always at the windows, enjoying the wonder of it all.

Thoughts of her mother made her throat clench. How her life would have been different had her mother lived was something she dreamed about at times. But it did no good. And her father. Here she was on her way to his valley, the special place he had never been able to return to.

Instead of climbing into the wagon, she detoured around it and wandered out to where Wind Dancer was grazing. Her father had found this horse for her and helped her train him. To be honest, he had trained both her and the horse together, which was why they seemed able to read each other's minds. She leaned against the black-and-white shoulder and let the tears flow.

Wind Dancer turned his head and snuffled her shoulder, holding her in a curve of comfort. When the tears finally dried up, she wiped her eyes and rubbed his ears, scratching down his cheek and under his mane. Heaving a sigh, she wandered over to the creek that chattered over rocks and sparkled in the sun that was beginning to head down in the west. What a pretty place to camp. It was a shame they would be pushing on in the morning. But now that she was confident they were heading the right way, she realized she was anxious to get on the road again.

Get back to work, she ordered herself. So she turned around and headed back to the wagon, mounting the steps and deciding which doors and drawers to start opening. She went back outside to pour some of the steaming water into a bucket and shave some of the precious soap bar into the hot water. She dug a rag out of the dwindling hoard and started with the cupboards at the front of the wagon. Some were empty, which made her wonder about Jason. It seemed that he had only slept there and had not really lived in the wagon, as she and her family had.

The next row down, she found more papers, a stack of aged white shirts, several ledgers, including ones that bore her father's handwriting, and a stash of contracts. In one packet she found two twenty-dollar bills. *Thank you, Lord.* They could buy supplies. In another, more money, but when she looked at it, she almost laughed. Confederate money was not worth the paper it was printed on.

When she had to light the lamp to see into the cupboards, she finished up the row she was on. She'd do the drawers another time. Eyeing the piles of paper work, she wished she could just take it all out to the fire and watch it go up in smoke. But what if she found something else of value?

A knock at the door and Chief announced that supper was ready.

"Thank you." She pulled out a drawer that she knew to be empty and shoved the stacks into it. Now she had two drawers of more stuff to sort through. But finding cash certainly was worth her time. She closed the door behind her and joined the others at the campfire.

A rabbit carcass was sizzling over the fire, and the soup Mrs. Hornsmith had sent was steaming in a kettle. The loaf of bread was on the rock that was their table, waiting to be sliced.

"You cut it." Chief nodded to the loaf.

Cassie picked up the loaf of bread and inhaled the yeasty fragrance. Nothing smelled as good as fresh bread. She took up the long-bladed knife and sawed off the heel, then three more slices. Bread was worth savoring and saving for the next meal. Wrapping the loaf back up in the towel, she returned it to the basket and opened the jar of preserves.

"Do you all want jam on your bread?" At their nods, she spread jam on each slice and handed them around. She then dished up bowls of soup and sat down to eat. While the others wolfed their bread, Cassie nibbled at hers, savoring every bite. Chief broke the rabbit into pieces, and they devoured that too. All those years she had taken meals for granted. Food, good food, just appeared at the right times. Her only duty was to go to the dining tent, dish up her plate, sit down, and eat. Thinking back, she could not remember a single meal that her mother had cooked. They always ate with all the other performers and crew, just like a huge family.

No wonder she was lonely now.

And they would all still be there if Jason had done a decent job of keeping the show going. Anger flickered like a flame and caught hold to burn underneath her awareness. It was a good thing Jason was gone, probably never to be seen by them again. Did the others feel the same way she did? Or had they gone on to work for other shows? Most of them were most likely having a hard time too, since most Wild West shows shut down until spring. Lockwood and Talbot had continued through the winter by moving south to the warmer climates.

"More soup?" Micah asked.

"Yes, of course." She picked up the ladle and refilled his bowl. "Anyone else?" As the kettle emptied, she dug into the basket to bring out half a gingerbread cake, which she split in four and handed out. She decided to save the pickles for another meal, along with the cookies and the hunk of cheese. Tomorrow they could have the leftovers. Thank you, Mrs. Hornsmith.

19

*I*f you cut up the elk, I'll bring down the applewood."
Ransom stared at his brother. While Lucas liked
hunting elk, once he gutted and hung the carcass, he liked to
leave the remaining work for someone else. Usually his older
brother. After all, who else was available? "I guess." *Which
means I have to put off cutting those trees another day.* And
they still hadn't run the fence line. "Fine. I'll do that, and
you ride the fence line at the same time as bringing down
the applewood."

Lucas gave him a disgruntled look.

Ransom heard his mother chuckle at the stove behind him.
It took some thinking to keep ahead of or even up with his
younger brother. Often he thought they should have named
him Jacob, the wily son of Isaac in the Old Testament. But

then, he didn't feel like the other brother, Esau, so there you had it.

Mavis laid a hand on his shoulder as she placed a new platter of sliced ham on the table. "I could go ride fence, I suppose."

"No. I'll do it." Lucas stabbed a ham steak. "Is this the last of the ham?"

"Yes. I still have lard to render, so we'll have chitlings for a while. Maybe I'll do that today, and we can have fried corn-meal mush tomorrow. It's so much better with those crunchy little bits in it."

"That old sow is getting mighty big for farrowing. She laid on three of her last litter. We should have kept one of the gilts." Lucas buttered and spread raspberry jam on a biscuit.

"Maybe we can trade half of the sow for a gilt." Mavis pulled another pan of biscuits from the oven. "More?"

"Yes, please." The only thing Ransom liked better than fresh-from-the-oven biscuits was fresh-from-the-oven rolls. He took two right off the pancake turner and dropped them on his plate, shaking his fingers.

"Hot?"

"Right." He grinned up at his mother, who had rolled her lips together to keep from laughing.

"Some people never learn." Lucas stuck a chunk of ham in his mouth. "You want to brine some of that elk, Ma?"

"Not a bad idea. How about one or both of the shoulders? We can smoke the haunches right away. I'm frying part of the tenderloin for supper. Good thing it's cold enough at night to freeze it."

Ransom sopped up the last of his fried eggs with the biscuit and heaved a sigh of contentment. His mother was known as the best cook in the area, and they ate the benefit of her talent all the time. Other than when Gretchen cooked, which thankfully was not too often. "Okay, let's get that carcass up on the cutting table, and then you head out." He nodded to Lucas. "The saw is hanging in the springhouse?"

Mavis nodded. "I'll sharpen the knives while you get set up."

"That's okay. I'll use the grindstone." Ransom pushed back from the table. "Come on, little brother. Up and at 'em."

The two brothers headed for the barn and, after letting down the winch, hauled the wrapped carcass over to the table they used for cutting meat.

"Let me scrub that first." Mavis met them at the table with a bucket of soapy water.

"Well, hurry. This thing is heavy." Lucas propped the carcass on the edge of the table to take the weight off his arms.

Mavis scrubbed and then sluiced the remainder of the bucket over the heavy-duty table her husband had built years before. With posts for legs and wheels on one end so it could be easily moved, the table was used at both the barn and the house, doubling as a serving table for their annual barbecue. She stepped back, and the men hefted the carcass in place.

"He's sure a big one."

"Probably a well-grown three-year-old, judging from his horns."

Lucas headed out to the corral to bring in his horse, and Ransom took the knives over to the grinding wheel to put an edge back on them. He sat down at the seat, lifted his feet to the pedals, and cranked the wheel up to speed. Holding the knife blade with both hands, he held it at just the right angle to the spinning wheel. Sparks flew and the wheel screamed as the knife returned to sharp. Ransom sharpened four knives, took out a whetstone, spit on it, and worked the blade edge in a circular motion to put the final edge on it. When he finished, the knives could slice paper or remove the hair from an arm. His father had taught him well.

His mother brought out several enameled pans so he could put the bits to grind for ground meat into one and the cuts in the other. He sliced the loin into steaks, left the brisket whole, and after cutting off a couple of roasts, left the remaining haunch to be smoked, along with the shoulders to brine and then smoke. He cut up the big bones for soup, tossing one to Benny to gnaw on. Ransom wrapped the haunches in the sheeting again and hoisted the bundle closer to the rafters for safety. Coyotes had been known to worm their way into the closed barn to ravage the meat. Carrying the two pans to the house, he set them on the counter in the kitchen.

"What smells so good?"

"Rendering the lard in the oven." Mavis pulled open the door and brought the shallow pan out to set on the top of the reservoir. With a cooking spoon, she dipped out the golden liquid and poured it into a bread pan, then slid the big pan back into the oven.

"Interesting how golden it is and yet it firms up white." Ransom dug under the counter in the pantry for the meat grinder and clamped it down on the edge. "You want me to grind?"

Mavis stared at him.

"No, I'm not crazy. I saw how hard you had to work at the sausage, so I'll grind if you want me to."

"Thank you. I'll cut, then."

With the two of them working at it, the meat was ground in time for a late dinner. Mavis had a kettle of soup simmering on top of the stove while the lard simmered in the oven. "I was going to bake bread, but this old oven can only do so much at a time." She set the soup-filled bowls on plates and carried them to the table.

"I'll fill that last crock with ground elk patties and pack it in lard. Good thing I'm doing both things on the same day."

"Put it in the root cellar or the springhouse?"

"The cellar. I have more potatoes to dig yet. The deer mowed down the chard row last night. It'll come back if we have enough warm weather yet this fall. Say grace, will you, please?"

Ransom nodded and bowed his head. "Heavenly Father, thank you for this food, for Ma being such a good cook, and for keeping us safe as we go about our chores. Amen." He looked up to find her looking at him with shiny eyes.

"Thank you."

"For what?"

Mavis heaved a sigh. "For being such a considerate son. Some woman is going to have a wonderful husband one of these days."

His snort was drowned in his first spoon of soup.

After they finished eating, Ransom pushed his chair back. "Tell Lucas that if he gets back before dark, to come help me cut those pine trees down."

"I hate to see you go out there by yourself."

"I'll be careful. I'm just going to wedge them before we use the crosscut saw to bring them down."

Ransom whistled as he saddled his horse and hung the ax

from the latigo. Swinging aboard, he trotted out of the yard and nudged the gelding into a lope. Maybe he should have encouraged his mother to come along. She'd not ridden since the time they rode up and got the deer. She'd had a great time then. He heard a hawk scree high above, so high it was lost against the sunlight. Often they saw eagles, especially farther up in the hills.

When he arrived at the stand of pines, he dismounted and tied his horse to a low bush. Taking the ax, he strode to the first tree he'd marked, decided which way he wanted it to fall, and swung the ax on the first cut on the side of the tree he wanted to hit the ground first.

He was on the third tree when his horse whinnied. Ransom tipped his hat back and looked down in the valley to see Lucas loping toward him.

"Hey, thanks for coming."

"You're welcome, but I'm on my way up to get the apple-wood. How many you planning on taking out?" Lucas asked, nodding at the stand of pines.

"Ten to start with."

"You do know this is the most insane idea you've had so far?"

"Don't get me started."

"I won't. See you back at the house." Lucas turned his horse away and headed farther up the hills.

Don't let him rile you, Ransom reminded himself. *Just don't. Now, why didn't Lucas take the wagon up there? Could have brought a lot more back that way.* Never would he understand his younger brother, not in a million years.

He remembered the day he and Lucas had been playing, against their father's orders, at the opening to the mine. They'd pretended to be miners and dug into the mine floor with their shovels. When the light glinted on a piece of rock in their hole, they laughed and said they'd found gold, certain that it was quartz. They carefully dug it out, but they couldn't show their pa because he'd said that if he caught them playing in the mine, he'd whip them within an inch. An inch of what they were never sure, but they weren't going to take a chance on finding out.

So they dug out their little rock and took it to the house to hide it in their secret place under the bed. Ma found it one day when she was cleaning and polished it up before showing it to Pa.

"Where did you find this?" he roared at the two of them.

"Don't know. Just with some rocks." Ransom tried not to flinch.

"And you?" Ivar glared at Lucas.

Lucas shrugged. "Just rocks."

Ransom was never sure if Pa believed them, but when he took it in to be essayed, it was real gold. They still never told him they'd found it in the mine, and Ivar always told people his boys had found it while out playing with some rocks.

To this day, Ransom dreamed that there was more gold where that had come from, even though Ivar had mineralogists come search the mine for any further sign of gold. They always said no, that rock the boys found was just a fluke. It had probably been dumped by a glacier or by a flooded creek or maybe a landslide, like so many other places where gold was found in the Black Hills years earlier. The nugget had helped pay for groceries one bad year.

As the light started to dim, he stopped notching trees and, hanging the ax in the latigo again, mounted and headed for home. He'd not seen Lucas come back with the applewood.

Hauling his saddle in to hang on the brace on the barn wall, he heard Gretchen talking to the milk cow. She sat with her forehead planted in the cow's warm flank, milk pinging in the bucket.

"I thought Lucas was supposed to milk tonight," he said.

"He was, but he hasn't come back yet."

"Sorry."

"Nothing new."

"How was school?"

"Fine. Jenna and me got in trouble."

"You got in trouble?" His little sister was not one to disobey or cause a ruckus.

"Jenna sent me a note, and I sent one back. Mrs. Micklewhite saw us. I knew better, but—"

"What was the punishment?"

"Stay after school and clean up the classroom. We had to clean the erasers, wash the boards, and even sweep the floor." The last was muttered with disgust. "I'm mad at Jenna still. It was starting to get dark before I got home, and Ma was worried. Now she's mad at me."

Ransom fought to hide a grin. Gretchen did not like people to be mad at her. "She'll get over it."

"But now I have a mark against me at school." She stripped out the teats and pulled the bucket off to the side. Heaving a sigh of disgust, she got to her feet and hooked the stool over the nail on the post. "She's not giving much milk anymore."

"She's due when?"

"Not until February. What'll we do for milk until Rosy calves in November?" Gretchen handed him the bucket and flipped open the stanchion to let the cow loose.

"See if we can buy some from—"

234

"With no money?"

"Gretchen, that's not for you to worry about." Together they shut the barn door and strolled to the well house.

"I'm not worried. It's just a fact." She opened the door into the stone building next to the windmill and stepped down inside. "Dark in here. You have a match?"

Ransom lit a lantern and hung it back on the wall, watching his little sister set out the pans for the cream to rise. She poured the milk through the strainer setup, and it flowed into the pans.

"Do we need to take some into the house?"

"No. Ma said we have a pitcher in the icebox." She motioned for him to leave and followed him out, shutting the door behind her. They heard Lucas whistling down at the barn as he stripped the tack off his horse. A stack of applewood branches and a section of the trunk sat beside the smokehouse.

"Smoking that elk?"

"Tomorrow."

"I could stay home and help you."

"Gretchen."

"Worth a try." She pushed open the door to the kitchen. "Mmm, smells good in here."

Ransom hung up his hat and coat and crossed to the sink to wash his hands. "Lucas is home."

"Good. Gretchen, help me get supper on the table, please."

"You want me to slice the bread?"

"Please." Mavis gave the brown gravy another stir and then poured it into the pitcher. "The steaks are in the oven, potatoes all drained and ready to dish up."

When all four of them had sat down at the table, Mavis smiled at each one of her children. "Thanks for the help. All of a sudden I got behind. Lucas, please say grace." She bowed her head.

Ransom caught a frown flit across his brother's face before he bowed his head. Why would that be? He'd also caught a glare from Gretchen. She was not happy with her other brother, that was for sure.

As soon as the amen ended, Lucas reached for the steak platter right in front of him and helped himself before passing it to Ransom. Suddenly aware of the silence, Lucas looked at his mother, who nodded toward Gretchen. "What's wrong?"

"Weren't you supposed to be here to milk the cow?"

"Sorry, but I was bringing the applewood down for the smoker."

"You never milk anymore. I got home late, and poor Bess was bellering at the barn door."

"That's not quite true, but . . ." He paused and stared at her. "How come you got home late?"

"Jenna passed me a note and Mrs. Micklewhite saw. We had to stay after school and clean the whole classroom." Gretchen poured some gravy on her potatoes. "I warned Jenna."

"What?" Mavis asked.

"That I won't be her friend anymore if she passes me notes again."

Ransom and his mother exchanged looks of surprise.

"I don't ever want to have to stay after school again." She tucked her hair behind her ear. "Lucas, you always have excuses for not milking. It was your turn."

Ransom dished himself some potatoes, passed the bowl

to his mother, and reached for the gravy. It was beginning to look like Lucas had offended them all.

"Hey, I said I was sorry."

"Sorry doesn't mean a thing to you. You just go on doing what you want."

"Gretchen." Mavis frowned.

"It's not fair, Ma, and you know it. He makes sure that whatever he is doing takes longer, just 'cause he hates to milk."

"I don't hate it."

"Yes you do. I heard you say so." Gretchen glared daggers at her brother.

Ransom kept his mouth shut. It was time someone else said something to Lucas besides him.

"Men shouldn't have to milk cows. That's women's work."

Mavis's eyebrows arched into creases. "Oh really?" She narrowed her eyes. "Since when did that matter in our family?"

"She's grown up enough now to understand things like that."

"Well, I thought I reared you all to help where help was needed," Mavis said, "none of this men's work and women's work. When the work needs to be done, we do it together."

"But, Ma, that's not the way the world works."

"That's the way it works here, and we will hear no more about this." Each word was clipped, as if cut with one of the newly sharpened knives. "If you don't want to milk anymore, then you'd better figure out a different plan. Talking to the two *females* in this house might be a good place to start. We believe keeping one's word is important."

"Can't a man eat in peace in his own house?" Lucas slammed his hands flat on the table.

Mavis leaned forward. "This is *our* house, Lucas Engstrom,

not just *your* house. And now, I think this has gotten out of hand. We will all calm down and finish our supper and enjoy our chocolate pie for dessert. Any questions?"

Ransom thought for sure Lucas was going to storm out, but he clamped his jaw shut and nodded. Surely this wasn't the end of the matter.

20

*T*he sun peeped over the horizon.

Cassie and her mismatched group creaked out on the road, setting the pattern for the coming days. After long days on the trail, they set up camp before dusk and ate the leftovers from Mrs. Hornsmith and whatever meat they'd shot or snared. In the mornings they ate a cold meal and drove as far as they could, following the instructions the pastor had given them. They bypassed the towns when they could, stopping only once to refill their water barrel at a local pump.

Runs Like a Deer became stronger and started riding up on the seat beside the wagon driver, bracing her splinted leg on the footboard.

Cassie watched her talking with Micah and realized that

the Indian woman saved special tidbits especially for him. One day Cassie caught a knowing look from Chief that made her smile. Might a budding romance be happening right before their eyes?

When she mentioned something about Runs Like a Deer to Micah, he looked at her in confusion.

"She's getting stronger," was all he said.

Driving through rain on the second day, Cassie wished she had stayed in the wagon. Water was dripping off her hat and down her neck, in spite of her wool coat. They all needed raincoats, but not only was there no money, there was no town nearby where they could find a store.

When they stopped, Chief and Micah rigged up a tarp attached to the wagon and built the fire at the edge of it, using wood they'd brought along that was dry. Hot coffee tasted mighty good, and being the last they had, even better. Cassie heated the beans on the stove in the wagon, and they all ate under the cover of the tarp.

"At least it isn't snowing," she said to Chief.

"Not yet."

"You think it will?"

He shrugged. "Possible. You like a cat."

"A cat? How's that?" She shivered at a gust of wind.

"Hate being wet."

Micah and Runs Like a Deer joined in with Chief's laugh.

Cassie tried to laugh with them, but laughing was difficult through clenched teeth. She shivered again. "Sorry. I'm going inside."

"You want me to bring you more wood?" Micah asked.

"Thank you, no. I can manage that myself." But he beat

her to the door and, after opening it for her, followed her inside, carrying an armload, some needing drying. He added wood to the stove, put the lids back in place, smiled at her, and left.

"Thank you," she said as he stepped out the door.

His nod said he'd heard her.

Cassie rubbed her hands together over the stove, and then rubbed her upper arms to get the circulation going. Hanging up her coat and scarf, she hooked her hat on the peg by the door. She pulled a sweater she'd found in a cupboard over her head and then removed her damp shirt from underneath it. The wool, although a bit moth-eaten, warmed her within seconds. She pulled her quilt out of the cupboard, wrapped it around herself, and then sat down at the table, where the lamp spread a pool of light as soon as the match touched the wick. Within minutes she'd stopped shivering and could feel the warmth from the stove on her face. It was too early to go to bed, and while she could hear her companions talking outside, she had no desire to join them.

Instead, she drew out the drawer that was stuffed with the papers she'd found in various hidey-holes and removed a stack to look through. Bills, some marked *Paid* and others said *Due Now* in large letters. *Please Pay* and *Overdue* marked others. All of those she stacked in one pile. They would make good fire starter. She paused. If she was half owner of the show, like Jason had said, was it her responsibility to pay these bills? Would creditors come after her? What would her father have done?

Her father wouldn't have let the show get into trouble like it did, that was for sure. She thought of all the tents and wagons and animals and all the supplies left behind. Who had all that now? Did some other show come in and buy it up? Wouldn't that money go to pay the bills? But how could it, if she had the papers with her? She rubbed her forehead. There was no one she could ask. But there might be someday. The stack of bills didn't take up a lot of room, so they would stay.

She returned to her sorting, draping the quilt over the back of the chair now that she was warmed up. Letters discussing travel plans and locations where the show would be performed went in another pile. For some reason she decided to keep those. On her third stack, she opened an old envelope and found the bill of sale for the wagon. Her father's signature sealed the transaction. That she put in the separate to-be-kept-for-sure pile.

Leaving the piles on the table, she climbed up on the open end of the bunk bed, ignoring all the things they had stored on the top bunk and reaching for the three drawers that butted up against the ceiling. Pulling them all out, she had to give a hard jerk on one that was stuck, but it gave up, screaming as it broke free. She climbed back down and moved the drawers to rest on the woodbox. Which reminded her she should add some wood to the fire. She dug two pieces out from the now covered box and stuffed them into the stove, impatient to get to the drawers. They looked like they'd not been opened for many years. Probably too difficult for Jason to climb up there.

Back at the table she quickly realized these were from the days when her mother was alive. She found letters from Norway, programs from the early shows, a daguerreotype of a young girl and her horse. Another of a very sober-looking couple, her mother and father on what must have been their wedding day. Mother was wearing a traveling suit of a light color, and Father was dressed in a dark cutaway coat with vest and cravat, both of them high fashion for the day. Had she possibly seen this picture as a little girl when her mother was telling her of her life in Norway? She didn't remember it. She sank down on the lone chair and leaned closer to the lamp to study their dear faces. What a dashing couple they were.

She put the picture down and went back to sorting. A small velvet box in the bottom in a corner caught her attention. She opened it carefully to find a ring in the slot. Holding it to the light, the stone seemed alive in the glow. An opal ring. Her mother's opal ring. She slipped it from the nest and onto her third finger on her right hand. She now had something precious of her mother's, something she'd dreamed of all these years. Not that she needed a memento to remember her by, but a treasure. Not for the value of it, if there was any, but something her mother wore and loved.

Putting it back in its nest, she closed the box and resolved that when she finished sorting, she'd pull her trunk from under the table and secret this down in a corner where it would be safe. Or should she put it back in the same drawer? Obviously no one ever went up there.

She found camisoles, shirtwaists, and various belts, gloves, and even a fan. She shook them all out, wiped the drawer, and packed them back where she'd found them. A packet of fancy hatpins reminded her how much her mother had loved hats. Although she'd never worn a western hat in the show, she had in the parade, but her real joy was fancy hats with feathers and silk flowers and ribbons and all manner of vibrant decorations. Cassie left the ring box on the table and climbed back up to put the drawers in their slots.

When the wagon chilled off, she got up and put more wood in the stove, opening the vents to help it catch more quickly. A knock at the door and Chief asked if Runs Like a Deer could come in to bed.

"Of course. It's not locked." She knew she sounded cranky, but instead of apologizing, she fetched another pack of papers from one of the lower drawers and started sorting it. She said good-night to Runs Like a Deer and kept on sorting. Some for the fire starter, some, like the bill of purchase for a black-and-white pinto gelding, also bearing her father's signature, went in the to-keep pile.

A five-dollar bill fell out of a folded paper. She read the paper and added it to the burn pile. When the room cooled again, she put the to-be-kept pile in one drawer and put the to-burn papers in the woodbox by the stove. Stretching, she caught back a yawn. Morning would be there before she was ready. Wrapped in her quilt and swinging into her hammock, she thought of the papers her father had signed. At least they were with her and not at the mercy of some unknown person.

"Thank you, Lord," she whispered, "for the man who was my father, for these papers to help me remember what a fine man he was. I'm not sure how he could be friends with Jason Talbot, but maybe when my father was alive, Jason was a better man."

BAR E RANCH

I am not getting angry with Lucas today.

Ransom stared at the ceiling. He could hear his mother in the kitchen already and Gretchen slamming the door on her way to the barn. By the time he was dressed and pulling his boots on, his mind had gone up in the woods to cut trees. One person could not use the crosscut saw alone. Had Lucas set the elk shoulders in the brine? He banged on his brother's bedroom door as he went by.

"He's out cutting up that apple tree to fit in the smokehouse. He's already started the fire in there," Mavis said, answering his question.

Great, so now I owe him an apology for thinking him a lie-abed? Ransom shrugged into his coat.

"Breakfast is nearly ready."

"Call us." His breath clouded white when he stepped out the door onto the back porch, which stretched half the length of the log house. Pulling his leather gloves on, he strode across the frost-crisped grass to the woodpile.

"You're just in time." Lucas settled the now limbless apple log into the log holder and grabbed the short crosscut saw off the woodshed wall. They took the opposite sides and fell into the pulling rhythm. He remembered his father yelling, *"Just pull. You push and you'll bind the saw up."* So people often called it the pull-pull saw. As they ripped the log into foot-and-a-half lengths, he watched his brother.

"You going to help me cut pine trees after breakfast?"

"I will, and then we have two places where the fences need repair." Fixing fence, like so many other ranch chores, was always easier done by two pairs of hands than one.

Lucas grabbed the other log and set it across the two Xs of the stand built especially for this job. They were chopping up the bigger branches by the time Mavis called them to eat.

Gretchen came flying down the hall and slid into her chair, finishing her second braid as she sat. Ransom said grace, and she dug into her bowl of oatmeal. "I might be late again today."

"Why?"

"I can't remember if Mrs. Micklewhite said one or two days." She made a face at her eldest brother. "And yes, I learned my lesson. I will not pass notes in class again."

"You knew better." Ransom hid a grin behind a spoonful of oatmeal. He lifted the bowl off the plate for his mother to slide two fried eggs and two slices of fried cornmeal mush onto it.

"That enough?"

"For now." He finished his oatmeal and reached for the warmed syrup pitcher. "We're cutting pine trees first and then fixing fence after dinner."

"So will you watch the smoker and make sure there's enough wood in it?"

"I will. You already have the meat hanging in there?"

Lucas nodded.

He must have been up mighty early, Ransom thought, taking a drink of coffee. *Amazing that he didn't bang on my door.* Lucas had spent his early years trying to keep up with his big brother. The day he won a footrace he'd shouted his glee to the heavens. Ransom may have pulled up a little to let his little brother win, but pride should have kept him from doing so. And yet he'd often taken the discipline of his father because he was the older and should have known better. Both boys well knew where the razor strop hung and what it felt like wielded across their rears when Pa got angry.

Gretchen drank her mug of half coffee, half milk and grabbed her plate and silverware to dump in the dishpan on the stove. Then shoving her arms into her coat, she kissed her mother's cheek and flew out the door to where her saddled horse was waiting.

Mavis smiled. "It was all I could do yesterday not to burst out laughing when Gretchen said she told Jenna that she wouldn't be her friend if Jenna passed a note again." She snort-chuckled. "When that girl gets something on her mind, it takes an act of God to change it. A lot like her pa that way."

"A lot like Pa for sure," Ransom agreed.

"Need a refill?" Mavis asked, coffeepot in hand.

"And some more of the fried mush," Lucas said as he held his cup up.

When his mother held up the pancake turner, Ransom nodded. "If there's enough."

"I made extra." Mavis served some to herself and sat back down. "Were there any more apples up on the trees?"

"Some at the top. The deer got all the ones on the ground."

"I thought a few more would be good. I've not made apple butter yet, and I hate to use the ones down in the cellar."

Lucas looked to Ransom, who nodded. "We'll bring them down at dinner."

"I could maybe make an apple pie if you do."

Apple pie was Lucas's favorite dessert.

"Do you think there are enough up there to have a cider party?" Both Mavis and Ransom looked to Lucas. He was the last one to have been up there.

He thought a moment. "Not sure. But if we announced the party, we could ask others to bring their leftover apples to press too."

Mavis nodded. "I've been thinking I'd like to have a party of some kind here. This would be ideal. There's nothing like fresh-pressed apple cider."

"Ma, it's not cider until it sits a few days and the bubbles start to rise." Lucas grinned at his mother. She always canned the first of the presses so it would keep. Apple juice left alone began to ferment. Hard cider was really fermented apple juice, the sugar all turned to alcohol.

"If you want, you could press some a couple of days early. Let me get a calendar. I'm thinking this Saturday might be good a time as any."

"That's not far away. No time for an announcement at church." Ransom didn't have a lot to say on this. They knew his feelings on parties and such. He'd run the apple press. That way he wouldn't have to carry on conversations with those of the feminine gender.

"Shame we don't have room for dancing."

"No, we are not moving the hay in the middle of the barn." Lucas grinned at his mother. "But if the weather holds, we could dance in front of the barn, like we have in the past. Dance enough and you'll keep warm."

"We could have a bonfire."

Ransom gave up. He could see that between the two this was indeed a done deal, and while his mother would say there wasn't a lot to do, he knew differently. He'd learned from experience. He got up to get the coffeepot and refilled all their cups. This could take awhile.

Later than Ransom had planned, the two brothers pushed

back their chairs and shrugged into their jackets. A few minutes later, mounted with saws, an ax, and gunnysacks for the apples, they headed across the pasture.

They ground-tied their horses far enough away to be safe from falling trees and carried one of the saws to the first notched tree. Setting the saw teeth with a couple of short, quick cuts, they settled in to pull the four-foot saw back and forth. Within a couple of minutes, the tree let out a groan and started to tip in the direction of the notch. They gave it two more licks and stepped back to watch the tall pine come crashing down, taking branches from the other nearby trees with it. Branches and pinecones flew up as the tree hit the earth with a mighty roar. All Ransom could see was what a good stack of beams to repair the mine shaft the tree would become.

"I hate to see that." Lucas tipped his hat back and wiped his forehead. "Guess the jacket needs to go." They hung their jackets on a perpendicular branch of the fallen tree and moved on to the next one. By the time they had downed ten trees, Lucas pulled out his pocket watch. "We better get to the apples."

"I was hoping to get some of the branches cut off, but this has been a good morning's work. We could skip the apples." Ransom knew the answer he'd get on that. He clapped his brother on the shoulder as they lugged axes and saws back to pick up their jackets. "Thought I'd bring the branches in and let them dry for firewood."

"You don't think we have enough cut already?"

"Depends on how cold the winter is." They flipped the reins up from the horses and mounted. "An apple sounds mighty good about now."

"Think I'll set a snare line for rabbits. Their fur should be real dense by now."

"Fried rabbit sounds good too."

When they got to the apple trees, Lucas climbed up in the trees while Ransom picked from horseback. It wasn't long before they had two sacks, one tied to each saddle horn. "Ma would have enjoyed this."

"That she would have, and you know, if we hadn't agreed to do this, she would have been up in the tree." They both turned to study the three remaining trees. "Enough for a cider party?"

Ransom nodded. "We'll get the rest tomorrow morning—bring a wagon up."

After dinner the two of them loaded a roll of barbed wire, a posthole digger, some cedar posts, and the rest of their equipment in a wagon and drove out to the places Lucas had found that needed repair.

"Surely that fence wasn't cut." Ransom stared at his brother. "Who would cut our fence?"

"I wondered the same thing." Lucas climbed down from the wagon and reached for the wire and wire clippers. "I haven't counted to see if we're missing any cattle."

"We'll do that before evening. Can you tell if anything has come through here into our fields?" While he was asking, Ransom was studying the area around the cut. No wagon wheel tracks. Only horse and cattle prints, but had some been driven out through this cut?

"I don't think so. I rode around the cattle looking for any different brands. Didn't find anything. The last time someone cut our wire, it was to let his cows in with our bull."

Ransom looped the reins around the whipstock and

climbed down. He pulled his leather gloves out of his rear pocket, all the while looking up and down the fence line. *Who would cut the wire?* Working together, he and Lucas cut three pieces of wire to loop at both ends and put loops on the cut piece. At the post, they used the wire stretcher to tighten the strands and stapled the excess into the post so the wires were taut again. With all their tools and spare wire back in the wagon, Ransom squatted down to study the tracks. He ranged farther from the cut and knelt down again.

"Come here."

Lucas joined him and examined the print Ransom was pointing to. "A shod horse. How'd I miss that?"

"Who around here shoes their horses at this time of year?" Since few of the horses were ridden off the ranch, the only ones they ever shod were the team that pulled the wagon to town or on errands.

"I don't know. It's not something you go around asking." Ransom walked a bit farther. "Here again."

"See anything unusual in it?"

"No, worse luck." Convictions had been made on an anomaly of hoofprints.

They walked back to the wagon, both of them studying the ground as they walked.

Once loaded, they headed across the field to another fence break.

"You going to see Sheriff McDougal, or do you want me to do it?" Lucas asked.

"I'll go talk with him while you go check with the ranches right around here. Ask if anyone else has had fences cut. We can count cattle as soon as we get done here."

"This one has a post rotted out. Maybe the bull pushed

against it or something." They'd not gone far before Lucas said, "You thought any more about selling this place?"

"No, and I have no intention of thinking on it."

"So what do you think? Let the bank take it over? That doesn't seem too smart to me."

"You know, Lucas, have you ever discussed this with Ma?"

"She wants to keep it for sentimental reasons."

"How do you know that?"

"That's just the way she is."

"Our mother sentimental? Why, she's the most practical person I know." They stopped at a post that was kept upright by three strands of barbed wire. "Have you pushed on the others on either side?" He nodded toward the rough-sawn four-by-fours.

"No. But she'll listen to you, Ransom. You know she will."

"Just go lean your shoulder into those other posts." Ransom sucked in a deep breath and, after letting it all out and hopefully the anger with it, pulled the replacement post out of the back of the wagon and leaned it against the wagon bed. He had the other supplies on the ground by the fence when Lucas strolled back.

"All the rest seem okay. Must have been a faulty post."

"You pull out the staples and I'll start digging a new hole." Ransom slammed the posthole digger into the ground, spread the handles, and pulled out a chunk of grass and roots. After digging a couple more times, he raised his voice. "How about using that pry bar on this?"

Lucas hefted the heavy iron bar that had a point formed on the end. Using both hands he raised and jabbed the pry bar into the started hole, then moved it back and forth before repeating the process to loosen up the dirt in the hole.

Ransom brought all the loose dirt out with the digger, and Lucas repeated his actions until they had a hole deeper than a couple of feet. Then they slammed the post into the hole and tamped the dirt in around it with the pry bar so it was packed securely. Ransom started putting things back into the wagon while Lucas hammered the staples holding the wire in place.

"Sure wonder who cut that wire. It's not like we have range wars like some other places."

"We'll know more after tomorrow."

Lucas dropped his hammer and the remaining staples into the bucket where they kept them.

On the way back to the barn, Lucas asked, "How you going to saw those trees into beams?"

"Hope to borrow Arnett's saw."

"Have you asked him?"

"No. Thought you'd like to do that."

"Ransom, why would I want to ask a favor when I think what you're planning on doing is downright stupid? There's not been any gold from that mine since 1876. And there wasn't a lot before then. Besides, we don't have the money to build a sluice or any other necessary equipment. Gold in the Black Hills is all played out. Everyone says so."

"That nugget we found came from somewhere."

"It was an accident, washed down by the creek or some such."

"Look, you don't know any more than what Pa said." Ransom's voice rose in spite of his good intentions.

"It's foolhardy, taking chances like that in an old broken-down mine." Lucas glared at his brother. "You're so stubborn, don't listen to reason."

"What would you do if we sold the ranch?"

"Go homestead in Montana."

"That's the stupidest thing I've ever heard. Ma already built one place. You think she wants to start over at another? Lucas!"

"I said you'd never listen to reason, and I'm right. Just listen to you."

"What kind of reason have you been talking? Just sell the ranch. Give it up and walk away. And I'm not any more stubborn than you are. I'm just trying to do what's best for us all."

"Let me off here."

"Good." Ransom halted the team, and Lucas vaulted to the ground, taking off across the pasture to where the rest of the horses were grazing. He swung aboard his gelding and galloped toward the barn. "Great, go off to town and get drunk again. That'll solve everything." Though he yelled loudly, he was sure Lucas couldn't hear him above the hoofbeats.

Steaming mad had a new meaning for him as he trotted the team up to the barn and backed the wagon under the shed roof. He unhitched the horses and walked them up to the big barn door to take off their harnesses. Hanging the harnesses on the wall pegs inside, he kicked at a bucket that was sitting by the door. The clang of that startled the horses, and he just barely managed to grab them before they took off.

"Easy, boys. Sorry to scare you. But if he was your brother, you'd be steaming mad too." He led them to the pole gate, pulled back the poles, and let them loose in the field. They kicked up their heels then lay down and rolled, kicking their big feet in the air like young colts. After returning to standing and a good shaking, they put their heads down to graze.

Ransom closed the gate and pulled out his pocket watch. With the clouds covering the sun, he needed to know the time. Milking time, and he'd seen no sign of Gretchen yet. So guess who was supposed to milk? As usual his younger brother had disappeared, conveniently so. He slammed the heel of his fist against the gatepost. Good thing Lucas had left, or he might have gotten the full force of his brother's fist. "I hate fighting! Going to Montana to homestead. What does he think he'd use for money?" Yelling at the heavens was not doing any good. He stomped off to the well house to get the milking pail. When were they going to count the cattle if tomorrow they needed to talk to the other ranchers and go to the sheriff? *So he leaves me with all the work! When is he going to grow up and think on someone besides himself?*

21

*L*ucas showed up for supper.

The rest of them were dishing up their plates when he washed his hands at the sink and took his chair. Ransom tried to not look surprised.

"Looks good, as always, Mor," he said, reaching for the meat platter. "I checked on the smokehouse. I'll add more wood about midnight."

Just as if our yelling match never happened. I was so sure he would head to town and drink out his troubles. Ransom studied his brother. Surely he had not let his idea to sell the ranch go. He would be back with another volley later. Like all the Engstroms, Lucas did not give up easily.

"What did you decide on the apples?" Mavis glanced between her two sons.

Ransom could feel her studying him. "I think there are enough, but not plenty by any means. The deer have been eating their fill. We can take a wagon up tomorrow, so you could come too."

"I want to go along." Gretchen looked to her mother. "Mor, I'm getting straight As. I could miss one day of school."

"So what would I write on your excuse for Mrs. Micklewhite?"

"You could say I was sick." Gretchen shook her head. "But I know you wouldn't do that." She thought a moment. "How about you need my help here at the ranch?" Her face fell when her mother shook her head.

"Well, that wouldn't be a lie, at least. I'd be helping. I can climb those trees better than anyone."

"Oh, I don't know. Lucas, here, did a good job playing monkey."

"I haven't lost my touch." He grinned at his little sister. "Next year we'll plan for apple picking on a Saturday."

"Other kids miss school for far less than this." She clamped her arms across her chest and glared at them all.

Ransom started to say, *Oh, let her come,* but a look from his mother stopped that idea. Instead, he cleared his throat and asked Lucas, "Did you count the cattle?"

"I did, and I think we're missing two cows, possibly a steer." He dug into his pocket and pulled out a piece of beat-up paper. "I wasn't sure how many feeders we had left." He handed the paper to Ransom. "This doesn't look good."

"What is happening?" Mavis asked.

"Someone cut the wire on the north fence. Found prints of a shod horse. We need to tell Edgar and see if others have been hit too." Edgar McDougal was the long-time peace officer and sheriff for the area between Hill City and Rapid City. He lived and had his office in Argus.

"Rustlers?"

"Looks that way, although it might be just someone who's desperate and needs meat to feed his family."

"But you don't believe that." Mavis stared at her eldest son. "All these years, and we've never lost cattle to thievery."

Ransom heard a whole history behind those words. This never happened when his pa was in charge. He pushed back his chair. "I'm heading in to talk with Edgar in the morning, and Lucas will canvas the other ranchers. If you write something up, he can invite them all to the party as he goes."

"I'll do that and take care of the smokehouse." Mavis stood and began clearing the table. "Maybe a party is just what we all need." She turned to Lucas. "Back to the apples, can we reach them from horseback or do we need ladders?"

"No ladders." He slitted his eyes. "You do not need to go up there and climb the trees. We'll take care of the apples."

Mavis rolled her eyes. "All right. I won't climb the trees, but I could take a wagon up there and stand in the bed."

Ransom shook his head. "Better if you let us worry about the apples." He turned to Lucas. "Why don't you ask everybody to bring any extra apples they have left, and jugs. With so many hands to turn the press handles, we can do plenty."

Mavis wiped her hands and left to get some paper.

"I was thinking that if I brought in another deer, we could do the pit-roasting, half at a time," Lucas said. "Or maybe do both halves at once, like we used to do with a half a beef."

"Sounds like a good idea to me. Talk to Mor." Ransom paused and looked his brother in the eyes. "But you have to take charge of one thing or the other, the cider press or the pit."

Lucas nodded. "I'd rather do the pit."

"It might have to be widened."

"Come on, big brother. I do have a brain, you know."

"Sorry." *But if you used it more, we might not have these heated discussions.*

On the evening of the third day from Belle Fourche, Cassie's entourage reached the outskirts of Rapid City and found a place to camp on a river that ran through one of the valleys that surrounded it.

The morning after setting up, she mounted Wind Dancer and followed the directions Pastor Hornsmith had given her to find his friend. She'd made sure the letter of introduction was in her pocket. Stopping only once for more specific directions, she found the church with the parsonage right next to it. Since it was about noon, she dismounted at the two-story clapboard house and tied her horse to the hitching post right in front of a picket fence. The gate squeaked when she pushed it open. Two steps led to the front door, where she knocked with assumed confidence. Never in all her life had she knocked on doors like this. Thinking no one at home, she turned away but then grabbed her courage and knocked again.

"Coming."

Cassie sucked in a deep breath, hoping that Reverend Hornsmith had been correct about this man. Perhaps she should have worn a skirt. Why had that idea not entered her mind until right now? Swallowing the lump in her throat took three tries.

When the door opened, she forced a smile to her quivering lips. "Good day, my name is Cassie Lockwood, and Reverend Hornsmith sent me to you." Should she shake his hand? *Mother, I don't know the polite thing to do.*

"Come in, come in. Any friend of Obediah is a friend of mine." The man stepped back and beckoned her in. "I'm sorry, I am Reverend Kemp. Come and meet my wife. Can you stay for dinner? If so, I'll have your horse taken care of."

"Ah, why thank you. I'm in no hurry."

"Good. Come with me." He led the way down a hall paneled in a dark wood and into a kitchen at the back of the house. "Mrs. Kemp, we have company for dinner. Meet Miss Cassie Lockwood. She's a friend of Obediah's."

"Oh, how wonderful. Did you get to meet his dear wife?" Mrs. Kemp wiped her hands on her apron and led Cassie to the table that was already set for two. "You sit right there, and I'll get another place setting. Would you like to use the necessary first? We do have indoor plumbing."

"Yes, please."

"Come with me." Mrs. Kemp led her back down the hall to a door on the right that opened into a room with a sink and a toilet with a large tank attached to the wall above it. "When you're finished, you pull this chain, and it will flush. There's hot and cold water at the sink."

"Oh, this is marvelous. Thank you." After her hostess left, Cassie followed the instructions, letting the warm water from the faucet flow over her hands. How she longed for a bath and a place to wash her hair. She stared into the mirror above the sink. Did she look as dirty as she felt? After drying her hands, she made her way back to the kitchen, forbidding herself to look into the parlor she'd glimpsed as she followed the reverend into the house. She dug the letter out of her pocket on the way down the hall.

The two of them were waiting at the table for her when she entered the kitchen and took her place. "Thank you." She handed the envelope to the reverend. "This is for you."

"Good. Let us have grace." They bowed their heads, and Cassie heaved a sigh of relief. As the grace continued and every blessing had been reiterated, her amen to join theirs was heartfelt.

Reverend Kemp peered at her over the glasses that perched on the end of his rather long nose. "Are you traveling through or planning on staying here in Rapid City?"

Would her answer make a difference in how they treated her? She banished the thought before it could take root. "I have a bit of a story."

"I see." He nodded to his wife. "Then I think we need to be fortified with some coffee while she tells us." Again the look over the glasses. "If you feel like telling us, that is."

"Yes, of course." After Mrs. Kemp had poured them all some coffee, Cassie mashed her potatoes with her fork and poured the gravy over both the meat and the potatoes. The fragrance of the meal made her wipe her mouth with the napkin before she could begin to eat.

"Reverend, let her eat first."

"Oh yes. Sorry."

When she'd cleaned her plate twice and refused a third helping, Cassie wiped her mouth again and laid her napkin beside her plate on the table. She told them who she was, where she'd come from, and where she was headed to. "We camped west of town, I think along the road that goes out to Hill City. I think we need to go there first."

"But I thought you wanted to go to Argus?"

"Is Argus a real town? I didn't know for sure. All that happened so long ago."

"Argus is more like a village, or at least that's what my father would have called it. *Village* isn't a term used so much in this country. My father came from Scotland. But in Argus you'll find stores and two churches, a school for children, and various other places of business. I know one of the preachers there, Reverend Brandenburg. A fine man and leading a good congregation. Argus is a town of farmers and ranchers. There used to be some mining in that area, but that is all long gone."

"I need to find my father's valley."

"I'm sure Brandenburg will be able to help you. You have no idea where it is?"

"I have what it says on the deed, and Chief remembers the look of the valley."

"What if someone else is living there?"

"But I have the deed."

"As you said, that was a long time ago. Things could change."

Cassie stared at him, her stomach tying itself in knots. What if he was right?

Cassie stopped at a store that Reverend Kemp had recommended to purchase cornmeal, coffee, and a small amount of sugar. They needed grain for the horses, but the twenty dollars she had might need to help them through the winter, so the horse feed would have to wait. In her pocket this time, she carried a letter to Reverend Brandenburg in Argus. She browsed the aisles as she waited for her supplies to be weighed and wrapped, stopping in front of the rain gear. She checked the prices and kept on moving. Never in her life had she gone shopping like this. While with the show if she needed a new costume, the show's seamstress made it for her, and before that her mother had sewn for her. She'd looked at samples of fabrics and then picked up her completed garments.

"Your order is ready, miss."

She returned to the counter. "Thank you. Can you put them in a sack so I can tie it to my saddle, please?"

"You come back when you need more." His smile made her nod.

"How far is it out to Argus?"

"About ten, twelve miles. We carry a wider range of supplies than the stores there. It's a small town. You headin' on out there?"

"Yes."

"Well, best of luck to ya."

As she left the store, she thought of her trip to the store in the town earlier in their travels. She'd learned a valuable lesson, but why did the lessons always have to be so expensive?

Back at camp, Micah was chopping wood while Runs Like a Deer worked on her mittens, sewing the pieces together, fur side in, with slender strips of gut. Two rabbit carcasses were sizzling on sticks leaning over the low fire.

"Sure smells good." She handed the sack to Micah. "We can have cornmeal mush in the morning."

"Good."

"Chief is out with the livestock?"

"And Othello. Two yearlings joined our herd."

"What?" Cassie looked over her shoulder as her feet hit the ground. "Did you say two cows?"

He nodded. "Yearlings, no brands."

"So how do we find the owners?"

"Chief says they're ours now. Law of the land." He stepped over and uncinched her saddle, pulling it off Wind Dancer's back. He dumped it on the horn and led the horse beyond the camp to hobble him in a patch of grass.

When he returned, Cassie had the foodstuffs put away in the wagon, and she was inspecting what all they had left of their stores. Flour, beans, dried venison, lard, and the salt and pepper in small packets. She should have bought more salt too. While she'd enjoyed the visit with Reverend Kemp and his wife, they'd not sent food along for the others. She stepped out on the steps.

"Did Chief catch any fish in the creek?"

"No, said none there."

"Really? I thought all rivers and creeks had fish in them."

"Not all." Runs Like a Deer looked up from her sewing. "Not in Black Hills."

"Did you used to come here?"

She nodded. "Black Hills sacred to the Indian tribes."

"What was the other name you told me earlier for the Black Hills?"

"Paha Sape."

"That's right. Do you and Chief speak the same language?"

"Almost."

"But you can talk and understand each other."

A nod. "How did you learn to speak English?"

"School on the reservation."

"And then you married and left the reservation?"

When she didn't answer, Cassie recognized she'd gone too far. Obviously Runs Like a Deer did not want to talk about the life she'd left behind.

"Not go back."

It was Cassie's turn to nod. She brought the bean kettle from the wagon and set it in the coals. The three legs held it up off the hottest portion of the fire. She stirred it with the long-handled wooden spoon and set the lid back in place. Tonight they would empty this pot. While she hated to admit it, she was getting mighty tired of beans. She reminded herself she'd had a marvelous dinner with the Kemps.

When Chief came in, he hobbled his horse and sat down next to Cassie. "Need a branding iron."

"Why?"

"Because our cattle have the LT brand, and any animal we add to the herd needs the same thing."

"Like the two that found us?" At his nod, she sucked in a deep breath. "Is that stealing?"

"Law of the land on open range. During roundup they brand the cattle, calves with same brand as cow. No one can say these belong to them, because they missed out on the branding."

"So how do we get a branding iron?"

"You have one made. Just like the show brand." He watched her face. "At a blacksmith."

"Oh."

He nodded. "Tomorrow."

"I have to do it?"

His nod looked a bit frustrated. "They are your cattle."

No, they are our cattle. She huffed a sigh. If this was the beginning of the herd her father had dreamed of, they were in pretty poor straits. Three Longhorn cows, one calf, four steers, and no bulls. Even she knew they needed a bull in order to have more calves. "Are either of the new ones a bull?"

"One."

This must be like the story of Abraham and the ram in the thicket. God providing in unusual ways. "All right. I'll draw the brand and take it to a blacksmith."

"Easy." He leaned over and with his finger drew an L in the dirt, and the body of a T in the middle of the lower part of the L. "Wind Dancer has that brand, so you can show him that."

After supper Cassie returned to her sorting. How much would a branding iron cost? Where was a blacksmith? She'd not noticed one yesterday, but then, she'd not been looking. While the pile of paper in the woodbox continued to grow, she found no more money or bills of sale. She finished the one drawer and started on the next, finding only socks with holes in them, gloves with the tips of the fingers worn away. Could they all be mended or should she just toss them away? While her first reaction was to toss them, something made her combine several drawers of cast-off clothing into one. One of the women in the show had mended things. Surely she could learn to do that too.

When Runs Like a Deer stumped her way into the wagon, she handed the mittens she'd been working on to Cassie.

"For you."

"Really?" Cassie pulled them on and clapped her hands together like a small child. "They're wonderful. Thank you." So soft inside. She pulled one off and stroked the back of the soft skin. "I can't believe how soft they are."

"Rabbit skin like that. Warm for winter."

"Do you have a pair?"

"I will make mine next."

Cassie pulled open a drawer, then changed her mind and put her new mittens in her trunk. She'd found traces of mouse in the cupboards and drawers. No mouse was going to chew on her new mittens. "Thank you."

"Thank you for my life."

Cassie looked into the woman's eyes. "You are welcome." Maybe they could become friends after all. She sure hoped so.

22

The next morning Ransom woke up sometime in the dark before dawn and couldn't go back to sleep. Rustlers and a party and getting ready for winter . . . And here he'd not even gotten around to patching his boots yet. The only way he could see was to sleep less. It seemed he was going full tilt from dawn to dark as it was. He dressed as quietly as he could, carried his boots out to the kitchen, and sat down by the door to put them on. He heard the floorboards creak before his mother entered the kitchen.

"Can't sleep?"

"Something woke me."

"You want a cup of hot milk?"

"No thanks. I'm going out to the barn and find those lasts. If I don't get my boots patched soon, there'll be water soaking

269

my feet." He looked at his mother in her flannel nightdress with a shawl thrown around her shoulders. "You go back to bed. One of us needs to get enough sleep."

"There are some small pieces of elk hide in my sewing room. I'll leave them on the table for you."

"Do you remember how Pa made the soles?"

"I think he used pigskin and treated it some way to make it hard. Let me think on that." She stood beside him, a hand on his shoulder. "Might be easier to buy the soles." She leaned over and kissed his cheek. "Good night, or good morning, whatever it is."

"Sleep in."

She waved as she returned to the hall.

Ransom heaved a sigh. He pushed against his thighs to stand and snagged his sheepskin jacket off the rack. Taking a lantern off the shelf by the door, he lit it with a match from the box on the stove and closed the door gently behind him.

Benny crawled out of his house on the porch, stretched, and joined him.

"You don't have to get up too, you know."

Benny nuzzled Ransom's hand and ran ahead with a yip. Benny was the second dog in Ransom's life. Abner had raised Ransom, making sure his charge was safe, in between herding cattle and guarding the place. But they'd buried Abner, at fifteen, under the maple tree where he liked to lie in the summer. They heard of a litter of cattle-dog pups sometime later and brought Benny home. He took charge of Gretchen and shadowed the men, loving to ride in the wagons with them and making sure no one trespassed.

"How come you didn't hear the rustlers?" Ransom asked him. Benny looked over his shoulder as if to say *Are you talking to me?*

Ransom hung the lantern on a post above the junk pile, where anything that didn't have a place got dumped. It had been growing in the last couple of years. He pulled off a broken rake, a three-legged table, and various machinery parts, and finally pulled out one boot last and then the other. Neither was attached to the board Ivar used to nail to the heavy workbench to support them. Rust roughened the steel post and the foot-shaped last.

He tossed the remaining things back in the pile. All he needed was a few handles for the rakes and hoes and the old axhead. For that he needed to go find an ash tree or an oak and trim a few straight branches off. Once they were seasoned, he could use the lathe to form the round handles. While handles for various tools were sold at the general store in town, his pa had always made his own, usually in front of the fire on a winter's eve.

By the time he had the lasts sanded and anchored down, the rooster crowing announced that dawn was there. He stared at the workbench, a picture of his father working there taking over his mind. Ivar moved with an easy precision, methodically going from one stage of a project to the next. When repairing boots, he always studied the whole boot first, turning it this way then that, testing the stitches. He would work the elk hide with his powerful hands, then lay it over the hole and study it again. By the time he finished by rubbing bear grease into the leather, the boot would be as good as new. He never smiled much, but when he held the finished boot to the light, Ransom remembered the look of pride on his father's craggy face. Pride in a job well done—that was Ivar Engstrom.

Ransom blinked a couple of times and went to let the cow in. She'd announced her presence about the time the rooster crowed. He forked hay her way, knowing that Gretchen would dump some grain in front of her before she sat down to milk. The rooster crowing again, the cow chewing her hay, Benny scratching with his foot thumping on the wood floor, all were sounds of a peaceful barn coming awake in the morning. Ransom held his breath, waiting for the sound of his father clearing his throat. A sound so familiar that it had to be ingrained in the posts and floorboards.

Benny jumped up and ran to the closed door. He heard Gretchen before Ransom did.

She pulled open the door and stepped into the light. "I wondered who was out here. You're up early."

"Couldn't sleep."

"Oh. Thanks for letting Bess in. Did you grain her?"

"No, but I will."

"Mor must have had the same problem. Bread is already on its second rising." She unhooked the stool from the post and sat down, talking to Bess all the while.

Ransom went outside and whistled for her horse. When he trotted up, he patted the brown neck, slipped a halter on, and led him out of the pasture and into the barn for a brushing.

"Are you feeling all right?"

"Sure, why?"

"Well, cow in, getting my horse—not your normal behavior, you know." When she got all she was going to get, she rose and, after setting the milk bucket out of the way, hooked the stool back in place. After rubbing Bess's favorite place, on the soft skin of her throat, she pulled the wood block up on the stanchion so the cow could back out and meander out of the barn.

Ransom tightened the cinch, and leading the horse, he

and Gretchen headed for the house. He took the bucket. "I'll strain that."

"You better be careful, big brother, you might spoil me." The lightening sky allowed him to see the twinkle in her eyes.

"Don't worry. I won't make a habit of this."

Later, on the road to Argus, Ransom let himself think about the mine again. What if they did find color? What if there really was a pocket or even a vein behind that cave-in? In spite of the metallurgists who said otherwise?

He snorted at his dreaming. When would they have time to mine it? Maybe that was a good thing for the winter. After all, the inside of the mine was supposedly the same temperature no matter what was going on outside. Getting to and from the entrance from the ranch could pose problems.

The old cabin. The thought made him smile. Of course. That was the answer. The cabin was only a couple hundred yards away from the mine. How long since they'd been up there? Was it in livable condition? Who had been up there last? Since that was the first home built on the property, his mother said she had a special place in her heart for it. It was thanks to her that the roof had not rotted out years earlier. It wasn't far from the apple trees. Maybe they'd do a foray up there before picking the apples.

He rode into town, waving to those who called greetings, and dismounted in front of the false-fronted building with the sign *Sheriff* in fading letters.

"Well, if it isn't Ransom Engstrom come to town. That hot place hasn't frozen over, has it?" The man wearing the badge stood and reached across the desk to shake Ransom's hand. "Good to see you, son. Have a seat. Coffee?"

"Thanks, but I value my stomach too much." Ransom sat down and propped his hat on the knee of his crossed leg. He leaned back slightly, glancing around the office. "You don't look too busy."

"And that's the way I like it, no trouble to go solving. Since I know how you dislike coming to town, it has to be something important that brought you in." Edgar got up to pour himself some coffee from the pot on the stove. He added a healthy dollop of cream and motioned to his cup. "Now, that is how you tolerate my coffee." He sat back down, setting his cup on a cup-sized block of wood. "Now, what's up?"

"You had any ranchers in here complaining about cut fences and missing cattle?"

His eyes narrowed. "So much for peace and tranquillity. I hate to say this, but you are the third. I was so hoping this was going to blow over." He scrubbed a calloused hand over his nonexistent hair, heaved a sigh, and propped himself on his elbows. "Fill me in."

After Ransom told his story, the sheriff pulled out a paper and pencil. "Run that by me again so I can take notes. You never saw or heard anything?"

"Nope, but I'm surprised that our dog didn't sound an alarm. He's usually real good about that."

"Interesting. And you say you saw shod-horse prints? Anything else?"

"Just a gaping hole in our fence. We're missing at least two cows."

"Why would someone go to all that trouble for two, three head?"

"The others say the same?"

"That's what the guys at the Rocking R said. At the Bar S they didn't know how many were missing, but there weren't tracks enough for a larger bunch."

"So, say they got between six and ten head. Where are they hiding them?"

"I don't know. None have been shipped out of here. I would have known about that."

"What about Hill City or Rapid?"

"As I said, I've not checked, because I thought it was just a fluke."

"Lucas is out checking with the other ranchers. Oh, and he's inviting them all to a cider party Saturday at our place. He's pit-roasting a deer."

"Sounds mighty good. I remember when I was a young feller and your pa would roast a steer in that pit of his. Best meat I ever tasted."

"If you have extra apples, bring them and a jug. We'll have a lot of arms to crank that press." The apple-cider press was another thing Ivar had built that was still in use. He'd ordered the gears from someplace east, and while they'd had to replace some of the staves in the basket, the grinder worked just fine.

Edgar turned and looked at the calendar on the wall. "How about we set a meeting for Sunday after church? Save everyone an extra trip. We'll see if anyone knows anything at all and devise a plan to catch whoever's doing the thieving. Cattle rustlers in this day and age . . . I thought that went out with the Old West."

"I'll tell everyone I come in contact with. I'm heading to the store and Reverend Brandenburg to let them know about the party. Spread the word." Ransom stood. "Sorry to be the bearer of bad tidings."

"We'll catch him, son. No matter how long it takes."

"I hope so, before someone goes off their rocker and—"

"Me too."

Ransom stepped outside and settled his hat back on his head. A rustler. Could you beat that? He groaned inside. One more thing to take care of—watch for rustlers.

With his forehead in the milk cow's flank, Ransom forced himself to calm down, or he knew she would put her foot in the bucket. He knew that from experience. The cow did not like angry hands milking her. When she switched him with her tail, he stopped and spoke gently to her, then resumed milking calmly and let the peace of the cow and barn flow over and around him.

When she was dry, he pulled out the bucket and hung up the stool. "There you go, old girl. Thanks for the respite." With the handle of the bucket over his arm, he let her out of the stanchion and watched as she backed up, turned, and meandered out the back door. As always, she would go get a drink, then graze for a bit, and lie down to chew her cud with the other cows. She and Rosy were the only ones trained to come to the barn to be milked; the others produced milk for their calves and then dried up to be ready to calf again.

Ransom shut the back door and blew out the lantern on his way out the front.

"Sorry I'm late." Gretchen stopped her horse near the door. "I stayed to help Mrs. Micklewhite after school. Figured it wouldn't hurt to get on her good side for a change."

"Good idea."

She removed her saddle and led her horse to the corral that had no water tank, where she let him go until he cooled down. "Take it easy, boy. I'll come back and let you out again." She slammed the poles into the gap between posts and turned to see that Ransom had put her saddle up. "Thanks. Where's Lucas?"

"Good question. He went out to talk with the other ranchers regarding that cut fence and see if others have had the same. I thought he'd be back soon after dinner."

"He probably came up with some excuse to go to town."

"Most likely."

"When is he going to grow up?"

Ransom bit back a burst of laughter, and when she laughed, he joined her. "You are wise beyond your years."

"Sometimes, maybe." They poured the milk into the pans and grabbed the jug of already skimmed milk to take to the house. Gretchen shook the jug to stir up what cream was left. "You find us a hog to butcher?"

"Not yet. Had to talk with the sheriff. Some other ranchers have had the same problem."

"Somebody cut the fence? Why would they do that?" They scrubbed the soles of their boots on the mat and went in the back door.

"Sorry I was late, Ma. I was helping Mrs. Micklewhite."

"That's fine, dear. Would you please set the table?" Mavis pulled a roasting pan from the oven and set it on the reservoir top. "We're having stuffed heart. Ransom, hand me that cutting board and a bowl for the potatoes." After she'd made gravy from the pan drippings, she set the platter of sliced meat on the table. "Do you think Lucas will be back?"

"I don't know. I can only suspect where he went."

"He's a grown man, son. You can't be responsible for him any longer." Mavis sat down. "Gretchen, please say the grace."

For a change Gretchen said the Norwegian grace her father had taught all of them when they were young. "I Jesu navn, går vi til bords . . ."

Ransom silently said the words along with her. While they'd all learned to speak Norwegian from their father, with his passing, they seldom used it any longer. He knew Gretchen did it to please their mother, who tried to keep some of the traditions alive. They all said the amen together, including a voice from the doorway.

"You're just in time, son. Get yourself a plate and silver." Mavis did not get up to serve him. "There's plenty here."

Ransom passed the serving dishes on to his sister, who held them until Lucas sat down. As far as he was concerned, Lucas could eat on the porch or not at all. But he didn't smell any cigar smoke on him or booze either. Where had he been? Curiosity was always a Ransom trait, but so was keeping his mouth shut. Except when his brother irritated the words out of him, which seemed to be happening an awful lot lately.

"So what did you find out?" Mavis asked when everyone had been served, including herself.

Ransom looked up. "Edgar said others had reported cut fences. He's scheduled a meeting for after church on Sunday."

"Which ranches?" Mavis asked.

"The Double Bar S and the Rocking R. No one else, so we might be catching this early. They weren't sure how many head were stolen but less than ten."

"That's still quite a few."

And where were you all afternoon? is what he wanted to

ask, but he didn't. No sense making supper uncomfortable for everyone.

Lucas smiled at his mother. "This is so good."

"But none of our stock got out?" Gretchen asked.

"No. We don't have them in that pasture right now, or they would have."

"Good. Please pass the potatoes," Gretchen said, with a nudge to Ransom.

"Oh, sorry. Did I miss something?"

"I already asked once." She took the bowl, helped herself, and passed it on to Lucas. "So how come you weren't here to milk?"

"Sorry. I got tied up."

"Tied up? As if you didn't see the sun going down? I even warned you."

"I know, but it took longer than we thought to load the saw."

Ransom passed on the bowl of applesauce. "What saw?"

"Well, I was over at Dan's, and I got to talking to him about his sawmill. He said he would either sell it to us or loan it to us if we needed it, that it would be easier to move the saw than to haul all the logs over there. So we got the wheels under it and hitched up his teams, and I hauled it home."

Ransom let out a breath he didn't realize he'd been holding. "You brought his sawmill home, here to our ranch?"

"Yes. I let his teams loose in the corral and threw them some hay. He said we can bring 'em back after we get the saw out to the trees."

Ransom stared at the ceiling. Leave it to Lucas. He could charm the squirrels out of an oak tree. "Do we have a time limit?"

"Nope. He said he's run out of timber, and no one's come

around to hire him. I have a feeling he'd just as soon get rid of it, but we can't buy it right now. I think he's lonely out there since his wife passed on."

"I have to apologize that I've not been a good neighbor. I'll send him a note and invite him to dinner." Mavis shook her head. "Is he coming to our party?"

Lucas nodded. "Everyone sounded pleased about a get-together."

Now they could cut the timbers and perhaps even some lumber to be used around there. One minute he wanted to pound his brother into the ground, and then he up and does something like this.

"Thank you, Lucas."

"You're welcome. We might need to talk to Emerson about looking at the sawmill. Dan says it needs a bit of work, but we can try it first." Emerson Hansel was the blacksmith in town, and he had a knack for working on steam engines, something that was slowly taking the place of his dwindling blacksmithing.

That was one of the things that bothered Ransom. Times were changing and machinery speeded up things like haying and harvesting. They'd hired a traveling crew to harvest the oats and wheat. Not that they'd planted huge amounts of either.

But their granary was full of oats, and the wheat had been shipped out on the train from Argus, except for what they kept for farm use. The corn had dried and filled the corncrib for the chickens and the hogs. The stalks would be thrown out for the cattle when the pasture was snowed under. Hopefully they'd have seed left for the spring too.

Gretchen prodded him again. "The bread, please."

"Thought we were going to dig that pit for the party this afternoon," Ransom said.

"Oh, that won't take long," Lucas said. "I'll see if I can get a deer tonight or in the morning."

Ransom heaved a sigh. Lucas always had an answer for everything, but Ransom hated to leave things until the last minute, a far different attitude than his younger brother's.

They'd finished supper when Mavis asked, "You want cream on your apple pie?"

"Not me," Ransom answered. "Just plain pie."

"I'll take cream," Lucas said. "Are those the apples we picked?"

"Some of them. The sauce too. I'll do the apple butter tomorrow."

Gretchen cleared the table while her mother cut the pie and served it. When they'd sat down again and all taken a bite with the requisite murmurs of appreciation, Mavis cleared her throat. "All right, what's this I hear again about you wanting to sell this ranch, Lucas? I thought we'd already settled that."

Lucas laid down his fork. "I don't see how we're going to meet the payments to the bank with the little cash we have. If they foreclose, we lose everything."

"That is true," Mavis said.

"Why would they foreclose?" Gretchen asked.

"Because we can't meet the payments. They foreclosed on the Double Y," he explained.

"Do you know how long that ranch had been in arrears?" Mavis asked.

"No."

"Do you know what their assets are or were?"

"No. But I don't think they wanted to move."

"Did they move?"

"Yes, and left it."

"Did you know they had another ranch in Wyoming and that they moved cattle and all their belongings there? That they tried to sell the Double Y and were not able to and so let it go back to the bank?"

"No."

"What is it you want to do rather than ranch here?"

"I . . . I thought of homesteading in Montana."

"You know, Lucas, if you want to go homestead in Montana, you have every right to do that," Mavis said. "But I don't plan on leaving here, and while I know things are tough right now, I've seen things turn around before, and I'll see them turn around again."

"But you need both of us here to work this place. There's more work than two men can do, let alone one."

"If you leave, we'll have to hire help, but we'll still make it." She leaned forward. "But I don't want to hear any more talk about selling out. Do you understand me?"

Lucas nodded.

Ransom sat staring at his mother. Where had all that come from? The legal terminology, the definite plans? Who was that woman at the end of the table?

She turned her gaze on Ransom. "Now, I understand your desire to open the mine again. I don't think it will be worth your time and all the work that will go into it, but I won't tell you not to do it. I would ask that you pray about it. The trees that are downed could be sawed for lumber we can sell so they wouldn't be wasted. There are other stands that can be thinned too. Your pa planned on doing just that after he read some papers on tree farming."

"He did?"

"He was a forethinking man. And he loved this place with a passion."

"All but the mine."

"He trusted what the professional miners told him. Had there been any chance there was more gold in there, he'd have gone for it. He even thought of blowing up the entrance to the shaft to keep anyone from being injured there." She leveled one of her stern looks at Ransom. "Your pa would not be happy that you are dreaming of opening that mine."

My pa might not be happy about a lot of things around here, but he's dead and gone, and I've been pretty much in charge for the last years. Until tonight. "But what if there is gold left in there? That nugget we found came from some vein."

"Most likely the one they worked until it quit. And after the cave-in, he never allowed anyone back in there. I'm sure he guessed at where you found that nugget." Ransom kept from looking at his brother by studying the crumbs left on his pie plate. "And did you know?"

She made a motherly face. "Let's say suspected. And now I know for sure."

"You think he figured it out?" Lucas looked as guilty as Ransom felt.

"I never asked."

23

*T*oday was the day.

Right after breakfast Ransom and Lucas moved the sawmill out to the stand of pine and set it up to be ready for cutting. But when they tried to start the engine, the smokestack went *puff-puff*, and that was it.

"Sure wish I knew more about engines." Ransom felt like kicking the black monster.

"I'll go see Emerson and ask if he'll come help us get it started. Need anything in town?"

"Not that I know of, but ask Ma." After looping the reins over the collar nobs and hitching the traces to the harness, they each mounted one of the heavy horses and rode back to the barn. They ate dinner, explaining what had happened, and Lucas picked up the list Mavis prepared, saddled his horse, and rode out with the teams in tow.

So much for digging the pit that afternoon. Ransom

watched him go, grateful on one hand that Lucas enjoyed going to town and frustrated with the lack of help around the ranch. He went back into the house and poured himself another cup of coffee. The cinnamon from the apple butter baking in the oven made the house smell delicious. "Any more of that pie?"

"Do you think I would bake only one?" His mother cut him a slab and set the plate on the table. Bringing herself one too, she sat down. "So did you decide what to do regarding the mine?"

He shook his head. "I didn't know you felt so strongly about it."

"Your pa always had good common sense. He was adamant no one go back in there. He came too close to losing his life there. I know that was part of it. He always said better the gold on the hoof than in the belly of the mountain."

"Well, the gold on the hoof isn't quite as brilliant as it used to be."

"No, but it is steady. Would you help me haul those spuds down into the cellar? Some of those big squash too. I got the cabbages hung up." She'd pulled the cabbages out by the roots and hooked them up to the floor joists, something she'd read about in her gardening magazine.

"Of course." Two barrels of apples lined one wall of the cellar, the carrots, parsnips, and rutabagas were packed in sand, and now the potatoes filled another bin, covered by several thicknesses of burlap bags to keep the light from turning the potatoes green. Sealed jars, filled with fruits and vegetables, syrups and jams, lined the shelves, and crocks sat on the damp earth floor under the shelves.

"I love to come down here," Mavis said, holding the lantern

high to spread the light around. "No matter what happens, we'll have food this winter."

"The dried beans and such are upstairs?"

She nodded. "And the dried herbs are hanging along the pantry beams. Everything smells so good."

"You and Gretchen can be right proud."

"I know. She's a trooper. I thank God for my children every day and pray you will always make wise decisions."

Ransom followed his mother and closed the outside cellar door behind them. One of the last things his father had done was to install the inside stairs to the cellar to make it easier to get to in the winter. Taking after their father was a good thing. After he had quit drinking.

RAPID CITY

The next morning, after brushing Wind Dancer, Cassie mounted and headed for town again. At the first corner she saw a livery stable and a sign for a blacksmith. How had she missed it yesterday?

"How can I help you, miss?" a burly man in a leather apron asked. "Horse need shoeing?"

"No, I need a branding iron. Ours got left behind." She pointed to the brand on Wind Dancer's rump. "Like that."

"I see." He walked to her horse's rear. "Is he touchy?"

"Not if he knows you're there." She patted the black-and-white shoulder.

"Easy, fella." He patted the rump and ran his hand over the brand. "And this stands for?"

"L and T. Lockwood and Talbot. Lockwood was—is—my father."

"I see. Where you headed?"

"Some land he owns in the Black Hills."

"Give me an hour."

"How much?"

"Say three dollars."

They branded the two calves that afternoon, with Chief running the show.

Cassie gagged on the stench of burning hair and hide. "How do you know how to do all this?" she asked.

"Who do you suppose branded the show stock?" He nodded to Micah. "Him and me and some of the others."

"Is George branded?"

"Nope. And I ain't about to try it. The others were branded as calves."

BAR E RANCH

Early the next day Lucas brought in a nice spike buck. After hurrying through breakfast, the brothers went out to the barn to finish dressing it out. With the carcass wrapped in sheeting and the liver and the heart soaking in brine in the sink, Ransom, Lucas, and their mother bundled up and took the wagon out to the apple trees. By the time they'd stripped the trees bare and picked up the few apples that the deer didn't get, the sun was high and warm enough to take off their jackets.

Mavis bit into an apple and, leaning against a wagon wheel, stared out across the valley. "This is one thing we never could figure a way to have at the house, and yet we didn't want to build a road clear up here either."

"What is that?" Ransom turned from setting the bushel basket in the back of the wagon.

"This view. I'd sit outside my front door of the cabin and look out across the valley just thanking God for such a beautiful place to live. But building the ranch house where we did was much smarter."

"Why'd you build the cabin up here?"

"To be closer to the mine. These apple trees were one of the things I was sad to leave behind." She waved her half-eaten apple. "Can't find an apple anywhere with better flavor."

"I'd like to go on up to the cabin if you don't mind." Ransom polished the apple on his pant leg and took a bite.

"I never mind going up there." She motioned toward the pine trees. "You thinned that stand well. It'll give those smaller ones a chance to grow." She tossed her apple core out into the grass. "Let's go."

What used to be a well-used trail was now barely visible as they climbed the hill behind the orchard. The boarded-up entrance to the mine beckoned his attention, but after his mother's stern warnings, he ignored it. He'd deal with that later.

An oak tree shaded the cabin, covering the ground around it with acorns and dry leaves.

"We should bring the pigs up here. They'd clean up those acorns right quick."

"Right, and some cougar would look on that as serving his

next meal up all nice and tidy." Lucas pulled the latch, and the door swung open. They stepped inside, blinking in the change from sunlight to dimness. Light through the two windows and the door was sufficient once their eyes adjusted.

"We cut the logs ourselves, and the neighbors came for a cabin raising. It was up in one day."

Ransom and Lucas walked around, looking for water stains and signs of animal habitation. One year they had found a mound of pine cones where a squirrel had gotten in and made sure he had plenty to eat in his palace. They'd blocked his hole by the fireplace and threw his store out. The rope-strung bed in the corner needed a mattress, and the whole place needed a good cleaning. But other than that, the cabin was aging well.

"What do you think?" Lucas asked after examining one of the windows to make sure the glass didn't need new glazing. The small cookstove wore a bit of rust, but the chimney felt secure, and there were no nests in the fireplace chimney. Lucas stuck his head in the fireplace to make sure.

Mavis opened one of the cupboards and a mouse leaped out. She let out a small shriek, making her sons laugh. "He caught me by surprise." She gave them both a reproachful look. "You would have jumped too."

"Of course, Mor." Lucas rolled his lips together to keep from laughing.

"You satisfied?" Ransom asked.

"I am. Let's go have dinner. The soup should be ready by now. I think I'll make dumplings. Your father loved dumplings."

Back at the ranch house, she mixed the dumplings and dropped them by spoonfuls into the bubbling soup. For a treat, she sliced bread and, putting butter in a frying pan, browned the slices slightly.

Ransom scrubbed his hands at the sink where, thanks to their windmill, they had running water. Then he dried them on the towel hanging there for that purpose. "After dinner I'm going to get the press in shape for the party," he said, looking at Lucas. "While you dig the pit. We ought to line that with rock or bricks to keep the dirt from washing into it."

"As if we need one more thing to do." Lucas pulled out his chair and sat.

"I'm thinking that fitting that cabin out would make a great place to stay if the weather turns bad when we're shoring up the mine," Ransom said, sitting down.

"I thought you gave up on that idea." Mavis set plates with bowls full of soup on the table.

"Mor, something is driving me. I need to work that mine. If nothing good comes of it, so be it, but there's something that says I have to try."

"In spite of your father's wishes."

Ransom nodded. "Right."

She stared at him. "Foolhardy."

Later, when Ransom was working on the apple press, he thought back to his mother's words. The barb hurt but she hadn't absolutely forbidden his reopening the mine. . . . Oh, and he'd forgotten to tell them that Emerson would come out on Monday.

24

*A*fter the promised cornmeal mush for breakfast with sugar on it for a real treat, Cassie moaned to herself, *If only there were milk.* All the things she used to take for granted, like milk on cereal, cream in coffee, fresh bread every day, pies and cakes for dessert, and eggs in the morning. Her mouth watered at the memories.

Today Micah was driving the wagon, something he'd been doing more and more, so she helped Chief with the livestock. One of the horses that spelled off the other team on the wagon insisted on snatching grass every other foot. When she flipped her looped rope at him, he glared at her and took off after the others.

Othello grinned up at her, tongue lolling.

"You want a ride up here, fella?" She stopped and patted

his spot on Wind Dancer's rump. Othello took two steps and a flying leap to land behind her, where he gave her ear a quick lick. Cassie laughed and turned to give him a one-armed hug. Dancer snorted and swiveled his ears. "All right, jealous one." She patted his shoulder and smoothed the small flips of his mane to the same side as the rest. "You handsome horse, you. What a trooper."

When Cassie rode up by the wagon, Runs Like a Deer's mouth fell open at the sight of the dog on the horse behind Cassie. Then she laughed. Cassie laughed with her. With the sun warming the crisp fall air and the smell of pine and fir trees drifting on the wind, she felt like letting Dancer gallop ahead of the wagon and yelling in the breeze. Instead, she kept him at a slow jog so that Othello would not slide off.

When they met another wagon, the small children in the back pointed at the dog and laughed in delight. The woman on the driver's seat nodded a greeting.

"Othello, you know what? People here are very friendly. Pretty soon we're going to see Pa's valley, and then we'll be home. A real home. For the first time in my entire life we're going to have a home that stays in one place. What do you think of that?"

Othello barked twice.

That afternoon, when a sign at the side of the road said *Welcome to Argus*, she dropped back with the wagon, and Chief moved the livestock up right behind it.

"You go ahead and see what it is like. Can we take the animals down Main Street?"

Cassie told Othello to get down and stay with Chief, then nudged Wind Dancer ahead, and they trotted into the town. A church on their left wore a sign that said *Argus Lutheran*

Church. And under that: *Reverend Brandenburg.* That was
the man she was supposed to meet. A man and a woman in
a buggy waved at her as she stopped her horse at the hitching
post. No one was at the church, but a man riding by pointed
to the pastor's house, one over from the church. Cassie rode
over there and stopped again at a hitching rail. After flipping
the reins around the silvered rail, she walked up to the house
and knocked on the door.

No answer. She knocked again. "We're back here" came
a call from the backyard. She took the path around the
house and found a man and a woman digging potatoes in
the garden.

"Welcome, young lady." The man wiped his hands on his
pants and crossed to greet her. "You need some potatoes?"

Cassie knew instantly that she liked this man. "I haven't had
potatoes for more than a month. That would be wonderful."

"Good, good. I'm Reverend Brandenburg, and this good
woman is my wife, Elouisa."

"I am Cassie Lockwood and I have a letter here from Reverend Kemp in Rapid City. He said he's a good friend of yours."

"That he is. We just don't get to see them very often." He
accepted the letter and read it quickly. "So you are looking
for your father's valley?"

"I am. We've come from Dickinson, North Dakota."

"We?"

"I left the others just out of town. We have some cattle, and
we weren't sure we could drive them through town. Besides,
I didn't know where your church was."

"How many are in your party?"

"Four, along with two dogs, horses, Longhorns, and,
well . . . three buffalo."

His mouth fell open. "Did you say buffalo?"

Cassie looked him directly in the face. "Yes. The bull's name is George."

"I see. And how will that—those—buffalo react to a town?"

"George has been through others. I think he thinks he's just one of the cows."

"Has your buffalo been corralled before?"

"Oh yes." *Do I tell him the whole story, or what?* Cassie felt pulled two ways. Keep on going to find the ranch. Or camp near town and go on tomorrow?

"We have some corrals over by the train tracks. You could put your animals in there and camp in the field next to the church."

"That sounds like a good idea, but we don't have hay or grain for our animals. They need to graze." *And I can't afford to buy any. Go on, stay . . . what are we to do?*

Brandenburg rubbed his chin.

"Surely there's enough hay over there to feed these animals," Mrs. Brandenburg said softly. "We can find someone to replace what they use."

"Thank you, ma'am. I'm just not sure what is best to do," Cassie said, nodding at the smiling woman. Go or stay? They were so close now.

"I think you should bring your people in, put the animals in the corrals, and join us for supper." She glanced at her husband with a gentle smile. "Not that you asked my opinion or anything."

Reverend Brandenburg smiled at his wife. "As usual, she has figured it all out way ahead of me. Please, do what she says. Mrs. Brandenburg loves to feed people."

Cassie struggled before she made her next question. "But two of my people are Indian. Will that make a difference?"

"Are they hungry for a home-cooked meal?"

"Oh yes."

"Good. Reverend will go with you to show you the way."
She patted his arm. "Won't you, dear?"

"Of course. But I don't have a horse. I'll be waiting for
you right here, so come on in."

Cassie stared from one to the other, and then heaved a
sigh of . . . what? Defeat or compromise? "Thank you for
your hospitality." She returned to her horse and mounted.
"It won't be long."

She set Wind Dancer to a lope and reached the others in
five minutes. "Come on ahead. Reverend Brandenburg is going
to show us where to corral the stock, and then we'll camp in
the field by the church."

Chief stared at her. "You are sure?"

"I am." *Lord, this seems to be a gift from you. Please, if
not, tell me to go on.* So close to the valley. Was she postpon-
ing the next step?

"We are all invited to supper at the pastor's house," Cassie
said, repeating the invitation to the stunned group.

Micah sat on his horse, keeping an eye on the stock, most of
which were lying down, chewing their cuds. The spare horses
were grazing along the fence line of a farm that bordered the
road. "You sure about us all being welcome?"

"Mrs. Brandenburg said for all of us to come. Pastor will
show us the way to the corrals."

"She knows we are Indian?" Chief asked.

"She knows." Cassie straightened. "So let's get a move
on." She turned Wind Dancer around and led the way into

the town of Argus. Reverend Brandenburg met them at the second corner.

"Turn left here and we'll go three blocks, then turn right for one block." He mounted his bicycle and pedaled beside her. "This won't bother your horse, will it?"

"Nothing bothers Wind Dancer. He's used to Wild West shows."

"I'll go ahead and open the gate. Please keep the cattle from grazing on the trees and bushes in people's yards."

Cassie dropped back to give Chief the instructions and then to help Micah keep the cattle moving. When they scented water, they picked up their pace and trotted right through the gates, cattle in one pen and horses in another. Micah dismounted to help the pastor throw in some hay. The water tanks were already full.

Cassie watched the horns clash as all the Longhorns tried to drink at the same time. While it sounded fierce, she knew they never injured each other. They stepped back when George decided to drink.

"How did you get buffalo?" Brandenburg asked.

"George was part of the show, but he's old and would not have done well in a new show. We know his weaknesses, so he came with us. The others followed him."

"I have a feeling you have many stories to tell."

"Actually, Chief is a far better storyteller than I am. I grew up in the show, so life away from it is all new to me."

"You really are or were the star of the show?"

"Well, the shooting and trick-riding part."

"Do you miss it?"

She thought a moment. "Yes, on one hand, but our traveling has taught me a lot of new things. I'm looking forward to finding my father's valley and settling down. He always wanted to raise cattle and Appaloosa horses."

"An admirable dream. Since the animals are all settled, we'll go to the house now. You can hobble the team there and your two horses. That field needs to be grazed off anyway." He led them around a block and to the edge of town where the house sat in the dusk. He showed them where to park the wagon, but when Runs Like a Deer was helped down from the wagon seat, he stopped.

"Can she walk to our house?"

"She has a crutch. The men will help her." Cassie dismounted. "Let's leave the horses tied up until we get back." She paused. "I really would like to clean up a bit before we come."

"You can wash up at our house." Reverend Brandenburg pushed his bicycle so he could walk with them when the animals were grazing. "Your wagon will most likely cause quite a stir in the morning."

"Would we be better to camp outside of town?"

"This way you don't have to worry about your livestock. People in Argus are used to cattle being driven to the railroad. They'll probably think this is a Gypsy wagon."

"More and more I'm wishing we'd taken the time and money to repaint the wagon." She followed him into the house, and he held the door open for the others. Micah and Chief picked up Runs Like a Deer and lifted her over the steps.

"Welcome, welcome." Mrs. Brandenburg greeted each of them and repeated their names as they were introduced. "I'm sure you'd all like a chance to clean up and then come right this way when you're done. I have supper all ready."

The fragrances of food drew them to the round table in the kitchen that was set for six.

"Why don't you men take the chairs near the windows. Runs Like a Deer, I think sitting here would be easiest for you." Mrs. Brandenburg pulled out the chair she indicated and helped her guest be seated. Chief and Micah had both removed their hats when they came in the front door and hung them on the hall tree. Cassie let hers hang down her back by the stampede string that she so seldom used unless she was in the arena.

She glanced around the room. If this was what all kitchens could be like, she realized that she did indeed want one. The more she was in people's homes, the more her memories of the cook tent faded. White curtains at the windows, several plants in the window, some with red blossoms and one pink and white. A framed sampler on the wall looked old. A braided rug lay in front of the sink and another near the cookstove. Clear glass knobs adorned the cupboard doors, cupboards that lined one wall clear to the ceiling.

"Thank you, Mrs. Brandenburg. This is so lovely and smells absolutely delicious." An ache started in her middle. Could something like this be part of her new life? She glanced down at her hands. So much for cleaning up. She should have insisted they scrub before they came. Cassie sat down in the chair indicated and pulled it in. Glancing at Chief and Micah, she swallowed a smile. While she was getting used to being treated like a guest, thanks to her newfound friends in the pastorate, her three friends looked decidedly uncomfortable.

"Let us bow our heads for grace." Reverend Brandenburg prayed simply, but Cassie had no doubt that God was listening.

The man spoke as to his best friend, blessing the food and the guests at his table, that their dreams may be accomplished. He thanked God for bringing them to Argus safely.

So did Cassie. She murmured an amen along with his and took the bowl that Mrs. Brandenburg started around. Potatoes, real cooked potatoes. The aroma alone made her mouth water. "What did you sprinkle on these?"

"Oh, that's just a bit of dill leaves, if you can call them that, from my garden. I do love the smell of dill." She looked to the others. "Please start the serving bowl or plate nearest you and help yourselves. Oh, and in our house we pass them to the right." Her gentle voice held no note of censure or criticism. One would think she entertained such a motley crew every day.

"Cassie, dear, is there anything else we need here?"

"Not that I can think of. We don't usually get food like this, especially if I do the cooking, so we are so grateful. They've been teaching me how to cook over a campfire—not that I ever cooked on a stove either. We always ate in the dining tent."

"Really?" Mrs. Brandenburg stared at her for a moment. "Well, I wish you could stay with me for a while. I would love to teach you how to cook."

Cassie stared at her. "You would do something like that?"

"Of course I would. What a fine time we would have."

"My wife is known for her good cooking. Why, she and Mavis Engstrom have contests sometimes to see who is best." He leaned forward. "Not a bad thing to have superior cooks in your congregation. We all eat like kings."

Mrs. Brandenburg *tsk*ed and wagged her fingers at her husband. "How you go on."

Reverend Brandenburg turned to the men, who were quietly cleaning their plates and refilling them at his wife's insistence. "Chief, what reservation were you from originally?"

"Pine Ridge."

"Will you be going home again?"

Cassie waited for his answer, but all he did was shrug. Was he going or staying? She would have to confront him another time. The thought of his leaving them made her stomach roll. She'd wakened some nights from a nightmare of him gone.

When their plates were empty, the Brandenburgs started the platter and bowls around again. "Help yourselves, please, although I do hope you save room for dessert too. I made chocolate pie—that is Reverend Brandenburg's favorite." She smiled at her husband. "This way you won't be forced to eat two pieces so it doesn't go to waste."

Cassie needed to loosen her belt by the time they were finished. While she and the Brandenburgs carried most of the conversation, the others had answered when spoken to.

"Thank you, ma'am," Micah said. "For all of us."

"You are welcome. I do hope you will come again."

"You'll be going on tomorrow?" Reverend Brandenburg asked.

"They stay. I will go looking," Chief said, not looking at Cassie.

Cassie stared at him. When had he decided this, and why had he not mentioned his idea to her? She pushed her chair back with the rest of them. "May we stay and help you with the dishes?"

"Oh no. That's not necessary, but thank you for offering. I'll have the reverend bring you some fresh bread tomorrow after I bake, and I have extra eggs that I thought you might enjoy. You might like to take them tonight and have them for breakfast. Oh, and we put some potatoes in a sack for you. They are by the front door, so pick them up as you go out."

Eggs for breakfast. Cassie could feel her grin splitting her face. "You are so generous. Thank you." Cassie accepted the basket thrust into her hands.

Mrs. Brandenburg patted her arm. "I do hope you find your valley and that it is near to us. We'd love to see you in church on Sundays. And if you are close enough, the offer of cooking lessons will be a standing one."

"Thank you." Cassie followed the others out the door. It occurred to her that she'd better dig out one of those skirts from her trunk. She'd better be dressed like a lady, even though Mrs. Brandenburg hadn't seemed to notice her pants. All the other women around might not be so forgiving.

They had left Othello to guard the wagon, and he welcomed them home with a yip and a dance. The other dog at least came out from under the wagon now, and sometimes even wagged his tail. She'd asked Runs Like a Deer what the dog's name was, but she looked confused and said she called him *Dog*.

After they hobbled the horses and before she climbed up the steps into the wagon, she stopped by Chief. "What do you mean, we are staying here and you are going on to look?"

"I think that best."

"Why?"

"No sense driving wagon and cattle all over looking for the place."

Cassie thought a moment. That did make good sense. "I could go with you."

"Someone needs to be here."

"Micah and—"

"You do not understand. Someone needs to be here." He stared into her eyes.

"But we are safe in town, by the church . . ." She slowed each word, trying to decipher his meaning. A slight shake of his head added to her confusion. "Look, Chief, I have no idea what you are talking about, but I can see this is very important to you, so I'll stay."

"Good." He knelt by the wagon and pulled his and Micah's bedding out of the box slung beneath the frame.

Cassie joined Runs Like a Deer in the wagon. "Do you need some help?"

"No. Those were good people."

"The Brandenburgs?"

She nodded. "Wish we had gift for them."

Cassie nodded. "That would be good. Runs Like a Deer, are you going to leave and go to a reservation?"

"You want me to go?"

"Not at all. I want your leg to finish healing so that you can do whatever you want to do. And if that means staying with us, all the better."

"But I am Indian."

Cassie stared at the part in the woman's hair, since she was studying her hands in her lap. "Why should that make a difference?"

"Many white people do not like Indians."

Cassie knelt in front of her. "Look at me, Runs Like a Deer. I am not like most or many white people, then. Chief is my friend. You are my friend. Friends are extremely important to me. Like the family I don't have." She paused. "Do you have family?"

"Not any longer."

"Then please, can we be family?"

The nod came slowly, but when Runs Like a Deer put her hand over Cassie's, the pact was sealed.

"Sisters?" Cassie whispered.

"Sisters."

25

The fire snapped and crackled.

Cassie stepped out of the wagon in the morning then reached back in to grab the basket Mrs. Brandenburg had sent with them. Peeking inside, she found a slice of ham in there too. She set the basket on the ground by the fire and told Othello to keep his inquisitive nose out of it. "We can cut up the ham and scramble the eggs."

Chief nodded and within minutes the breakfast was ready.

"I should have made biscuits," Cassie said.

"No time. Water the horses at the corral. Put the team in with the others. Keep Wind Dancer here."

Micah nodded. "This is good." He held up his plate.

"Hey, Ma, Indians," a boy shouted from the street.

"You stay away from them. Come here to me right now."

Cassie spun around to see a child dragging his feet back to his mother's side. The woman's eyes opened wide when she saw Cassie. "In our churchyard. Well, I never." She spun around so fast her skirt fluffed and huffed back the way she had come.

Cassie stared after her. What was that all about? She walked a few steps to see up the street. The woman was making a fast line to Reverend Brandenburg's house.

"We need to leave here today." Chief went for his horse and within minutes had him saddled and ready to leave. "Stay close to the wagon."

Cassie watched him leave. Of course she had read in newspapers about the Indian problems, but that was some time ago. When she did give it any thought, she figured fighting was still going on in Texas and Arizona, not in the Dakotas. Her father and Jason Talbot had always treated their Indian workers just like everyone else. While the Indians had kept more to themselves than the rest of the performers and crew, there had never been any conflict, at least not that she knew of.

Runs Like a Deer poured Micah another cup of coffee and raised the pot, looking at Cassie. She shook her head. Was this what Chief was trying to tell her last night?

She walked out to where Wind Dancer was grazing, swung aboard, and rode him over to the corrals to give him a drink. Two boys were sitting on the corral fence watching George and the Longhorns. She slid to the ground, swung open the gate, and led her horse in for a drink at the trough.

"You sure got a pretty horse, miss," one of the boys called. "What's his name?"

"Wind Dancer." She leaned her rear against the lip of the trough and smiled at the boys. "He's a mighty smart horse."

"Does he do tricks?"

Another boy climbed up to join them. "That's a real buffalo."

"His name is George. He used to be in a Wild West show."

"A buffalo named George?" His eyes widened.

"Yep. He's pretty old now."

Wind Dancer turned his head and dribbled water on her arm. "Thanks." She pushed his nose away. "Drool on the ground, not on me."

The boys giggled.

She led Wind Dancer out of the corral and shut the gate. "I wouldn't get in that corral, if I were you. George isn't used to kids much."

"You with that fancy wagon over by the church?"

"I am."

"Those Indians yours?"

How did one answer that question? Cassie chose to ignore it and swung back up on Wind Dancer. She waved. "See you."

A group of people had gathered near the wagon and fell back when she rode up.

"This your wagon?"

"Yes."

"You part of a Wild West show?"

"Used to be."

"What are you doing in Argus?"

"Just passing through."

"Good thing. Does Reverend Brandenburg know you're camped here?"

"He told us to camp here." She eased closer to the big man who was asking the rude questions. She dropped her voice. "Are we doing anything to bother you?"

"You being here is a bother."

"Why?"

"You got an Indian with you."

Dancer sidled nearer, forcing the man to take a step backward. "Look, mister, we're here by invitation. We'll be moving on later today or early in the morning. Are you a member of this church?"

"Well, in a way. But I lived in this town a long time, and we don't allow Indians to take up living here." His voice sported a bluster as big as a north wind.

"How come you're the only one complaining?"

"Somebody's gotta speak up for the folks."

Cassie glanced around to see some of the other adults looking at the ground or at each other from under their hat brims.

"Good morning, Miss Lockwood. I brought the bread the missus promised you. Right from the oven. Looks like I should have brought more. Glad to see you folks welcoming our visitors. Why, did you know this young lady used to be a trick rider with that wonderful horse of hers?"

"You were with that Wild West show?" another man asked, pointing at the wagon. "I saw that show one year up in Fargo. There was a trick-riding girl who could shoot clay pigeons out of the air and an apple off her dog's head." He looked around at the others. "That could be her."

"It was. Glad you were able to attend. That show has disbanded now, so you were fortunate." She glanced up to see a good-looking young man on a horse at the rear of the crowd. He touched the brim of his western hat with a gloved hand, his smile bright like the sun. Unlike the other man, this one indeed said welcome.

Cassie smiled back and watched him turn and ride away. The whole thing lasted less than half a minute. She dismounted and took the loaf of bread. "Thank you."

"You were doing just fine," he whispered. "You might think of putting on an exhibition sometime. It would go a long way to making a place for yourself here."

"I'll keep that in mind."

"Mith, can I pet your horth?" a little snub-nosed girl asked.

Cassie squatted down to the child's level. "Why, you certainly may." She signaled Wind Dancer with her hand, and he bowed down on one knee, his head right near the little girl's hand. She beamed at Cassie and smoothed the forelock.

"He likes to have his ears rubbed." Cassie showed her how, and the child followed her actions. When Dancer stood upright again, a young woman put her hands on the little girl's shoulders.

"Thank you, miss. That was right generous of you."

"Thank you, mith. I never patted a horth pretty ath him before." The little girl took her mother's hand and waved as they left.

Cassie looked up to see that most of the crowd had faded away. She glanced over to Reverend Brandenburg, who was standing by Runs Like a Deer. "I'm going to hobble Dancer. We have coffee in the pot if you'd like a cup."

"How about later? I need to get my sermon ready for Sunday." His smile made her nod. "And a little child shall lead them?"

"I guess. Who was that blowhard?"

"One of our few not-too-savory characters. He's usually sleeping off the night before at this time of day, so I was surprised to see him here."

"I guess there are people like that everywhere."

"Sad to say. But most of the people of Argus are fine, upstanding Christian folk who welcome strangers and help one another out. Chief is out searching?"

"Yes. He left early."

"You know you are invited to stay as long as you need to?"

"Thank you, but I'm sure we'll be pushing on."

"Don't leave without saying good-bye."

"We won't."

Sometime later when she heard a horse trotting up the street, Cassie looked up to see Chief riding in. He had to have found the valley to be returning so soon. How could her heart be leaping and her stomach clenching at the same time?

Cassie was almost afraid to ask. She studied the sober look on Chief's face. Good news or bad? Her throat tightened. He was back early. Surely he wouldn't have returned without finding something. *Lord, help me.* "So . . ." Her voice squeaked, so she cleared her throat and tried again. "So what did you find?"

"I found the valley."

"And?" *Come on, Chief, get it out.*

"I found a good place to camp."

"Fine. What about my father's valley?"

"There is a ranch there."

Now what would they do? She turned away and climbed the steps to the wagon, the need to be alone stronger than her curiosity. Someone was ranching on her land, the land she held the deed for, the land her father had bought and paid for. Tears burned behind her eyes, making her nose run. This was too deep a matter to cry over. If someone was already living there, what were they to do? Winter could hit any day, as Chief had reminded her on their way down from Belle

Fourche to Rapid City. They not only needed a place to set the wagon but pasture for the animals.

You can always go find another Wild West show to star in. The voice sounded close enough to be real. "Right. I could do that. But that means I would have to leave the others. What would happen to them?" She shook her head. Here she was arguing with an unseen voice.

Her mother had always said God had a plan for her life. But if He did, He sure wasn't giving clear directions. Her mother also said to look for answers in the Bible, something Cassie had not been doing ever since they'd left the show. So how would she do that? Just flip open the Bible and voilà, there it would be? She leaned her forehead against the bedpost.

Her father always said, *"Take the next step. All God is asking you to do is to take the next step."* The next step for them was what? She made a mental list of the possibilities.

Do we all go out there now?

Do Chief and I ride out there?

Do we go on to Hill City and come back another time?

The questions rattled around in her brain like a child's toy. There were good reasons for any of them. For all of them. She took a deep breath, assured herself that she wasn't going to break down in tears, and went back outside.

"You get on out of here before we have to make you leave." The loudmouth from the morning was back and had brought some friends.

"We could stay here another night," Cassie said to Chief.

He crossed his wrists over the saddle horn, rolled his eyes toward the trio at the street, and waited.

Lord, what is it I am supposed to do here? We aren't doing anything wrong. Why do people act this way? We came all this way, and now I'm terrified. She sucked in a deep breath and let it out. "How far is it?"

"Four or five miles."

"And you're sure it's the right place?"

"Yes. The three upright rocks have not changed."

"Hey, little high-and-mighty show star, you hear me?" The man turned and said something to a man beside him who looked about as disreputable as the first. Loudmouth was obviously the leader of the pack.

"Need to get out of town," Chief told Cassie. "Found good place to camp. Valley will wait." Chief dismounted and tied his horse to the wagon wheel. "Before bad trouble."

Cassie rubbed her forehead with her fingertips. This morning could happen again, only in the middle of the night if some men got liquored up. Like the blowhard. She'd seen men who were drunk, or rather had heard them. Drunkenness was cause for firing from the show, but they couldn't always control the townspeople where they performed.

"Get ready to leave, and I'll go talk with Reverend Brandenburg. We can pick up the rest of the cattle on our way out." She strode off, knowing that the reverend had left the church and gone home an hour or so earlier. What a shame that they couldn't stay there. But Sunday was coming, and the people who attended the church would need a place for their horses and wagons. She knocked on the door and waited.

"Well, Miss Lockwood, what a nice surprise. No, maybe not. You're planning to leave, aren't you?" He stepped back. "Can't you come in?"

"No, I think not. I just wanted to thank you for the

hospitality and tell you that the valley I hold title to is four to five miles out of town. Chief found it, but there's a ranch already there."

"I see. Is it on the main road?"

"I don't know. He found us a place to camp. Uh . . . I've never in my life asked anyone this, but could you pray for us? I really don't know what to do here."

"Of course we will." Mrs. Brandenburg appeared by her husband, wiping her hands on her apron. "And if your land is no further away than that, you'll be able to come to church. Why, a ranch family out that way, the Engstroms, will be wonderful neighbors, and they are staunch members here. Fine people."

"Thank you both." Cassie nodded and turned to leave.

"Would you like me to go with you?" he asked.

Cassie paused and gave it some thought. "Maybe later, but right now we need to get out of town before there's trouble."

"They're back?"

She nodded. "He brought his friends."

"Go tell the sheriff," Mrs. Brandenburg told her husband.

"No, please. We don't want to cause trouble. We'll just leave, and all will be well."

"Do you know where your camp will be?"

"No, but when I know more, I'll let you know. Thank you again." She nodded to both of them and left with a small wave. Talk about the different kinds of people in a town. She'd seen that in their audiences through the years, but today it hit home harder than any other time. How could they live near a town that held such hatred?

She walked swiftly back to the field and mounted Wind Dancer, since Micah had him saddled for her. They were just finishing hitching up the team, and Runs Like a Deer drowned the campfire with water from the barrel.

"I can drive the wagon," she said.

"Without hurting your leg?"

She nodded. "Easier for three to get the cattle."

Cassie nodded her agreement and looked to the two men. They shrugged.

Since Micah's horse was in the corral, he helped Runs Like a Deer up to the driver's seat.

With far more ease than Cassie had supposed, they brought the animals out of the corrals, and she and Chief kept them moving while Micah saddled his horse and caught up. They took the back streets out of town and picked up the road to Hill City on the other side of town. They'd driven several miles when Chief indicated a road off to the right that led into some pine trees.

He led the way and the cattle followed, with George bringing up the rear. Someone had camped there before, as there was a fire pit in a small clearing. A creek bounded one side and a steep rocky bank the other. Micah climbed up to the wagon seat and backed the wagon into the spot by the fire pit.

By the time they'd finished setting up camp, long shadows were graying the trees. Cassie wandered out to where the cattle were grazing and made her way to George's side. He lifted his head to stare at her and snorted gently. "You been enjoying the trip? This is about as close to the wild as you're going to get." He tipped his head to the side so she could reach his ear. "Sure glad no one bothered you when we were in town. That could have been bad." If it could be said a buffalo can purr, George would have been doing just that.

He sighed and lowered his head so she could dig into his heavy coat and scratch the poll of his head, but his favorite place was his ears. "You'd lose your reputation as a big bad bull buffalo if people saw you like this. Sorry, I have no carrots for you." When he dropped his head to graze again, she leaned against his shoulder.

"Here we are, so close to the valley and I have to wait. But the problem is, George, I'm scared. What if they run us off? What if . . ." She knew that what she was doing was worrying, but after all they'd been through . . . "Do you think that deed is still good?"

That was the big question. Back in the wagon, she lit a lamp and, getting her mother's Bible out of her trunk, laid it open on the table and removed the deed from the envelope. She leaned closer to the light and read it again. Nothing had changed.

Nothing but the fact that she was now camped nearby rather than on a train to the next show. Something was gnawing at the edge of her mind. Did Chief know more about all this than he was letting on? She laid the envelope back on the Bible and meandered outside. The others were sitting around the campfire. Micah had dragged in a hunk of wood for Runs Like a Deer to sit on, and she was sewing another pair of rabbit skin mittens. Micah was carving on a long piece of wood, and Chief was telling a story.

She listened until he finished and then asked, "Chief, why do I feel there is something you aren't telling me?" Cassie leaned against one of the wagon wheels when her knees didn't want to hold her up.

He blinked. "But that is all of the story." He stared at her. "You mean about valley." He didn't ask a question, just laid the comment out there flat and unadorned.

317

"Yes. Were you with my father when he bought the land?"

"No. But I was guide for Lockwood and Ivar when we found valley. They were looking for gold mine. There was one on side of the hill that someone had left. So they filed on it."

"And found gold."

He nodded. "Not a lot but enough to buy land."

"Why didn't you tell me?" She watched the shutter fall over his face, and he shrugged.

"Better this way. Thought you would find another letter in all those papers."

"I've been through everything. I have the deed. If they are trespassing . . ." *Oh, Lord, I don't want a legal fight over the land. But this is my father's valley.* "You are sure this is the right valley?"

"I am sure."

"So what do you think I should do?"

"Go see people who are there."

Cassie nodded. Why did that sound so easy? And looked like a rugged mountain to climb?

26

*T*oday is the day.

Cassie lay in her hammock, listening to birds in the trees behind the wagon start their morning chatter. A horse snorted. One of the cattle bellered. Chief or Micah was chopping wood for the blaze snapping in the fire ring. The fragrance of woodsmoke teased her nose. She raised her head to look over the edge of the hammock. Runs Like a Deer was lacing her moccasin on her good side. They'd covered the other foot with firmer leather, and she left it on.

Maybe they should check her leg to see if it was still tender. Perhaps there was a doctor in town, but then, what could he do but probably the same. When the other woman left the wagon, Cassie rolled herself out and dressed as quickly as possible. The cold made her hurry. She'd already pulled on her britches before deciding that since she was going to the ranch today, she should probably put on a clean shirt. She

319

checked the trunk and the cupboards she had appropriated for herself. Not a clean shirt to be had. How could she go out there looking like a . . . a . . . The word escaped her.

Why was it that the thought of riding up to a strange place and announcing who she was made her want to throw up? She could wear one of her show shirts, but that would be too much.

She brushed and braided her hair before heading out to the fire, where she could smell coffee cooking. Not having a mirror made checking her face for cleanliness more than a bit difficult.

"Will you be ready soon?" Chief asked.

"After we eat."

He nodded.

"Bread, eggs, venison," Runs Like a Deer said, looking up from stirring the eggs in the frying pan. "Soon."

Maybe she shouldn't eat. What if it didn't stay down?

"I'm going to heat water to wash some clothes."

"Why? Pound them on the rocks in the creek."

Cassie shook her head. How quickly could she get a shirt dry? If only she had flatirons in the wagon to iron one dry.

BAR E RANCH

Remind me to never agree to host a party again," Ransom muttered.

Gretchen giggled. "You know this is the way it always is. Mor wants everything perfect for company." She gave the chimney to the final lamp one last lick. The smell of kerosene made his nose burn as he filled the bases.

"Why do we need all these lamps anyway? We're going to be out by the barn mostly."

"I know. We do the lanterns next."

"Where's Lucas?"

"Down feeding the fire. The venison smells so good. People are going to be raving about it for a long time to come."

"You two about done?" Mavis called from the kitchen.

"Just starting the lanterns." Gretchen motioned for her big brother to help put the lamps back where they belonged and held the door for him to take the two largest ones.

"If other people are bringing food, which they always do, why is Mor cooking so much?"

Gretchen rolled her eyes. "You know she would die of embarrassment if there wasn't enough food. Fill the lanterns and go ask her what else she wants done."

When he stepped off the back porch where he and Gretchen were working, Lucas called from beside the smoking pit, "Let's move the benches to the dancing area."

"Be right there." He headed for the barn, where they stored the benches on hooks on the walls. Anything was better than whatever his mother would find for him to do next.

Near as he could tell, everything was in place before the first wagon drove up. Since the plan was to eat supper before the dancing and serve dessert at the middle break, folks started arriving about four o'clock so they could be there to help lift the meat out of the pit. The spit was a contraption with a crank that Ivar had created to make it possible to turn half a steer or hog or, in this case, a deer.

Some of the men and older boys gathered around the cider press with the apples they had brought. As they turned the crank on top of the press, the juice poured out between the slats and into a tub with a spigot on one side. Others filled jugs at the spigot and another stood ready to refill the basket.

The women set their covered dishes on the long tables set up between the cider press and the pit and then checked with Mavis to see what else needed doing. The rustlers occupied the men's conversations, while the women chatted about the ending of the gardens and the canning and plans for the quilting bees to start up again. Mavis made sure the coffeepot was hot.

"Go tell the men that they need to start the fire before it gets dark."

When the Brandenburgs arrived, Mrs. Brandenburg set her things down. "Did you hear about our guests in town?"

Mavis noticed that Lucas, who had been passing behind them, stopped to listen. She turned from filling the coffeepot with fresh water. "No, what happened?"

"They were driving a fancy wagon, and the young woman came by our house with a letter from a minister friend of ours in Rapid City. Said her name was Cassie and she was, or rather is, a trick rider from a Wild West show. A sharpshooter too. She had three friends with her—an old Indian man, a young Indian woman, and a white man. Can you beat that?"

Lucas continued on his way, whistling a tune.

"So where are they now?"

"I don't know. Camping somewhere, I guess. Beckwith and his cronies started giving them a real hard time, so she came by to say they were leaving. They'd been camped in the field by the church. She's a real nice young woman. I hope they find the valley they are looking for and stay around here."

"I heard she was wearing britches," someone else said with a shake of her head.

Mavis didn't say anything to that. She wore britches outside plenty of times. They were much better for riding and working in the garden. But a Wild West show. *I wonder what her last name is.* She banished the thoughts for later. Right now they had people to feed. "Could someone holler out to the men to come help carry the food down to the table?"

CAMPSITE

Cassie hung one of her shirts on two long sticks above the fire. There were no flatirons in the wagon. She'd gone over every inch. Heaving a sigh, she wished she had started the stove in the wagon. Perhaps the shirt would dry faster there.

Chief rode back into camp. "Lots of wagons going to the ranch."

"You suppose they're having a party or something?"

He shrugged. "Go soon?"

"We can't go if there are a lot of people there."

Chief raised his eyebrows and shook his head.

"Well, we can't. That's all there is to it." She removed her shirt from the sticks and flipped it over a rope line Micah had strung from the corner of the wagon to a tree. At least she'd have a clean shirt to wear tomorrow. Clean and dry.

They had moved the butcher table out of the barn, and when they laid the roasted deer on top of it, a sigh went up from those around. Lucas had made his pa proud, Mavis heard someone say.

"Pastor, can you say the blessing?"

"I'd be glad to." He waited a moment for silence. "Our Father in heaven, we thank you for this family who so graciously planned this celebration for us. Thank you for the bounty of our land that has provided much of our food tonight and for the hands that prepared it. Thank you, Lord, for all the many blessings you so freely bestow upon us all. For all these things we praise you and bless your holy name. Amen."

"Get your plates, folks, and help yourselves."

Lucas and Ransom cut the meat and placed slices and pieces on all the plates held out to them. They stripped it down to the bones and dropped those into a tub at their feet. Mavis would cook all the bones in the morning to can as soup stock. Ransom sneaked a bit of meat for Benny, who sat right at his feet waiting for something to drop.

"Good to see you, Ransom," Lissa said with a smile as she held her plate out.

"Glad you could come. We usually plan things a bit farther ahead, but this is a good gathering anyway."

"It is. I'm glad there will be dancing too. We just don't seem to have many parties anymore."

Dancing. Ransom groaned inside. Maybe he could slip away . . . but no, he knew his mother would have his hide if he did. Hosts were not allowed to leave their own party.

There was just a plateful of meat left over, which they set

on the table along with the other food for those who wanted some later. After all, dancing made one hungry.

And thirsty, he decided as he refilled the crock with cider. He tossed some more wood on the bonfire, as the chill was settling in. The fiddles tuned up and the dancing began. He found himself standing next to Miss Lissa, and what could he do but ask her to dance.

"Thank you." She smiled and he took her hand and led her out into the group of moving couples.

"Really good food," she said. "The venison was a welcome treat."

"You've not had any?"

"No. Pa can't get out and hunt like he used to, and Aaron isn't much of a shot. His eyes aren't the best, you know."

"I'm sorry. I'll tell Lucas to bag you one." He stumbled just a bit. "Sorry." *Please don't make me talk anymore.* If only he dared say that to her. He pretended he didn't hear her next comment and swung her around on the edge of the dancers. When the music finished, he walked her to the benches, where some folks were sitting and visiting. "Thank you."

"Thank you." She turned as Lucas tapped her on the shoulder and danced off with him.

Ransom watched them go. She'd have more fun with Lucas anyway. Ransom danced the next one with his mother, who had a faraway look in her eyes. "Something bothering you?"

She looked up at him, a smile changing her face. "Nothing, really. Thanks for all your hard work to make this happen so quickly."

"You are welcome." But he could tell something was on her mind. Maybe she would talk about it later, after everyone left.

He'd just refilled the cider crock again when Miss Lissa came up to him. "You know, Ransom, if you'd rather not dance, we could just talk. You know, like we used to before . . ."

Before they both grew up? "I'd like that."

They moved over to the bonfire and sat down on one of the benches.

He studied the dancers, hoping she would take the lead.

"I hear you had your fence cut."

"We did. The rustlers seemed to stay in the same area. All three ranches are this side of town. So strange that they took only a couple of head from each place."

"You staying for the meeting after church tomorrow?"

He nodded. "Got to get to the bottom of this. I heard a couple of guys getting hot under the collar because of it. All we need are a group of vigilantes—"

"Sheriff won't allow that."

"What if it's someone trying to stir up trouble?"

"Who? No one would do something like that." She paused and stared at the fire. "Would they?"

"Don't know. The thought just ran through my mind. Something to think about, though." Ransom got up to throw more wood on the fire. "Mor said we weren't to talk about rustling tonight, but that edict sure hasn't stuck."

"Not even with her sons. That's all everyone wants to talk about, that and the fancy wagon that came to town."

Before long they took a break for dessert, and when that was over, Brandenburg stood up to call another square dance.

Ransom took Miss Lissa's hand. "Let's dance this one. I do all right on the square dances."

"You do better than all right on all the dances. I don't know where you get the idea you don't."

They joined the square and no one had time to talk, just the way he liked it.

When the last of the guests left after helping put all the benches and tables away, washing dishes in the kitchen, and making sure all the food was put away, the Engstrom family relaxed in the living room. Ransom flopped back on the cowhide-covered sofa. "I am shot, but Mor, your party went really well. Everyone said so, as you know."

"They did have a good time, didn't they?" She turned to her other son. "You're in a mighty good mood, Lucas. What cheered you up so fine?"

"Ma, I met the woman of my dreams."

"Someone new?"

"That girl you were talking about with Mrs. Brandenburg? I saw her last time I was in town. I hope we can invite her out for dinner or supper one of these days." He paused, a frown growing between his eyebrows. "Maybe they're only passing through." He heaved a sigh. "I sure hope they stay around."

She smiled and shook her head. "Say, that venison was the hit of the party."

"Nothing but the bones left." Lucas stretched his arms above his head. "How come Miss Suzanne wasn't here?" he asked, grinning at his brother.

"Don't know and didn't ask."

"She went to visit an aunt somewhere." Gretchen turned from sitting on a pillow in front of the fireplace and petting Benny.

"How do you know all that goes on?" Lucas asked.

"I listen. People forget that kids have ears too."

Lucas looked over at his mother. "How'd we get such a bright kid?"

"Hmm?" She yawned. "Think I'll go on to bed. Thanks again, all of you for all your help. Even the lanterns looked nice." She half smiled at Ransom, dropped a kiss on Gretchen's head, and left the room.

Ransom looked at his brother, who stared back at him. Mor was always the last one to go to bed. Something was going on.

CAMPSITE

Cassie stared into the dying fire. Tomorrow was another day. Midmorning would be a good time to go. Let them finish breakfast first. Her stomach roiled again, sending a bad taste to her mouth. *Please, Lord, help me get through this, whatever this is.*

27

assie's hands shook as she gathered her reins.

Sleep had eluded her, and when it did finally come calling, it brought nightmares. Her stomach threatened to erupt at any time. Perhaps she was getting sick. She grasped the saddle horn and stuck her foot in the stirrup, only to miss and get a good jarring when it hit the ground. What a dismal way to start a morning.

She could feel Chief watching her, the others as well. When she returned, she'd have to apologize for being so cranky. She leaned against the stirrup leathers and forced herself to take a deep breath. Swinging aboard, she followed Chief out the lane to the road and turned right.

"This is road to Hill City."

Maybe they should go back, get the others, and drive on to Hill City. At least she might find a flatiron to use there so she wouldn't have to wear a wrinkled shirt. She tried to watch the scenery, but every second her heart pounded harder.

"How much farther?"

"Not far."

They had gone down a hill and around a bend when Chief said, "That road up there."

"You're sure?"

"You see in a minute."

As they drew closer, he pointed toward the hills on the skyline. Three huge rocks, nestled right next to each other, pointed toward the sky. The lane led straight toward them. Two silvered tree trunks held another across the lane, the ranch name, Bar E, carved into the horizontal log. *I Engstrom* was carved in smaller letters off to the right.

"Ivar Engstrom was your father's best friend."

"Best friend? Why would he take over my father's valley, then?"

"Don't know whole story. Will learn it." He turned his horse into the lane and rode up to the buildings. "You coming?"

"Yes. No. Yes."

Wind Dancer snorted and pulled against the reins.

My father's valley, but someone is living here. His best friend. Her heart thundered. Her throat went dust dry. Did she dare ride up this lane? She could see bits of a log house through the trees. She loosened the reins and let Dancer catch up with Chief. They jogged up the lane, fenced on both sides. Narrow rocky ridges, studded with pine trees, came to matching points on either side of the road, as if once there were a natural gate there. Past those points, the valley opened up, leaving the three rocks marking the far end of the valley. No wonder her father dreamed of this place all those years. A log house nestled at the foot of a low hill with a barn and corrals ahead on the flat. Cattle grazed off to the left, and ahead, beyond the buildings, they could see fields that had been harvested.

"It's beautiful."

Chief grunted.

Cassie turned Wind Dancer up toward the house. At the hitching post she dismounted and, taking all of her courage in hand, along with ordering her stomach to behave, mounted the steps and knocked on the door. She waited. A dog growled at her from the edge of the porch. No sound from inside the house. She knocked again, harder this time. Maybe they were out back.

When there was no answer, she turned back to Chief and shrugged.

Not home. "What day is this?"

"Sunday."

"Of course. They are at church. Reverend Brandenburg said they were faithful members and fine folk."

But did he know they had stolen her land?

ARGUS

"Order. Order! Let this meeting come to order." Reverend Brandenburg rapped on the wooden podium in front of him.

Amid shushings and whispered orders, the crowded room finally quieted.

"Now, we've called this meeting, as you know, because some folks have had fences cut and cattle stolen. So let us

331

bow our heads and pray. Heavenly Father, we thank you for this lovely fall day, for all the folks gathered here from both congregations, because this issue concerns us all. You know what is happening, for nothing happens that you don't know. Today we ask for wisdom and clear thinking as we talk about what we need to do. Thank you for your presence here. Your Word says that where two or more are gathered in your name, you are in the midst. We thank you for your promises. In your Son's holy name we pray. Amen."

When the folks settled again, he continued. "Today, our sheriff, Edgar McDougal, will chair this meeting. Sheriff?"

Wearing his badge on his Sunday coat, the sheriff took the podium. He glanced across the now silent room. "I hate to be standing here like this with the news that we have to talk about. We've never had any rustlers here, at least none that we know of, and I'm sure sorry it has happened now. The interesting thing is that only a couple of head were taken from each of the three ranches. Had the fences been repaired again, it most likely wouldn't have come to anyone's attention until roundup next spring. I'm willing to bet the cattle thieves were counting on that."

"Call a spade a spade, Sheriff. They're rustlers!"

"Now, let's not go getting all riled up. We know this must have occurred within the last three weeks. I know that's pretty general, but most of us don't check the fences every day unless the cows get out."

Nods of agreement answered him.

"So my first question, and one I want you to think on, is this: Have you seen any strangers around here recently?"

"That fancy wagon with the trick rider and the Indians."

"That was this week, and they are no more thieves than I am." Brandenburg shook his head. "We mean weeks ago."

"We've checked with the freight trains in both Hill City and Rapid City, and no one has reported shipping any cattle lately. We gave them the list of brands and asked them to watch for those brands or any doctored brands."

"If they butchered them out, they could ship hanging halves, and we'd never know. Or sell them to meat markets or even to private customers."

"Thanks, Swen, we thought of that too, and the law officers are on the lookout."

"They could have driven them farther out," someone else added.

Ransom wished he had sat in the back so he could see who was talking. He glanced at his mother, who looked as perplexed as he felt.

"What I am asking each of you to do, and I know this just adds to your chores of getting ready for winter, but could you please send someone out to check your fence lines."

Someone groaned from the back.

"I know, but it would help to know if this is widespread. And keep a close watch. If you can, move your stock closer to the house at night." More groans. "The sooner we catch these cattle thieves, the sooner we can all relax."

"When you catch 'em, string 'em up," someone called out. "Make an example." Someone else muttered an agreement.

"When we catch them, they will be prosecuted to the full extent of the law." The sheriff stared down the man owning the voice of inciting viciousness. "We'll have none of that here. Not in my region."

The man frowned and looked to the floor.

"So, everyone, keep your eyes open. If your dog barks at night, check it out. Hear any strange noises, see if you can figure them out. You see or hear anything, let me know immediately. Anyone have anything else to add?" He scanned the room. "Then, Reverend, please close this meeting."

Brandenburg stood up. "Let's all stand and say the Lord's Prayer and then you are dismissed." He waited and then closed his eyes. "Our Father which art in heaven . . ." On the amen, folks began moving around, greeting one another and talking in hushed tones.

"You think Benny tried to warn us and we ignored him?" Gretchen asked her brothers.

"If he did, we owe him a big bone for an apology." Lucas turned and greeted Betsy Hudson, standing with her folks in the row behind them, waiting their turn to get in line to leave.

"So your place was one of those hit?" Her smile would make one think she was inviting him for dessert.

"Sad to say, yes." He smiled back. "Did you have a good time last night?"

"I most certainly did. We all did. That venison was delicious. You throw the best parties."

Plenty of people congratulated the Engstroms on their party the night before as they all made their way out the door. The consensus was a return engagement.

"Did any of you catch the last name of those people who camped by the church?" Mavis asked on the way home.

Both Lucas and Ransom shook their heads.

"I looked at that wagon, but I don't remember what the lettering said."

"All he remembers is how pretty the girl was." Gretchen

334

gave Lucas an elbow in the ribs. The two of them were sharing the bench behind the wagon seat.

"I do hope the dinner isn't all burnt up by now," Mavis said. "We have a lot of cleanup to do, even though folks helped us with some of it. That's the only thing I dislike, the cleaning up afterward."

"Getting ready runs a close second," Ransom muttered to himself. *When will I ever get back to making my beams?*

Monday morning. Maybe today he could get back up to the pine trees and cut off all the branches so the logs would be ready for the sawmill. Ransom was still amazed that Lucas had gone ahead and not only asked about the mill, but brought it home. Was his good deed a possible apology for the lecture Ransom had delivered? If only that would be true. It would sure ease both his and his mother's minds.

He poured himself a second cup of coffee and raised the pot to see if Lucas wanted a refill too. At his nod, Ransom brought the coffeepot back to the table and, after filling Lucas's cup, set the pot on an empty plate on the table. He'd set a hot pot on that table years ago, and the burn ring still showed—one way to learn a permanent lesson.

"What are you two planning today?" Mavis asked from the counter where she turned out the risen dough onto a floured board to be kneaded again. The thump and swish of her hands kneading the bread dough was the only sound until Lucas poured hot coffee into his saucer and slurped it.

"I'd like to get back up the hill if Lucas will ride the fence line and then come and help me."

"You two all right?"

They both shrugged. "Why?" Ransom asked.

"Because you're tiptoeing around each other like two tom-cats meeting for the first time."

The brothers both shrugged, and Lucas smiled at his mother. "Don't worry, Mor, all will be well."

"All I have to say is you better come to some kind of under-standing. And soon." She flipped the dough over and dusted more flour on it.

Ransom gave a short nod and pushed his chair back. Setting his dishes in the dishpan, he checked both woodboxes and shook his head. Filling woodboxes was a never-ending job.

"I'll saddle the horses." Lucas shrugged into his sheepskin coat. "Don't count on us back for dinner."

"Hard to work on an empty stomach."

When Ransom finished hauling in the wood, she handed him a flour sack. "That should hold you."

"Thanks, Mor."

CAMPSITE

Cassie dithered about when to leave. After breakfast? No, after dinner. She nursed a cup of coffee, trying to talk her-self into going back to that ranch house. What more did Chief know that he wasn't telling her, and why was he being secretive?

It was midafternoon when Chief brought the saddled horses to the wagon. "You ready?"

"No. Yes. I don't know."

336

"Get it over with."

She nodded and mounted up. She'd smoothed some of the wrinkles from her shirt with a hot rock, but cold as it was, she needed her coat buttoned up anyway. Maybe out here a wrinkled shirt wasn't so bad.

The ride wasn't nearly long enough. When they turned in under the tall sign, she brought Wind Dancer to a stop and stared at the valley and the hills surrounding it.

"It's beautiful."

Chief grunted.

Catching up with her guide, she tried to memorize all she could see. Today the cattle were on the other side of the lane. Some of them raised their heads and stared, as if not much caring for strangers.

Cassie turned Wind Dancer up toward the house. She heard a horse's hooves behind them and looked over her shoulder to see a young girl galloping her horse up the lane. She waited.

"What a beautiful horse you have," the girl called, bringing her horse to a stop a few feet away.

"Thank you."

"Did you come to see my mother?"

"Is your father here?"

"No. He died a long time ago." The girl pointed toward the house. "Go tie up your horses there. I need to put mine away, and then I'll be right up. Ma must be home. There's smoke from the chimney."

Cassie and Chief looked at each other, shrugged, and did as the girl said. A long porch covered more than half of the face of the house, which looked hunkered down, like it had grown up there with the rocks and trees. A stack of split wood took up a good portion of the wall to one side, while two rocking chairs waited on the other. They dismounted and flipped the reins over the rail.

Cassie's feet felt nailed to the ground. She looked at Chief, who was looking up the valley, where two riders were crossing the far field.

Come on, feet, move. This can't be any worse than entering an arena surrounded by spectators. She took one step and then another, keeping her feet going forward instead of turning and running back to Wind Dancer and riding at top speed out of this valley, whether she owned it or not. She felt in her pocket for the envelope with the deed in it. Still there.

She mounted the two steps to the porch and half turned to leave, but Chief was right behind her. Trapped. Cassie swallowed and crossed to the door of wide pine boards. Her hand had to be commanded to knock, just as her feet had been to walk.

Chief reached around her and rapped on the door with his knuckles.

"Coming," called a female voice. The door opened and a tall woman, her hair in a bun and her dress covered by a floured apron, smiled at them. "Come on in." She stepped back and beckoned them in.

But you don't even know me. Don't look so welcoming. Cassie nodded and stepped forward.

"How can I help you?" The woman's voice felt as warm as the heat from the rock fireplace across the room.

"I . . . I am Cassie Lockwood."

Her eyes widened, and a smile creased her face. "Cassie Lockwood. Is your father Adam Lockwood?" Her voice softened.

"Yes, he was—is—my father, but he died five years ago."

"So they are both gone." She left staring at Cassie and looked to the man slightly behind her. "John Birdwing, is it really you?"

Chief nodded. "Hello, Mrs. Engstrom."

"So I am no longer Mavis?"

"That might be impolite. Is that your girl we met?"

"If you nearly were run over by a girl on a galloping horse, that would be Gretchen." Mavis reached out one hand to Chief and the other to Cassie, her smile as wide as the blue Dakota sky. "Welcome home."

Acknowledgments

Whoever knew we would have something called Facebook as a getting-to-know-you place and also as a research tool. When I got stuck on something, like the Rosebud Reservation in South Dakota, I posted my cry for help on Facebook, and those with great information and contacts got right back to me. I, of course, lost the list of names. I think the computer ate them, but here is my public expression of gratitude to all who helped me.

Melinda and her family drove us through the Black Hills and shared the history of the area at the same time. What a fun way to do research—fun rock picking too. We found the valley for this series on that drive, all but the three rocks at the end of the valley. They were somewhere else, but for the story I moved them.

As always, I ask people that I meet to tell me their family history. What great tales I hear and often use them in my books.

My Round Robin writing buddies brainstormed in characters with me, *quirky* being the key word, and then helped with the research at the Cowboy Museum in Oklahoma City. What an incredible adventure that place was. The statue of a drooping Indian on his horse in a storm took my breath away. I've dreamed of a story for George for many years. We do love buffalo.

I met Rebecca on Facebook. She's written devotional books using her experiences with horses to illustrate spiritual truths. She has a mule named Wind Dancer and graciously allowed me to use his hame for Cassie's partner in trick riding and shooting. Wind Dancer so fits the striking black and white pinto we saw on our travels.

I work with the most incredible team at Bethany House Publishers, a division of Baker Publishing Group. So much of book publishing takes place behind the scenes—editorial, art, marketing, and all the rest. You give your all, and I can never thank you enough.

Blessings,
Lauraine

Lauraine Snelling is an award-winning author of over 60 books for adults and young adults. Her books have sold over 2 million copies. Besides writing books and articles, she teaches at writers' conferences across the country. She and her husband make their home in Tehachapi, California.

More Heartwarming Fiction in Large Print